STEVE WRIGHT

GREY, RED, BLUE... GONE

To Barbara — August 2021

Best of luck with all your writing endeavours

Respectfully,

Steve Wright

The Book Guild Ltd

First published in Great Britain in 2021 by
The Book Guild Ltd
9 Priory Business Park
Wistow Road, Kibworth
Leicestershire, LE8 0RX
Freephone: 0800 999 2982
www.bookguild.co.uk
Email: info@bookguild.co.uk
Twitter: @bookguild

Copyright © 2021 Steve Wright

The right of Steve Wright to be identified as the author of this
work has been asserted by him in accordance with the
Copyright, Design and Patents Act 1988.

All rights reserved. No part of this publication may be
reproduced, transmitted, or stored in a retrieval system, in any form or by any means,
without permission in writing from the publisher, nor be otherwise circulated in
any form of binding or cover other than that in which it is published and without
a similar condition being imposed on the subsequent purchaser.

This work is entirely fictitious and bears no resemblance to any persons living or dead.

Typeset in 12pt Adobe Jenson Pro

Printed on FSC accredited paper
Printed and bound in Great Britain by 4edge Limited

ISBN 978 1913913 113

British Library Cataloguing in Publication Data.
A catalogue record for this book is available from the British Library.

*For Suzanne, who continues to inspire,
and in memory of Fritzy,
for believing in the contentedness idyll.*

Steven Wright has published several articles in academic journals and two works of non-fiction, but *Grey, Red, Blue ... Gone* is his first novel. He lives in the Yorkshire Dales National Park with his wife, Suzanne, a studio potter, and two rescue cats.

CONTENTS

PREFACE VII

ONE	CHICAGO	1
TWO	SEATTLE	18
THREE	SEATTLE	29
FOUR	NEW YORK CITY	41
FIVE	SEATTLE	77
SIX	SEATTLE	87
SEVEN	FISKARDO	106
EIGHT	LONDON	121
NINE	THE COOP AT NETHERBY HALL, CUMBRIA	140
TEN	LONDON	156
ELEVEN	SEATTLE	166
TWELVE	FISKARDO	178

AFTERWORD 234

PREFACE

Throughout life I reflected the country that made me. After George W. Bush's unilateral invasion of Iraq followed by Donald Trump's upending of American democracy, a few years later, everything changed. My nation had become unfamiliar. It no longer stood for the ideals learned during my youth nor what I had spent five years defending in my early twenties; certainly not what I had believed as a young adult. But then I was different, too. Boyish optimism and youthful eagerness had given way to middle-age disillusion, educated cynicism and natural lethargy. I felt cheated, maybe even betrayed. I no longer belonged.

Life is rediscovering what we returned to the sea.
TASSOS STATHAKIS
IONIAN FISHERMAN, 1899

ONE

CHICAGO

I WANTED TO LEAVE. Quarantined in a hotel conference room with thirty-eight self-effacing archivists deciding the content of the annual meeting programme had taken a toll. Debating the numerous threads comprising the fabric of American life has merit, but if not monitored closely the discussions can descend to a level of benign repetitiveness. Archivists are a shy lot by nature and appear unassuming until provided an outlet for opinions. Suddenly the bashful become bold and the meek find their voice. After suffering through ten hours of debate it appeared that the illusion of inclusion had triumphed.

Finally over, I braced myself against the bitter cold of Chicago and scurried to Jilly's, a classic jazz club on Rush Street. I wanted to lose myself against the backdrop of Frank Sinatra's music and single-malt Scotch. Almost fifty-two, I needed to reflect on life, inventory accomplishments and analyse failures. I leaned against the bar and ignored the banter of several floozy-like women who kept bumping me to garner attention. As Sinatra belted out 'Don't Worry 'Bout Me', I drifted. Halfway through the number someone touched my shoulder.

"Pardon me—"

"Go ahead, take my chair. I've been sitting all day. Don't need it. Let me remove my coat and hat."

"No, no, my friend Helen and I only arrived from London and she is simply shattered and wants to return to the room, but I've requested a favourite song. Would you mind sitting at my table until it's played, to keep the odd-balls away?"

I surveyed the young woman, certainly British by her accent – tall, fit, red, auburn-like hair and blue eyes with a glint of lapis.

"Why not? It'll give me a break from inhaling too much Scotch. Let me welcome you to America—?"

"Sara, I'm Sara Hawes from London. And you are—?"

"Edward, Edward Lee from Seattle, Washington, in the Pacific Northwest, close to the Canadian border."

We shook hands.

"What are you drinking, Sara? Let me buy you a 'welcome to America' drink."

"A 'Jack Daniels on the rocks', please. I had to say that. It's so American. We don't ruin Scotch or whisky with ice in England."

"Of course you don't. You're purists. Traditionalists. Not a problem. I'll ask the barman."

Helen looked tired and declined another drink. As I approached the bar I thought to myself, *I don't know what 'America' is anymore. Long ago we stood for something admirable. Bush, Cheney and company and their bevy of hacks and charlatans, turned that ideal on its head. Pure apostasy. Hell, we even add ice to fine Scotch!* When I returned Helen, whose last name I learned was Cooke, had on her coat, ready to depart. She told Sara she was sorry but couldn't keep her eyes open any longer. They said their goodbyes. I offered a cursory nod.

"So what song did you request?"

"'My Funny Valentine' – hopefully they'll play Chet Baker's version."

"Ah, vintage West Coast Cool. Let's hope they do."

With drinks in hand we toasted to her having an exciting time in Chicago despite the bitter cold. Little time passed before we took turns summarising our respective lives. It felt like what I imagined a CIA or MI-6 interrogation to be. I volunteered first.

"I'm almost fifty-two years old, freshly divorced after twenty-three years of marriage. I earned an ROTC scholarship to attend university in exchange for serving five years as a captain and helicopter pilot in the US army during the early 1980s. Armed with a BA and MA in history, I manage archives of businesses, government entities, prominent individuals and families, and non-profits. I've published several articles in professional history journals but nothing of great import. I wonder sometimes whether I'm half intelligent and half charlatan or completely incomprehensible. Anyway—I'm an avid runner. Like jazz. Enjoy good wine, single-malt Scotch and fish fresh from the sea. I'm disillusioned with America and Americans. Its foreign policy and desire to dominate has been defined for generations as sentimental idealism. And the average American, to my way of thinking, is an overripe, provincial bore. I try exceedingly hard to limit contact. They exasperate me. Difficult listening to anything they say. Let's see, what else? My parents are dead. My brother and I haven't spoken in eleven years. A great friend from army days died in a plane crash twelve years ago and my best friend in Seattle, an architect, has terminal cancer and isn't expected to live but a few years. So overall you'd probably consider me a depressing tale of woe. I call it life."

Amazing I could summarise an uneventful life so effortlessly. She took exception, however, to my self-pitying lament.

"That's a bit dour, don't you think?"

"I'm soured on life right now. Perhaps it will sweeten over time. So what about you, Miss Hawes?"

"Well, like you I enjoy jazz otherwise I wouldn't be here. I also enjoy running, but prefer long-distance walking – fifteen, twenty, thirty miles. A few years ago I walked the entire length of the River Thames. Fine art fascinates and relaxes me. My office is directly across the river from the Tate Britain so I visit sometimes during the infrequent lunch break. Just sit on a favourite white leather couch and admire the Lowry's. I've been with the Metropolitan Police for almost nineteen years or, as Americans understand it, Scotland Yard. I'm currently a detective with the child murder team. I joined when I was twenty. Having grown up in the north of England, which seemed a long way from the big city, I wanted desperately to escape, and the police force was exactly what I needed. I've had a few serious relationships. They went awry for various reasons, but all had something in common: none matched my expectation of what a relationship should be. I have two sisters. Julie is three years older and works as a cabin steward for British Airways – on long-haul flights. The other, Clare, is eight years younger and works as a primary school teacher in our hometown. Julie unfortunately was diagnosed with breast cancer four months ago. She's had two surgeries and receiving chemotherapy now. The prognosis looks good but one never knows. Funny, but before I joined—"

Perhaps a bit impertinently I interrupted, telling her I had battled cancer – testicular cancer – seventeen years earlier.

Caused by excessive exposure to high-frequency vibrations in the helicopter cockpit. In addition to an enjoyable eight weeks of chemo I had two surgeries, one to exact the tumour, the other that gutted me like a fish from underneath the sternum to below the navel. I felt suddenly that I had conveyed too much personal information.

"You probably didn't need to hear all that."

"Let me see your scar."

"See my scar?"

"Yes, let me see your scar."

"Here in the bar? At this table? With all these drunk people carousing around?"

"Of course, they're too focused on their drinks."

I surmised this woman was used to people lying or telling stories so I indulged her. I unbuttoned my blazer and lifted my shirt high above my chest. She took her index finger and followed the surgical zipper down to my navel. When finished, I dropped my shirt and tucked it into my trousers.

"They did slice you. Must have taken ages to heal."

"I was doubled-stitched so no air could escape! Before I interrupted, you were going to say that something was funny…?"

"Oh, yes, before I joined the police I taught pottery to teenagers at a Vermont summer camp. I really enjoyed it. The countryside, the kids, the camp environment. Fab. I took my first pottery class when I was four and continued until I left school at eighteen. It's something I've always liked and excelled. The freedom, the artistry and the oneness with nature. What's the ancient Greek concept, 'Earth, Fire, Air and Water'? That's me. When I retire from the Met – ah, Scotland Yard – I want to set up a pottery studio. Not necessarily as a business but in the guise of a struggling artist. Who knows, I probably *will* be struggling. Anyway, I remained in America and worked as a nanny for a couple with three children in Boston, close to Harvard. I enjoyed it. Met some great people. If I could have stayed I would have, but US visa restrictions prevented it."

It was getting quite late and, while I wanted to continue talking, I faced the reality of a day-long meeting beginning at 8-am. Sara pre-empted me fortunately. Jet lag had kicked in. She longed for her bed.

"Are you in town tomorrow night?"

"Oh, yeah, got a full day but I'll certainly return in the evening. It's my favourite Chicago haunt."

"So will I, as will three more detectives from the Met. They arrive late tomorrow afternoon. Would you want to meet up?"

"Sure, that would be fine. About 8-pm?"

Bundling up we braced for Chicago's cold and left Jilly's. Before entering the hotel, she paused and giggled a bit.

"Change of plans. I'll meet you at seven tomorrow morning at that restaurant – The Original Pancake House."

Her gloved finger pointed directly across the street to what resembled an oasis of 1950s America.

"Whaaaaat? Really? Okay. I'll be there, but I can't stay more than thirty minutes. My meeting begins at eight."

"Don't worry, I'll be waiting! Good night."

"See you in five hours."

I walked down Rush Street and turned right onto Michigan Avenue to face a headwind even polar bears would find challenging. I tilted my body forty-five degrees to minimise direct impact and made my way to the conference hotel on Wacker Drive. I slept like the dead.

Minutes later my alarm sounded. *Why did I set the thing so damn early? Oh, Christ, I promised that Brit I'd meet her at some pancake house at seven.* I limped out of bed, stumbled to the shower, dressed quickly and left the hotel. Realising I had about twenty-five minutes I decided to walk, hoping it would wake me and engage my legs in preparation for a day of immobility. When I arrived at The Original Pancake House my hair was frozen solid; tiny icicles dangled from curly hair follicles. As I entered only two tables were occupied, by a homeless woman and two Chicago Metropolitan Sewer workers. The ginger-haired, British lady I met last evening – Sara, I believe – was absent. Despite innate pessimism, I tried to remain optimistic and ordered a black coffee from an exceedingly nice, middle-aged woman whose uniform reflected those worn by waitresses in restaurants where my parents and I had celebrated birthdays and my infrequent stellar report cards from elementary school. As soon as she brought the coffee I cupped it between my cold hands. The warmth was immediate. Fifteen minutes passed and still no ginger-haired woman. Now I became angry. She made me drag my sorry ass out of bed, walk in extreme cold, order coffee in a Buddy Holly-like, throw-back restaurant and all to be the proverbial 'no-show'. *I won't have it*, mumbling to myself. *I'm going to drag this woman out of bed so, like me, she can experience early-morning Chicago.*

I told the waitress I'd return, only have to cross the street and see what's happened to the young lady I had promised to meet. I put a few dollars on the table to cover the coffee but reiterated I *would* return. I crossed the street, entered the Sutton Place Hotel and approached the desk clerk.

"Could you ring Miss Sara Hawes's room, please?"

After a few seconds' checking he informed me there was no guest registered in that name. I couldn't recall her friend's first name but vaguely remembered the last. "Well, then, perhaps it's under 'Cooke'. Could you try that?"

"Yes, she is a registered guest. Would you like me to ring?"

After a few rings I heard a muffled but inquisitive, "Hello?"

"Yes, sorry to wake you, but this is Edward Lee. I met you briefly last night. Is Sara around or has she left?"

Not receiving confirmation – one way or the other – she passed the phone, muttering, "It's that bloke you met last night."

Obviously startled and a bit embarrassed about not showing up, Sara apologised immediately.

"Give me five minutes. Let me comb my hair and throw water on my face."

I told her she wouldn't have difficulty finding me as there were only three others in the restaurant.

"Good, I'll surely find you. Brilliant."

I didn't know what part was 'brilliant', being late or that there were only three customers. I returned to my table whereupon the proficient waitress poured another piping-hot cup of coffee. This time Sara did not disappoint. She entered from the side entrance but looked bewildered and stopped a passing waitress. The waitress pointed towards me.

Sara sauntered over.

"Lord, I forgot my spectacles. Stupid. I have poor distance vision, but here I am finally. How are you, Edward? Again, I'm sorry for not being on time. It's not like me at all."

I liked how she enunciated 'all': sounded like a heavily accented 't' followed by a lengthy 'allllll' and ending with a distinctive 'ahl', all in quick succession. My dutiful waitress approached and poured us coffee. Sara ordered a cheese omelette – as if she had preconfigured it in her mind – but because I only had about ten minutes remaining I stuck with coffee.

"So what was it about Bush unilaterally invading another country?"

Not waiting for a response, she interjected as to not give me too big a cow pad to chew on.

"Blair wasn't any better. Awful, simply awful. And, of course, now Obama's been elected… thank goodness!"

She paused, and as her lips touched the rim of the coffee cup, she looked at me as if seeking confirmation.

"Well, it was the complete manifestation of America's arrogance of power. I was against it and will remain so unless historians, decades from now, prove it the right course. I doubt they will. Bush, Cheney, Rumsfeld and company squandered whatever universal goodwill America had garnered after 9/11. I doubt it will return in my lifetime. It took two decades to recover from the Vietnam debacle and now Iraq. The situation is beyond depressing. Enough to drive one to drink. A vice, you may have noticed, I've embraced without qualms. Senator Robert Byrd's speech to the Senate the day before the invasion was unforgettable. It's the most impassioned but melancholy speech I have heard a politician deliver. He chastised the Senate for abrogating its duty to the American people by not openly debating the issue. He lamented that the cherished image of America as a 'benevolent peacekeeper' was gone. I've memorised his parting comment: 'America's friends mistrust us, our word is disputed and our intentions are questioned.' Pretty powerful, I thought. His tone had a genuine sense of foreboding. And it has all come to pass, I fear."

"What do you think of Obama? Can he change the dynamic?"

"Oh, I absolutely love him! I voted for him. I'll never forget the first time I heard him speak. He was running for a US Senate seat in Illinois and gave the keynote address at the 2004 Democratic Convention. The keynote sets the tone for the whole convention, the nominee and the ensuing campaign. I was riveted. It was so emotional. And I remember thinking, *This guy will be a contender in the future. He'll run for president in ten or fifteen years.* Well, Sara, I was partially correct... I wish him well, but the ugliness of American racism will raise its ugly head. It's our original sin, you know."

"I don't understand America's race problem. What does the colour of a person's skin have to do with competency?"

"It doesn't obviously, but America – even during the colonial period of British rule – found it easy to rationalise black inferiority and institutionalise slavery. Many don't realise that Britain controlled the colonies for over 150 years. Even the French had imposed slavery in Louisiana prior to American purchasing the land from Napoleon in the early 1800s. And, of course, throughout the Antebellum Era the South articulated a variety of spurious reasons to justify slavery. It came to head in 1861. To my way of thinking, the American Civil War was the child of slavery."

"Well, Edward, to be honest I'm not too familiar with American history, but I am smart enough to realise the issue and many others are complex and have deep and conflicting roots."

"You're right. When you think you understand an issue or the motivations of a government something happens. What you once believed is no longer credible. I'd have to say, prior to 9/11 most Americans liked and respected Blair. He was articulate and smart. He and Clinton saw eye-to-eye on many international issues. But when he threw in with Bush, I and millions of others were struck dumb. I don't know if their relationship was forged by some pseudo-religious fundamentalism or what, but it was distressing to say the least. Interesting you keep asking about current events. Not exactly something one discusses in 'polite company'. Are you interested in politics and foreign affairs, Sara?"

"Oh, yeah, always have been… and we haven't even touched the economic collapse. One of my A Levels in senior school was contemporary politics. I wanted to gauge your knowledge level. I know this sounds presumptuous, but most Americans are not too interested in current affairs. To be blunt, they're pretty damn ignorant. Haven't determined if this is caused by arrogance or genuine disinterest. I cannot judge an entire nation by the action or inaction of the few hundred I've met but... well, at least that's been my experience. Maybe I'll tell you my 'American experience' when I worked in Bosnia for the UN a few years ago. It made my head spin."

Deep in conversation, I'd forgotten the time. It was 7:45! I had fifteen minutes before the meeting started. As I stood to leave the waitress arrived with Sara's omelette – the largest I had seen east of the Mississippi River – it filled the entire plate. Sara looked shocked while uttering a boisterous, "Lorrrrrd, I'll never finish this!" Wrestling to put on my coat and hat, I reconfirmed with Sara we'd meet around eight. I placed a few more dollars on the table and left. Knowing I'd never make it across the Chicago River in fifteen minutes, I hailed a cab. Being so early on a Saturday morning, traffic was non-existent on Michigan Avenue. I arrived at Wacker Drive with four minutes to spare. I entered the conference room, slumped into an uncomfortable dinner chair and hunkered down for a nine-hour meeting with a bevy of self-absorbed archivists.

The meeting adjourned around 5:30-pm. Several committee members asked if I'd join them for dinner but I declined. I had liquidated my 'be nice and show an interest' quota hours earlier and decided, before returning to Jilly's as promised, I'd eat dinner at what arguably is the finest seafood restaurant in the Midwest – Shaw's Crab House. I found a seat in the bustling cocktail lounge facing the raw bar. The original décor dating from the 1930s was tattered but genuine. The New Orleans-type trio playing trad jazz standing off to one side added authenticity. The universality of 'Jelly Roll' Morton's 'Black Bottom Stomp' and 'King' Oliver's 'Speakeasy Blues' couldn't be denied. And, of course, Hemingway's quote from *A Moveable Feast*, handwritten on a small chalkboard suspended from a wall – "*As I ate the oysters with their strong taste of the sea and their faint metallic taste that the cold white wine washed away, leaving only the sea taste and the succulent texture…*" – enhanced the realism. My food choices may have disappointed Papa – iceberg lettuce with blue cheese dressing, grilled rainbow trout almandine with horseradish potatoes and French beans, and a Midwest-sized slice of Key lime pie – but he would have liked the wine: a 1999 Sancerre, full bottle.

Emboldened by the festive atmosphere and warmed by the wine, I paid the bill and made my way past the Wrigley Building, heading north on Michigan Avenue towards Rush Street. I arrived the smoke-filled Jilly's a few minutes after eight. True to her word Sara was sitting at a tall table against the right-hand side wall. I approached her, unsure of my intentions.

She introduced the fresh arrivals from London who, like Sara, occupied tables set strategically against the wall so they could survey the crowd. I asked what they had done since arriving in the 'Windy City'. Not much, it turned out. They only had registered and went immediately to dinner with Sara and Helen at the Cape Cod Room in the Drake Hotel.

"Ah, quite a Chicago institution. It's been around since Prohibition. I think Joe DiMaggio and Marilyn Monroe carved their initials in the bar when they dined there after getting married."

I stopped when I realised I was boring them. Monroe they could grasp, but not 'Joltin' Joe. I changed course and, to create an air of familiarity, shared stories of London. Despite redirecting the conversation, their demeanour indicated they sought a contemporary establishment – traditional jazz and big band swing bored them. On immediate reflection, however, I thought it may have been prearranged for Helen to depart with the girls in tow so Sara and I could be alone. I wished them an enjoyable time. The chubbier lady leaned towards Sara and, unaware I could hear, whispered softly, "He's gorgeous." If Sara replied, I couldn't hear the response. I took Helen's seat directly across from Sara and surveyed the room for a waitress. We needed a drink.

Forgetting where we left our earlier discussion, Sara wanted an explanation of what an archivist and historian did exactly. She had never met one before.

"Most are frustrated, non-PhD historians. We love history, want to practise it professionally but for reasons involving brains, finances, courage or a combination of all three, failed to follow through to completion, to earn a doctorate and find a university teaching position. An archivist is the gatekeeper of history, so to speak, who decides what is kept and what is discarded. The process is deliberately slow. It is a responsible vocation if taken seriously. As I used to say to potential volunteers: at its base the work amounts to hours upon hours of tedious boredom separated by minutes of pure ecstasy."

"Sounds a bit saucy."

"That was my intention. Exactly. You're paying attention. As my boss at the Historical Society often said, 'I can't believe I pay you to read other people's mail.' I love it nonetheless because when the collection is finished you're the acknowledged expert about a person, event, institution or business. Then comes the challenge of delving into the nitty-gritty, making the collection relevant – curating an exhibit, publishing a scholarly article or, in some cases, a book. It's a solitary vocation. You must be disciplined, self-motivated and focused on completing the work. If you're easily distracted then it…"

Suddenly a squatty man wearing a moth-eaten tweed cap approached and mumbled to Sara. I didn't understand what he asked but I heard her reply:

"Oh, yes, I'll be here most of the evening. I'm enjoying it. Love the music."

I didn't like his looks. He'd been drinking too much and talked how I imagined a 1930s gangster sounded – with a mouth full of marbles. As 'Begin the Beguine' started I asked Sara if she cared to dance.

Once on the floor Sara leaned towards me.

"By the end of the evening..." Then someone bumped me and apologised, but during that brief break in conversation I wondered what Sara was going to propose. I turned back around so Sara could finish her thought.

"By the end of the evening I am going to get that man's tweed cap. I want it!"

I laughed but didn't know what to think. A Scotland Yard detective 'stealing' a stranger's tweed cap? Surely, I thought, she's joking. If successful and he wasn't thrilled with her conquest, we'd be found the next morning floating in the numbingly cold Chicago River. Well preserved but dead.

As we made our way off the dance floor and through the crowd, I felt an urge to touch her waist. The smoke-filled room and her bulky winter clothing partly obscured what I presumed to be elegant curves. I placed both hands on her hips. She didn't recoil. We returned to our seats to find our newly ordered drinks as well as the man with the tweed cap. Perhaps he was a former Chicago gangster whose bullying days had passed. He seemed infatuated with Sara and was not going away. Maybe she reminded him of Rita Hayworth or another red-headed siren from long ago. His motivations were difficult to read. His speech challenging to understand. And, of course, his persistent hovering motivated Sara only further to acquire the coveted tweed cap.

Whether pre-planned or a spontaneous thought, Sara asked 'tweed cap man' to dance with one condition: she could wear and keep his cap. He uttered a barely audible, "Yes," whereupon they proceeded to the dance floor. I watched incredulously as Sara placed the cap on her head and twirled the little man like a falling maple leaf seed to Sinatra's 'You Make Me Feel So Young.' Sara had made his evening. The dance over, he escorted her to the table, kissed her cheek, shook my hand, bowed gently and left. Because of the way he walked around the bar, I thought he might pursue other young women, but he didn't. I watched as he pulled a huge, half-smoked stogy from his pocket and put it in his mouth prior to greeting the Chicago winter… without his tweed cap.

Flushed with success and feeling confident, Sara showed me the estate agent brochure on a cottage she wanted to buy. She hoped to close the deal in a month. It was of waddle and daub construction built in 1490 and located in a quaint village alongside the River Darent seventeen miles outside London. It had an open-hearth fireplace, a low entry door and incredibly low ceilings on the ground floor. She'll have to stoop low to enter the place, I thought, but it looked cosy. It seemed quintessentially English to a foreigner. And to think it was constructed two years before Columbus discovered the 'New World' enhanced its mystic. I told her I was delivering a conference paper on British author Robert Graves at St Johns College, Oxford, in July and, if possible, would like to check out her 'new' house. She responded, "Yes, why not?" but I detected more doubt than certainty. Nevertheless, she suggested we exchange emails and home addresses. She provided her current address as well as the potential new address without any prodding. I felt good. I had made a new acquaintance, someone to commensurate with as I rebuilt my life.

When the bartender announced last call, Sara and I decided we'd have one final drink in her hotel lobby. She approached the head bartender on the way out and handed him the tweed cap.

"There was short, bald, older man who, I'm sorry to say, resembles a 1930s gangster with whom I was talking and unfortunately left his cap. Is there any chance you might know him and keep it until he returns?"

The bartender looked at Sara.

"Oh, that must be Guido's. Sure, I'll see him again. He's a regular. You're spot on about the gangster description. Don't apologise. He spent ten years in Joliet for money laundering, resisting arrest and felonious assault."

We didn't bundle up, just darted around the corner and into Sara's hotel. The barman seemed irritated we ordered a drink, but Sara was a guest so he had little choice. Sara modelled her newly purchased winter boots that extended to just below the knee. She propped her right foot on the edge of the glass table and asked my opinion. What else could I say but, "Nice." Their thick construction prevented me from determining her ankle width, something most women would argue to be the typical pursuit of a shallow man. We finished our drinks after the barman informed us he was closing for the evening. Because it was 2-am, Sara and I agreed to say goodbye. Her flight wasn't until early evening so she could sleep late and Christmas shop with friends. I had a noon departure so I'd have to rise early. I followed her to the elevator. I had to think quickly. I liked this woman. She was humorous, intelligent, attractive and might have more to offer. I'd see her again hopefully – perhaps in July – so I didn't want to spoil the past two evenings. After pressing the elevator button she turned around. I shook her hand and, in the customary European manner, kissed both cheeks.

"Sara, it has been enjoyable. Thank you for making what promised to be an abominable Chicago weekend so memorable. I hope your friends enjoyed it and that America, despite its propensity for noise and hype, was hospitable. Have a safe flight home and good luck with the home purchase. I'll be in touch."

"Thank you, Edward, for being a perfect host, especially after I pressed you into service. I'll think about summer. Perhaps we could meet."

She entered the elevator and, before the door closed, turned around, waved and smiled. She was gone. Her response left me flummoxed. Did it reflect acute interest or benign politeness?

TWO

SEATTLE

I RETURNED FROM CHICAGO the following day to find my condo unit intact – except the shared closets. When I discovered in June my wife had been involved with a younger man for the previous nine months, I asked her to leave. I started divorce proceedings immediately. Bizarrely she left a full wardrobe – perhaps angling for reconciliation or hoping I'd transfer condo ownership as a reward for bad behaviour. Maybe he had splurged on an entirely new wardrobe. Who knew? Whatever the reason I felt it an imposition. I presented an ultimatum of sorts prior to departing for Chicago: if the clothes weren't gone by my return, I'd donate the lot to a woman's charity. It worked. Not a trace remained. The clothes of a forty-seven-year-old woman had vanished.

After twenty-three years I was on my own. I canvased the 885 square foot unit, loosened my tie, lit a cathedral candle, dimmed the lights and keyed-up Miles Davis's album *Kind of Blue* – specifically the track titled 'So What'. Partly as a sign of newly acquired independence and perhaps as a form of adolescent revenge directed towards someone who never appreciated the essence of American jazz. I poured a neat, single-malt Scotch and eased into my mohair club chair. I needed to replan my life. Her deceptiveness was a contemplative infidelity, not an irrational whim. What I thought stable had collapsed. My nostalgic continuity for the past had clashed with the realistic uncertainty of the present. I had entangled myself too deeply with ideas of how life ought to be. I needed to jettison these saccharine platitudes and accept life as it is. It was a new era with different problems to which I lacked answers. And I was damn sure I didn't know the questions. But I was certain of a few things. I didn't need anyone. I didn't want anyone. I longed to be alone and, cautious not to offend anyone, thought it best to ration public interactions. Aloneness can be highly stimulating, I thought. I loved my bookish, bucolic and solitary lifestyle. I had no desire to prove my masculinity despite friends admonishing me that, *It's the twenty-first-century, Edward*. Sod them, I thought – nothing but an excuse for bad behaviour. And besides, cancer had culled me a bit as if punishment for some past indiscretion. This inadequacy also offered opportunity. What I had fantasised about for decades as improbable now seemed possible. I began to appreciate how setbacks often contained the seeds of their own reversal.

In the passing days I reorganised my flat, discarded old photos, reviewed correspondence and trashed or donated to charity duplicative household items. The selfish experience proved enlightening, enabling me to prioritise and to redefine what was important – not to society, not to deceased parents, not to a disinterested brother, not to a non-existent partner but to me alone. While conducting this emotional cleansing I uncovered a dozen or so postcards my grandfather had written during the Great War. I had discovered them at the bottom of his army footlocker years earlier when my parents and I were reorganising my grandmother's apartment after her death. Finding them of historical and personal interest I had stashed them – uncharacteristically for an archivist – into an unlabelled, acidic folder and forgot about them. I opened the yellowed folder and began reading. Most of the sepia-coloured cards depicted images in the small French country town of Mussidan in Bordeaux. On the top of one card showing Mussidan's main street my grandfather, Clifford, had written: *X marks where I was standing when I heard the Armistice had been signed, 11 Nov 18. Reached Mussidan about two o'clock.* The message provided little additional insight other than predicting logistical manoeuvrings planned for the coming months. He signed off in what I discovered later was his characteristic salutation, offering love to his wife, Josephine, and his mother. I thought it important historically and only could imagine how local villagers reacted. I wondered also about my grandfather's feelings that afternoon and whether he celebrated into the early morning. Knowing the American army, his unit probably was restricted to camp, unable to revel with locals. Towards the bottom of the stack were two postcards with images not from France, Germany or England but from the Greek village of Fiskardo, Cephalonia, dated 28 June and 6 August 1919. Not exactly a characteristic location, I thought, for the demobilisation of an American soldier.

One of these sepia images consisted of a panoramic view of a romantic-looking fishing village consisting of about seventeen homes nestled in a pristine cove. The other depicted two homes, one bordered the water with a fishing boat moored parallel to it with a second home immediately behind. The area looked sparsely populated and economically poor. My grandfather's message on the first card indicated he and Stavros had arrived safely in Fiskardo. *The weather is exceedingly hot and the smell of fresh fish magnificently pungent*, my grandfather wrote. *Having a relaxing time. Stavros's family has made me welcomed. Visited the ruins of a sixth-century Christian Basilica. Love to you, Josephine, and to Mother.* The second postcard from August offered a scant more information. *Stavros's father took us fishing in the Ionian Sea. Greek people wonderfully friendly. Food different but fresh. Wish I could remain but have orders to Le Havre. Hopefully I'll return one day. Stavros and I won't forget our shared war experiences. Will remain friends. Your Yank is coming home. Love to Jo and to Mother.* I wondered how the fishing village looked today. Had cookie-cutter resorts proliferated and transitioned it into a tourist mecca, or had it remained largely underpopulated and unspoiled? I wanted to explore further.

Suddenly the phone rang.

"RESPECT."

"Fritzy! How the hell are you? Damn, great hearing your voice. Sure, I can attend a seminar this evening. Fontana, table eleven at eight. Not a problem. See you then."

It was my good friend and 'adopted' older brother, Chris Sunderland, who, when together, preferred his porn name, 'Fritz Skyline'. My porn name was 'Buttons Cottonwood' – derived from the name of your first pet followed by the name of the street in which you grew-up – I answered to it but used it less frequently than Fritzy. He had business cards printed which he'd drop in the proverbial fishbowl at restaurants and retail stores hoping to win free meals or gifts. Chris loved when they'd call asking to speak to 'Mr Fritz Skyline'. He found little difficulty keeping a straight face throughout the conversation. A skill, I thought, unmatched in the annals of comedic hucksterism.

I walked down Second Avenue to Blanchard and into the courtyard of Fontana where I saw Fritzy's thirty-year-old bike leaning against the iron fence next to the fountain. As usual he had arrived early. His wife, Eleanor, to whom he had been married for over twenty years, had suffered a sudden stroke a few years earlier and died. A classically trained harpist, she performed regularly with the Kamuela Philharmonic on the Big Island (Hawaii). Fritzy was devastated and hunkered down in complete isolation for eight months. When he emerged he appeared gaunt and undernourished. His deep, emotional void has not been filled by anyone new.

As I crossed the threshold the owner, Gian Carlo, greeted and showed me – as if I needed to know – the way to table eleven. Chris promptly stood up and offered his trademarked hug, first a firm handshake followed by a pull towards him and a heartfelt embrace. Such an act wasn't given freely. He reserved it for a select few. I felt fortunate. The tragedy of life, I thought, was nothing existed in pure form. Even personal friendships often were blurred by competitiveness and insecurity; however, with Fritzy it was genuine. It was pure. Chris had ordered the wine already and poured me a full glass of Montepulciano. Some might have been offended they had not been consulted about the selection, but not me. Fritzy had developed a theory that house wines of private/family restaurants always would be good. It had to be. They could not risk offering poor quality. I tried his theory a few times and, sure enough, he was correct. Best of all: house wines usually were the cheapest.

Despite fighting lung cancer he looked well. His lanky frame remained firmly upright. His eyes sparkled and he hadn't lost what I called his 'shit-ass grin'. Chemo treatments hadn't taken their toll… yet. His salt-and-pepper hair was thinning but intact, remaining wiry and wild. His breathing had improved, enabling him to take a flight of stairs with minimal difficulty. He confessed regular afternoon naps had become *de rigueur*; in fact, they were indispensable. He had completed negotiations recently for designing a medium-size condo on Queen Anne Hill that he was excited about. Chris admitted, somewhat sheepishly, that his architectural assistant would perform a majority of the design work. He took a sip of wine and as he placed the glass on the table his eyes covered over. Here was a man who understood the tentativeness of life. He might never see the project completed.

He adjusted his steel-rimmed glasses.

"Okay, Buttons, fill me in on Chicago. Was it as bad as you had anticipated?"

I bored him with a few archival topics, transitioning quickly to events at Jilly's. I told him about meeting Sara Hawes, our interesting discussions and late nights. He thought it fine but didn't see it as viable. Long-distance relationships worked in movies, theatres and literature, but real life imposed countless obstacles.

"Couldn't agree more, Fritzy. I like being alone. I enjoy my own company and have no wish to become involved with a woman who is twelve years younger and eight time zones ahead of me. Nonetheless, with Christmas approaching I may wish her well on the impending house move. She has no one and neither do I. That's not a big commitment, is it?"

"Suit yourself, Buttons, but be careful. You are emotionally vulnerable and ripe for sinking into a relationship where pain will be your best friend. You own your pad, are debt-free, right?"

I nodded plaintively, realising the chaser was about to come.

"You need to travel someplace you've never been – preferably warm – soak up the sun, get your nob worked on, overindulge, enjoy life and remain flexible. Be free for once in your God-damn, overly disciplined, predetermined life. Take a bite out of the ass of life, for Christ's sake!"

He wasn't finished. It seems years earlier in the summer of 1969 when he was a senior at university his girlfriend decided the gig was up. A budding architect would not provide the excitement she craved. Chris was devastated. Fortunately he heard about an outdoor concert being held in a few weeks near Woodstock, New York, so he headed across country in his VW van. There he joined the other 399,999 people intent on defining their generation. He remembered hearing Richie Havens, Joan Baez and CCR but couldn't recall listening to Crosby, Stills, Nash & Young or Joe Cocker. To this day he couldn't understand why – too much marijuana, not enough sleep or his befriending a senior from Brown University. Whatever the reason, he and the Brown co-ed left the concert together and departed for Greece.

"It sounds cliché now but I found myself during those six weeks in Greece. It wasn't the sex with Charmaine – Charmaine Silver, God she was highly polished sterling – although that was damn good. And it wasn't the intensity of our shared newness. It was the country, the people, the sun, the blue sea and the antiquarian isolation. Greece's beaches were fantastic but if you wanted to get naked, which Charmaine and I did regularly, you are relegated to using an unwelcoming coastline. But I must say, Buttons, the ruggedness enhanced the sex. It helped feed a selfish delusion whenever she became boisterous. I couldn't decipher whether she enjoyed our romp or was a cragged rock jabbing her hip or shoulder blade. Hard to believe now, I know, but I was too shy to ask which it was. But Greece to me was, well... as if I had returned home and knew it for the first time. You're an historian, Buttons, care to hear my take on modern Greek history?"

"Fritzy, I always enjoy your thoughts… they're enlightening, provocative and even entertaining sometimes."

"Don't, Buttons, you'll get me excited. May I continue, please? The loveliness of the people belies the trouble modern Greece has experienced since the 1821 revolution. While the people lean towards being classically romantic, sustained economic difficulties, dependency on foreign powers for defence and security, and pervasive political corruption conspires regularly against the people. I won't even touch the difficulties it's had with monarchs and church hierarchy. Perhaps that's why Greeks are friendly to foreigners; they recognise the potential of mankind, though they've experienced it only marginally. I don't know, Buttons, I muse often about Greece. The cradle of ancient democracy is a conundrum. Always in a state of flux but always deeply profound."

I couldn't believe the coincidence. I told Chris how I had rediscovered my grandfather's postcards from the Great War and thought seriously about taking a trip in late spring to the fishing village he had visited before returning to America. He affirmed my idea.

"You will receive more in return from Greece than you'll give."

"Any idea whatever happened to Charmaine? Did you remain in contact?"

"We wrote each other for several years. And then her conventional life became unconventional. She moved to Greece after earning her master's in Ancient History. Within a year she became the curator of jewellery at the Archaeological Museum of Thessaloniki. Then unconventionality slipped in. She met a Greek guy who worked as a cabin boy on a yacht belonging to a shipping tycoon. You know, the clandestine-type one reads about in *Vanity Fair*. Anyway, Charmaine quit the museum job to be welcomed aboard as manager of the ship's bar. She and the cabin boy married eventually. The last I heard – and this was several years ago – they still were sailing the Mediterranean and managing about fifty yachts for the same tycoon who, I'm guessing, must be quite elderly. Envisage an old-age composite of Anthony Quinn and Aristotle Onassis."

"You've got to admire her risk-taking. Bet a book is demanding to be written."

"Knowing Charmaine, it'll be a humdinger and then some."

After another hour Gian Carlo brought the bill and a half bottle of Vin Santo – on the house – facilitating an easy transition to deeper conversation. This kind gesture enabled me to focus on Chris. Make him the subject.

"You remind me of my father, Fritzy, in the stoic but brave way you're handling illness. No complaining. No anger. No bitterness. If I possess half that character I will judge myself a success. I don't know who but someone once said, *A person finds their true character when they stare into the abyss.* Well, by God, you are and you've found it!"

"Thank you. That means a lot. I remember from previous table eleven seminars how much you respected your father. I don't have any examples as you know from which to seek inspiration. My grandfather – the governor of Rhode Island – was killed in a plane crash. My dad dropped dead in the office and my mother decided to 'check out' – no note, no sign, no anything. So I'm kinda left approaching death as part of life's adventure. Who knows, it might be exciting. In some bizarre way I'm looking forward to it. I'll try and give you some kind of sign, so pay attention. Can't promise, of course, but I'll certainly try and blow as many notes as I can from Gabriel's horn. It won't be ecclesiastical, probably more like Miles Davis's pre-acid days."

Chris and I thought it time to leave when the kitchen staff joined Gian Carlo in the adjacent dining room. After he unlocked his bike he turned and hugged me in true Fritzy style.

"Enjoyable, as always, Buttons. We must do it again between Christmas and New Year. Promise? And think about what we've discussed. I won't exit until I know you're on the 'road less travelled.'"

"If that's the prerequisite, Fritzy, then by God, it will take decades to find that path! And, yes, let's meet up again before 2008 belongs in the history books."

I watched as he put on his black beret, mounted his bike and coasted down to First Avenue. A dense fog had moved in over Elliott Bay engulfing the grey city, muffling all noise except the mist hitting my spectacles. I turned and walked towards Second Avenue thinking of the future – his and mine. I knew how I wanted to live life; I just wasn't doing it. I needed to vanquish all vestiges of idealism and emerge on the other side as a man without beliefs. Inhabit a life void of illusion. As I poured myself a Scotch, lit a candle, keyed-up Art Blakey's 'Moanin' and slumped into my favourite chair, I realised Fritzy had encapsulated my problem perfectly. The past had been blasted to hell. It was gone. Not only was the old order not idyllic, it was dead. A significant portion of my life had turned out to be something entirely different from what I had thought. It had been a fraud. I had been a fraud. I needed to kick over my tiresome house of life and become what I had wanted to be all along: unconventional. But could I? This internal conflict – the proverbial battle within – remained a contentious but potent force. As I finished my drink the view from the window had become obscured by total whiteout. To maintain level flight in my army days I would have transitioned immediately to instruments. Perhaps my personal life had reached a similar crossroads. Should I proceed without a plan and fly simply by instinct – by the seat-of-my-pants – or should I use instruments, guaranteeing a safe but predictable course as I had done throughout life? It was a queer time.

THREE

SEATTLE

A FEW DAYS BEFORE Christmas I sent Sara an email thanking her for 'pressing me into service' and transforming my Chicago weekend. I wished her luck with closing on the fifteenth-century cottage. It was returned immediately: 'undeliverable'. I verified the address. I had entered it correctly. Tried again. Bounced back. I became disappointed and agitated simultaneously. She had played me. Her response beside the hotel elevator had reflected nothing except British politeness. In my prior life I would have left it alone and moved on, but life wasn't the same now. I needed to handle it differently. Her tactic – if that's what it was – could be countered. If I had thought about it longer, I would have realised I was reacting – over-reacting actually – to how my ex had dismissed me. It wasn't anything Sara had done. I certainly wasn't close to the girl. I didn't know her. Why was I upset? As I told Chris a week before, I don't mind being alone. I enjoyed my company. If true, why the hell was I concerned if a woman ten thousand miles away purposely gave an incorrect email address? Was I that crushingly insecure, desperate for female companionship, or just scarred by events? Too much in a hurry to see if women found me appealing, or simply an immature way of proving masculine relevancy? That was her choice if she didn't want to keep in contact… fine, but whatever the reason, I wanted to hear the rejection outright. At a minimum I needed to read it on paper or view it on a screen. She should be confronted. As I made abundantly clear in Chicago, I only had time for truth.

I accessed the Metropolitan Police's website. Fortunately it provided a general number. Taking into account the eight-hour time difference I waited until 3-am PST. After two rings I got through. I explained my situation. The directory listed two Sara Hawes: one in finance, the other in SCD-5. I asked if SCD-5 was the child murder team. The operator confirmed it was. He put me through. The phone rang once.

"Yes. Sara works in this department, but she's in the canteen having coffee with an associate. Can I take a message?"

I had to make a decision. Do I weasel-out as I would have done in my prior life or do I act aggressively the way I needed to be today, now, at this instant?

"Yes, Sir. My name is Edward Lee from Seattle, Washington in the States. I have been trying to contact Sara but the email address she provided bounces back."

"Certainly, Mr Lee. Not a problem. I'll make sure Sara receives it. She should return shortly."

I had hedged my bets and shifted responsibility to her. She needed to know I had tried to make contact but didn't want to appear desperate. I did not leave a phone number. It was up to her to make contact. I considered no response a response, too.

I woke a few hours later and checked email. I had received

a brief response: *I know you have been trying to email. I am just sending a short message to see if I can get it to work. I am out of the office all afternoon but if you can email back I will be able to reply tomorrow. Hope all is well. Sara*

Good, I thought; her response indicated a smidgen-sized desire for contact. More revealing, however, was the address was slightly different from what she had provided in Chicago. Had no idea if this was intentional but she had responded so, after resending my message, I slouched contentedly into my comfortable chair, threw a Pendleton blanket over me and fell asleep.

Mixing insecurity with stubbornness had paid off. In the coming days I received an eclectic array of messages from Sara: her house purchase was progressing nicely; her job interview for a new assignment went exceedingly well; and, she remained opened to an early summer visit. *I would like to see you and I hope we will be great friends. I'll think about the spring and let you know.*

I was unprepared for the straightforward answer. What really surprised me, however, was the message she sent three days before Christmas. Sara not only wished me – as the only other person she knew spending it alone – a 'Merry Christmas', but thought it good to chat before she visited her parents in the north.

Since Sara suggested a phone conversation I decided I should be the one to pay for it. We arranged a convenient time and, unlike the email gaff, the number was correct including the international codes. We chatted for one hour and forty-seven minutes about everything that mattered and anything else that didn't. I remember it as one of the finest Christmas presents I ever had received. After we hung up I realised something exciting might emerge... something exciting – however temporary – might emerge.

Barely a week into the New Year Sara emailed suggesting instead of waiting until June or July we meet sometime in March, perhaps in New York City. *I wasn't dismissing the visit to the UK at all. I just thought it might be good to visit some jazz venues in NY. I'm free from 11 – 21 March and was thinking about booking three nights, as I can always amuse myself for a bit depending when you will be about. Let me know your thoughts. Oh, by the way, I'm out with a friend to celebrate her thirty-fifth birthday. I might possibly be home by 10-pm which, I think, is lunchtime for you. If I'm not too inebriated I may try to call. What I am saying, in fact, is if I am drunk I am guaranteed to try to call. Speak later, Sara.*

While excited about possibly meeting three to four months early, a sense of concerned unease came over me. Perhaps I had misread her tone of voice by the elevator. What I had concluded after the wrong email issue as benign politeness may, in fact, had been acute interest. If true, why change the venue to America? Why move the date forward? Was she hiding something and, if so, what? Was she married? Was she living with another guy? Was she a lesbian or perhaps a bisexual? What was her motivation? I couldn't excise these colourful if perverse thoughts from my mind. It had been a quarter century since I had dallied with women and was confident the parameters had been revolutionised in my absence.

By the end of January we had organised the New York meeting, four days and three nights. On an earlier business trip to the city I had walked by a boutique hotel called The Library and thought if not on business it would be a wonderful place to stay – small, unique, perfectly located and reasonably affordable. Each floor was dedicated to a particular literature genre – mystery, fiction, biography, art and design, even erotica. I forwarded Sara the information. And I decided simultaneously to crack the puritanical shell in which I had lived my entire adult life: would she share a room? I received a reply two days later. *I like the idea of The Library. I will have another look and let you know; as you said, getting flights sorted is the main thing.* A non-definitive response, for sure, but as innocently immature as my request appeared, asking a pseudo-stranger to share a hotel room for three nights equated to breaking the rules of a lifetime to make different ones for a new life. Eight days passed before she responded. She titled the email 'The Library', and as I clicked on the message I thought I may have overreached. *Edward, I have thought about it and... yes, okay, let's book The Library, why not. I am not sure I am the easiest person to share a room with but you will see. I do tend to prowl about in the night and I don't sleep well but I will try to behave – a few Jack Daniels should knock me out.*

Well, I'll be damned. To use Chris's – and Robert Frost's – phraseology, I had taken my first steps on the road less travelled. Nothing serious needed to emerge from this relationship. I expected nothing. I was content solely because it was different – intellectually and culturally. How many American men had a female friend in a foreign country? She laughed differently. She smelled differently. She turned a phrase differently. Most importantly, she expressed a joy of life far removed from the tiresome triteness of American women. Perhaps she'd repair my damaged psyche and reignite my physical legitimacy.

Business required a trip to New York City in early February, so I took full advantage of the opportunity: researching restaurants, jazz clubs, bars and museum exhibitions we could visit. I found myself in the Blue Bar at the Algonquin Hotel the evening before returning to Seattle. The hotel's resident cat sat on the last stool at the bar so I decided to keep him company and sat at the table immediately facing him. I disregarded the five-hour time difference and updated Sara on my findings.

She answered the phone sleepily but after a few seconds came around to a pseudo-cognitive state.

"I hope you don't mind, Sara, but I did a little pre-planning."

"It's 3:15 in the morning. Couldn't you have waited until at least half three?"

I didn't know if she was serious so I waited for the full onslaught. It never came.

"Go ahead, darling, I'm propped-up, covered-up and eager to hear your thoughts."

Her statement was laden with words that kept my mine occupied long after I hung up.

"Well, for a fancy night out I made a reservation at the Carlyle Hotel to hear Jane Monheit, a young jazz standards singer. It's a small, intimate dinner setting – maybe fifty seats max, very 1930s. She's popular, so I took the initiative and made reservations. If disappointed, let me know and I'll cancel. It's my treat, kind of a payback for asking me to sit at your table at Jilly's. How does that sit with you?"

"I'm not familiar with her but it sounds brilliant. Provides the perfect excuse to buy a new frock. Go on then."

"Well, I visited the Lever House restaurant located in a classic modernist building constructed in 1952. While appearing a bit avant-garde, it could be an intimate place for a leisurely lunch, after the 'ladies who luncheon' and the business moguls have departed. I also found a small French brasserie on Madison Avenue – The Crocodile – that looks fabulous."

"A bit of Paris in New York. Brilliant."

"I found some quaint bars, most of which are inside hotels. Bemelmans Bar in the Carlyle looks fantastic, dark amber tones, expensive but pure class. And the King Cole Bar at the St Regis is, well, a place, I'm sure Zelda and Scott frequented."

"With all this reconnaissance activity and reminiscing about your Jazz Age friends, did you find time to attend any business meetings?"

"Burned it at both ends, Sara. Damp moss will never grow on my ass."

"That offers a visual. I like what I'm imagining."

After we said our goodbyes I ordered another dry martini. The black cat, whose name the bartender told me was Bix Beiderbecke, hadn't moved. His sleekness and pomposity melded perfectly with the room's ambiance. The only improvement would be if his green eyes were blue.

I sent Sara an apologetic email before going to bed. *So sorry I woke you, but I knew with my impending schedule next week I would not have a chance any other time and I didn't want you to think I was ignoring you. You sounded sleepy – rightfully so – but you recovered nicely. Impressive… sorry, 'Bloody Yanks'.*

When I woke the following morning Sara had replied. *Just remembered that's the second time you have woken me up — long may it continue. No problem at all. I'll get my own back in NYC. X*

During my flight home I contemplated Sara's comment when we spoke in the Blue Bar. Referring to me as 'darling', as well as her 'eagerness' to hear potential plans for our New York City rendezvous, made me smile. The 'X' after her signature confused me. What did that mean? While our innocent banter may have reflected a developing relationship, I was old enough to appreciate that dissatisfaction could arise after the initial – almost adolescent excitement – meshed with adult realities.

After I returned to my condo and completed the chores associated with being gone five days, I accessed email. To my surprise Sara had sent a message while I was in transit. *I think you have forgotten waking me up the first time; it was when I failed to appear for our breakfast meeting. Actually Helen was woken first but you know what I mean. I think that may have been one of those toss of a coin moments. You know that sometimes you are in two minds as to what to do. I wonder how close you were to not calling the hotel. I as am so glad you did. Anyway hopefully speak to you soon. Sara X*

There was that 'X' again – I must ask Chris its meaning. This message added oxygen to a newly lighted fire. I was being led by spontaneous events for one of the rare times in life. My twenty-five-year absence from experiencing another woman coupled with a twelve-year age difference were beginning to destabilise my tiresome house of life. Exactly what was required if I wanted to discard a much-maligned deterministic lifestyle.

Her email required a response so to guarantee genuineness I sent it in haste. No overriding strategy only matter-of-fact honesty. *I really believe we are going to have a phenomenal time together in NYC, Sara. Why? I don't know – intuition, I guess. Our phone conversations and emails are always positive, full of wit, humour and mutual respect. I'm really looking forward to a great four days! I'm so glad you approached me at Jilly's and, yes, you are* absolutely *correct: I tossed the coin early that Saturday morning to call you for breakfast, and it came up 'heads' – to go ahead and do it. We've connected and it's great. I adore your positive outlook and sense of humour. Truly intoxicating. You are a doll. Respectfully, Edward*

She responded the following morning. *I am really happy I came to speak to you in Chicago. I will never forget it. As Helen said she was leaving soon and I looked around and something told me to come over and speak to you. You were not the only person who was alone and the place was packed. I will never know what made me pick you. Speak soon. Sara X*

Over the next three weeks we exchanged emails and talked on the phone, touching a litany of subjects that evolved into an unadorned closeness. She wasn't enthralled by musicals – too much enthusiasm and overacting; sushi made her squirm;

embraced sarcasm; loved being a dyed-in-the-wool vegetarian; considered herself a proficient but basic cook; drank the archetypal British gin and tonic with lemon; frustrated by computer technology; and, perhaps most importantly, enjoyed her own company, which meant Sara wasn't insecure.

As the mid-March departure date approached Sara's emails helped me recall the romantic innocence of youth. Each message seemed awash with feverish excitement:

I have no experience of sharing a hotel room with an American historian and have no idea which pyjamas to bring. I wouldn't wish to embarrass myself.

I think it would be a great idea to dump our stuff and go for a walk in the park. What do you think?

We'll have so much time in NY to talk; of course you could change your mind if my pyjamas are not up to scratch.

Can't wait to see you. If I get any more excited about the trip I will pop (I hope that does not have rude meaning in the US). I have to be so careful!

Please feel free to chat me up anytime this weekend.

Crazy day. I will email more before bed. I have a couple of urgent things to do. One is to eat.

I am going to dash out of the door in a minute with a coffee in hand. For this reason only I cannot write and reply to you now. I will promise to pour my heart out when I get home.

> *I am sitting listening to Louis Armstrong's 'La Vie en Rose' reading your wonderful email. Does life get better than that? (I suppose a cup of coffee or a glass of wine in my hand would make it perfect.)*
>
> *You asked me what we will do if we have a splendid time together. I know what you mean, but I think we will just have to leave it to the angels. They have looked after us so far.*
>
> *In my quiet moments today I have been thinking of you. I hope your day is going well.*
>
> *Life is good and you are wonderful.*
>
> *Thinking of you, all good things.*
>
> *I cannot wait to see you, talk to you face to face and have some laughs. I feel I have known you for a long, long time. Won't it be wonderful to be in the same time zone and discuss our socially embarrassing musical tastes?*

An unexpected breakthrough came two days before the big trip.

> *Thanks for chatting me up again. I just feel the need to talk and talk with you. See you soon. Love Sara X*

I wasn't prepared for the salutation. It warmed me but was it presumptuous? How should I interpret its meaning?

> *Anyway this is it. At times I thought it would never come. I can finally say **see you tomorrow**. I am very excited. I*

feel like a child who has been given the best present in the world but has to wait to open it. I am happy and I feel comfortable, excited and content all at the same time. I can't wait to be with you. We may both make a scene at JFK but I will try to contain myself. Tomorrow. Sara X

The evening before departing I sent Sara a message she could read before leaving Heathrow. My nerves were as tight as a banjo string so the subconscious kicked-in, titling the message, 'I'm Beside Myself.'

*I wish I had an adequate vocabulary to articulate my current feelings and emotions about you and the trip. I have not felt such anticipation, elation and excitement in years. I'm simply beside myself with happiness. We shall have an absolutely brilliant time. I just know it. How many individuals do you know that talk for two and a half hours on the phone and regret ringing off, still feeling there was more to discuss? We will have all the time in the world the next four days – no deadlines, no distractions, no schedules, no work and **no** phones. It shall be simply you and me, living large and experiencing each other. You enthral me, Sara. I'm intrigued… totally. With affection, Edward.*

A plethora of unanswerable questions cluttered my mind. I put Dave Brubeck's 'Take Five' on continual repeat to ease my anxiousness. What *am* I doing? Is this relationship remotely realistic? Should I consider it a series of one-night stands with the same woman? Is this my fate: a pseudo-Bedouin-type lifestyle dominated by various women from disparate places? Wouldn't it be more practical to develop a relationship with a woman closer to home, say Portland or even Vancouver,

British Columbia? Canadian women have pleasant accents. But what happens if we are wonderful together? What if the personality reflected in her conversation and emails is genuine? Is it possible to create a relationship more meaningful than simply overcoming the logistical excitement of international travel? I searched for answers but my Scotch glass was empty. Lacking fuel, I suspended my lesson in cognitive dissonance and set the alarm so I wouldn't miss my predawn departure.

FOUR

NEW YORK CITY

Halfway across the nation – probably above the Dakotas – I suspended a long-held belief of Ernest Hemingway's that it's hell to drink before noon. Exhausted from limited sleep and nervous as a freshly neutered cat, I asked the stewardess for a double, neat Scotch. She looked mildly concerned but became sympathetic when I told her the situation.

"Buzz if you need another, Mr Lee."

"Thank you. I've been out of commission so long I must determine if the axiom pontificated by alcoholics is true: booze increases courage."

"If on my return flight I hope to see you drinking champagne."

Upon landing I turned on my phone. Sure enough, Sara had sent a text. Arriving thirty minutes earlier, she had sailed through immigration and was waiting by luggage conveyer seven. She'd meet me by whatever conveyer handled the

Seattle flight. I made my way to number sixteen and while waiting for the luggage I looked for Sara but couldn't find her. I felt confident I'd recognise her. It only had been three and a half months. Where was she? I retrieved my suitcase and hang-up bag, turned around and saw her peeking from behind a wide support column. Our eyes met. Her infectious smile made me laugh.

"Were you checking me out? Didn't remember what I looked like, huh?"

"Well, actually, I knew the essence of you, Edward, but wasn't absolutely sure. I'd recognise that smile. You don't have any fat on you. If you had looked dodgy I would have boarded the next flight home immediately! But you don't and I didn't so kiss me."

We noticed the cab driver continued viewing us in the rear-view mirror as we made our way through Manhattan to our hotel.

"You two look good together. Really nice. Happy. Like celebrities."

We looked at each other and smiled.

"Thank you, that's very kind. I agree 'we look good together', but only this lovely lady is the celebrity. Not me."

Sara blushed, smiled and uttered what became her trademark response to my hyperboles: "Don't be ridiculous." With extreme emphasis on 'ridiculous'. Our emails, phone conversations and occasional cards had laid the groundwork for a relaxed ride into the city and the hopeful promise of four memorable days.

While checking in and obtaining our room key, the hotel clerk smiled and wished us an enjoyable visit.

"Hope New York is good to you both. Enjoy. If you don't mind me saying, you both look smart together."

What did we look like? How did we act towards one

another? What had prompted these comments? Perhaps the cabbie and hotel clerk thought we were in the throes of a clandestine trans-Atlantic affair that needed affirmation. Once in the elevator and before reaching our room on the 'Fiction Floor' we decided to play along. Yes, it was a trans-Atlantic affair. A further extension of the 'special relationship' that's existed between the US and the UK since World War II.

Before unlocking the room door we put down the luggage and looked into one other's eyes. Nothing was said. She placed her arms around my shoulders and drew towards me. The touch of her body, the warmth of her breath and the smell of her perfume lingered after our lips parted.

"Are you certain the clerk didn't assign us a room on the 'Erotic Floor'?"

"Yeah, I'm certain. As we left the elevator I noticed a large portrait of Michael Ondaatje holding a copy of *The English Patient*. Romantic novel, yes, erotic... I don't think so."

Although small, the room fit our needs. Sara unpacked immediately, placing her clothes neatly inside the top two dresser drawers.

"Do you mind using the lower drawers, Edward? They are a bit larger and would hold your clothes more easily than the narrower ones on top."

"I'm easy. That works fine for me. I tend to live out of my suitcase anyway when away from home."

I watched as she refolded and placed an unending number of knickers and bras inside the dresser. While it became obvious that two drawers would be insufficient to store her 'intimate' attire, the smell of smoke slowly filled the room as she removed additional items from her suitcase.

I began to laugh.

"Did you retrieve your garments from the fireplace?"

"Don't be rude. Whatever are you talking about?"

After admonishing me she sniffed a few items. She started laughing.

"Oh, Lord, I never realised smoke from the Inglenook inundates everything. I must have been smelling like this for over three months. No one at work ever told me! What are they like?"

"Well, I think it's great. A bit of the English countryside inside a posh New York hotel. What I'm more curious about, Sara, is I thought our rendezvous was only four days. I think you may have brought every undergarment you own."

"Please don't judge me by my knickers. I couldn't decide what mood I'd be in at any given time so I brought them all. You're going to think I'm a silly old cow, aren't you?"

She started laughing, enabling me to join in without answering. If foraging for a harbinger, that was it.

With logistics completed we decided to open a bottle of red wine. We had agreed weeks earlier to bring photos of ourselves growing up as well as our parents, grandparents, siblings or anything else deemed important. We thought it also a good idea to bring ten favourite music CDs to play on the room's machine. Sara's pictures confirmed she had owned that infectious smile a long time. And she looked hauntingly similar to the sepia photo of her great-grandmother who had died during the infamous 1918 influenza. Her reaction to a photo of me as a young lieutenant with my first platoon made her laugh. "What were you, about ten?"

It was the CD selections where our similarities intersected. It was uncanny. Both of us brought Miles Davis, Frank Sinatra and Louis Armstrong; however, I was extraordinarily impressed that she owned a Chet Baker album. I didn't think it possible for a thirty-eight-year-old woman to own his music. Where she had the diaphanous Kate Bush, I had the eponymous Bruce Springsteen. Where she heaped praised on her countryman, Phil Collins, I shared a similar pseudo-nationalism for John 'Cougar' Mellencamp. But our generational differences also were present. Her affection for Coldplay was matched by my infatuation with Debbie Harry and Blondie. Surprisingly it was the soundtrack of the 1981 PBS television series *Brideshead Revisited* that crossed generational lines and initiated lengthy and humorous discussion of the book's theme, the characters and the country estate in Yorkshire, a destination Sara had visited frequently as a young girl. We repeated lines almost verbatim of our favourite characters including Charles Ryder, his 'pansy friend' Anthony Blanche, 'Boy' Mulcaster, 'Ma' Mayfield, Lady Cordelia, Julia and, of course, Sebastian.

We decided to go for a snowy walk in Central Park, having exhausted our trove of favourites from *Brideshead*. As darkness replaced the winter sun that had become shrouded behind the city's tallest buildings, we remained close to the perimeter, deciding not to venture deep inside the park. The walkway had been well travelled so we enjoyed a path free of slush.

"Can you believe we are walking together in Central Park? I can't get my head around it. I'll never know why I approached you. Something told me you were safe but not boring. Alone but not lonely. Well mannered but not a nob. A drinker but not a drunk. And well dressed but not fussy."

"Maybe it's your training. The ability to size-up people quickly and oftentimes accurately. Whatever the reason I'm glad you did. I needed a diversion, something characteristically un-American. Wonder how it will end?"

"Edward, don't try to predict. Enjoy us now, today and the next four days. You shouldn't attempt to determine the future by wondering how it might play out. Relax. You'll develop high blood pressure."

"I'd welcome high blood pressure if it meant I could jettison the crap I've got."

She grabbed my arm, forcing me to stop. She turned and looked at me directly. "What? You never told me about a heart condition. What's that about? How serious? Can it be fixed or regulated?"

"Sorry, dammit. It just slipped out. Few people know. I keep it to myself mostly. Chris knows, my boss here in New York obviously and now you. It's referred to as supraventricular tachycardia. I didn't want to tell you. Thought you'd befriend me only to take pity. And to be honest, after our emails and conversations the last three and a half months, I played that correctly. You are a feeling person, Sara, favouring the underdog or those with issues. I didn't want to be placed in your heart-shaped wicker basket labelled 'sympathy.'"

"Silly boy. Honestly. So tell me, what's the 'skinny' – to use my favourite American expression?"

"Well, about four months before we met I received a saccharine laden email message from 'the other woman'. It obviously upset me, I guess, because as I turned off the machine and rose from my desk I felt my heart pounding through my ribcage as well as the proverbial 'elephant on the chest' pressure. I laid down on the bed a bit but the rate didn't subside. I took the elevator to the lobby and told the concierge to call an ambulance. I was pacing the floor when the emergency personnel arrived, who were surprised I was erect and walking around. They sat me in a lobby chair and read my pulse: 287 beats per minute. They chatted to each other and decided I'd never survive a trip to the emergency room. They would have to 'reboot' my heart by injecting amiodarone hydrochloride directly into my veins which they hoped would slow the rate. The drug actually stops the heart beating for about a thousandth of a second or so and restarts it at a slower rate. Fortunately it worked, but more was on the horizon. After two days of tests I was diagnosed with Wolff-Parkinson-White syndrome, a congenital defect where an accessory electrical conduction path surrounds the heart. I won't bore you with specifics except to say that after a three-hour surgical ablation procedure I was cured supposedly; however, the surgeon warned intense and unreleased emotional stress could initiate another incident without warning – light-headedness, dizziness, followed by a rapidly increasing heart rate. I'm done if it continues out of control. Of course, the biggest irony is that after undergoing five years of class two physicals as an army aviator, the medical corps never diagnosed the problem. It would have been catastrophic – for me and the co-pilot – if my heart had tripped out while flying. So, there you have it. You had no idea at Jilly's I was a medical mess."

"Even if I knew these issues in advance I still would have asked you to my table. So you've got a dodgy dick and a dickey ticker. Just means we've got to crack on."

"Well, I don't know. One or both may become insurmountable obstacles you won't want to deal with over time. But, hey, until that date arrives… I certainly love your humour. First class."

"Humour is indispensable in cleaning up after man's inhumanity to man. Let's hope it works on you, too."

"Don't want to subject you to undue pressure but I hope it does as well. One thing I was proud about was my heart rate. Don't know if you remember or not, but in the movie *Casino Royale* after James Bond was poisoned by Le Chiffre during the poker game his heart rate rose to 136 beats per minute. Bond saved himself by injecting the exact drug I had. I know it's only fiction, but I can state now unequivocally – to all who will listen – that is the only time I'll outdo 007. Sometimes dark humour gets you through the bad times. Takes the edge off."

"Ah, yes, my friend Edward Lee from Seattle always comparing life events to a personal hero – whether from history, literature or the cinema. I don't understand it but I find it naively refreshing."

"To borrow your term, Sara, I think I'm becoming a 'figure of fun.'"

"Oh, no, not you, Edward. I could *never* be sarcastic."

"Another comical event occurred after surgery. It was late night – about eleven – and the nurses insisted a friend pick me up. They wouldn't release me until they knew I was in someone's care. I have numerous acquaintances but the only true friend is Fritzy. I wasn't going to disturb a man late at night who is battling cancer. So… I faked the call. Told the nurses he was meeting me in the hospital lobby in about fifteen minutes. They seemed convinced and signed my release. I proceeded to the lobby and, without looking left or right, headed confidently out the front door. Now keep in mind, Sara, I had been doped up, clearly circling the airport as I headed down First Hill towards downtown Seattle. A few people were out and about but it appeared deserted. All I remember is the city lights, twinkling in soft focus, ensconced behind an ethereal background – which obviously was the Oxycontin talking. I made it to my condo eventually where I drank two neat Scotches while enjoying Miles Davis's 'Recollections'. Certainly the first and probably the last time I'll participate in a psychedelic road trip."

"What are you like? I'm hoping that was a one-off. You could have killed yourself or been messed up mentally. Stupid boy. Honestly."

"Messed up mentally, huh? Well, you'll have a few days to determine whether the authorities should cart me away in a starched white jacket."

We shared a laugh and wanted to continue walking but,

with the approaching darkness and a bitingly cold wind approaching from the west, decided to return to the hotel. We dropped off our coats and agreed that because of nerves and the sheer excitement of being together we'd forego dinner and beat feet to the rooftop bar. Not the healthiest option – empty calories, of course, unless one included the lemon slice. Being the first couple in the bar we had a selection of seats, gravitating effortlessly towards the tufted leather sofa that was angled slightly, enabling a view of the city from the bay window and the bar area. Sara ordered a gin and tonic, of course, while I decided to keep the Bond comparison alive one last time and chose a Vesper martini.

"Thank God you didn't say 'shaken not stirred'. I would have started wondering all kinds of things if you had."

"Of course not. That would have been too pedestrian for my taste. And besides, I prefer Vespers stirred. That said, I'm sure I'll provide numerous opportunities for you to wonder things before the four days are up."

"I'm up for wonderment... all kinds."

"That sounds like an advertisement from a…"

"How would you know?"

"Ahhhhh, I read a lot?"

"I don't know *everything* about you, Edward, but enough to appreciate that's not your style. In fact, that lacks any style at all. And you're a horrible liar!"

Soon people – mainly couples – began filtering into the bar, clearly indicating the venue wasn't limited to hotel guests. Most appeared to have come directly from work; however, there was one couple seated nearby that clearly weren't hotel guests nor co-workers enjoying an evening cocktail. Sara and I determined they were in the throes of an affair and chose The Library because it was far from their respective places of work eliminating all chances of being recognised. He was dressed in a dark suit and conservative tie while she wore a slim pencil skirt and a blouse so exposed I feared she'd catch cold. While of similar age to me and Sara, they demonstrated a level of physical familiarity that appeared newly found. Like us – except the man was wearing a wedding band. His female ingénue was *sans* rock. Both owned bulging leather briefcases, state-of-the-art mobile phones which they checked often but not with synchronicity and refreshed their neat whiskies regularly. Sara thought it would be fun as we enjoyed our libations and shared conversation to watch their movements, their facial expressions, their touchiness and compose a story. I agreed, so for ninety minutes we engineered a plot with fictitious but spontaneous dialogue. The finale was pre-empted when the couple caught on to our shenanigans and left in a huff. Their abrupt departure indicated we had been correct: personal guilt had increased fear. Or maybe they considered us too obnoxious and went elsewhere. I opted for the latter.

We rose early the next morning and went for a run through the snow-covered paths in Central Park. The blue skies and brilliant sun worked in tandem to minimise us thinking about the cold. While I wore a long-sleeved shirt, sweatshirt and full-length running trousers as well as gloves, Sara opted for the tropical look – short-sleeved, nylon shirt, running trousers that ended below the knee, and no gloves and no hat.

"Not to sound patronising but will you be warm enough? Would you want my long-sleeved running shirt?"

"No, I'm fine. I don't sweat much. I never seem to lose body heat. I wear this all the time regardless of weather. I'll sport a waterproof if it's pouring rain, otherwise this is it, Edward. Thanks for offering, but I'll be absolutely perfect."

We maintained a decent pace and ran a respectable distance, especially considering our alcohol intake the night before and the late hour we dozed off. By the time we finished at the tree-covered walkway called The Mall we had completed seven miles in under fifty-six minutes. Sara was in fabulous shape. I was running purely on emotional adrenalin. True to her word Sara wasn't sweating when we stopped, but she was shivering. I offered my dry but cold sweatshirt and she accepted. She hugged me, partly out of gratefulness, I guess, but also to replenish lost body heat. After trotting past General Sherman's statue lording over the Plaza Hotel and the Pulitzer Fountain, we continued down Fifth Avenue, dodging snow piles that blocked the crosswalks until we reached the hotel. We welcomed the warmth of the lobby.

We decided Lever House Restaurant would be a perfect venue for a late lunch. The business and financial 'masters of the universe' – who helped usher in the Great Recession – would have departed, leaving only society ladies planning their next self-aggrandising fundraiser and couples like us enjoying selfish time together.

"Thanks for allowing me to nourish my fetish and experience this monument to modernism. It's a classic, Sara, completed in 1952 by the eponymous firm of Skidmore, Owings and Merrill. The blue-green glass and stainless steel curtain wall, as well as being on Park Avenue, made it iconic."

"How do you keep all this straight in your head? I have difficulty remembering phone numbers and computer passwords."

"What makes you think I'm not making it up?"

"You're not a fibber, Edward."

After the waiter seated us we took in the restaurant's interior design. We both thought it resembled something between a late-1950s spaceship and the set of the 1960s television series *The Avengers*.

"Except for not wearing tight-fitting boots and colourful jumpsuits, you bear a striking resemblance to Emma Peel. I think you fit in here nicely."

"Oh, don't be ridiculous… Emma Peel. What tosh. Only slightly less misogynistic than Sean Connery's portrayal of Bond. Lorrrrrd." Whereupon she offered a delightful giggle.

By the time we had finished our cocktails and served food we were alone, except for the attentive waiter, who uncannily understood the situation. He'd seen this scenario dozens of times before.

"I know you're disappointed in the police nowadays. What does that mean long-term? Will you remain until retirement? Can you last until retirement?"

"Let me correct you. I'm *not* disappointed in the police as a whole. I love the force. I respect my team and receive a lot of satisfaction from bringing a proper wrongin to justice. What I am disappointed in is, well, when you begin the career you're not aware of future frustrations. Through experience, however, you learn there never will be adequate funding to do everything well all the time. Only to do some things well some of the time until the political wind changes. For example, the child murder team at Tintagel house. The team was set up by our incredibly innovative boss. We worked for eight or nine years developing expertise. Some of the cases we worked on actually changed existing law. We were cutting edge. Then suddenly other types of crime were perceived as more important, causing the entire team to disband. Just like that, everyone was parcelled off to other departments. Difficult to accept all that acquired knowledge is now lost… gone. I'll predict that in five or so years they'll decide adult murder teams lack personnel with the proper background and expertise to investigate complex child deaths. And then the whole process will begin again. Different people reinventing the same wheel. It drives me crazy. And I've seen it numerous times before. It happened with street crime, methods of investigating sex crimes, even teams dealing with domestic violence. Probably will be worse now during the recession. In addition to losing experience, buildings will be sold and assets lost. And if they start cutting salaries and benefits, large numbers of people will leave or take early retirement. It will take new officers ten to fifteen years to become proficient detectives. Incredibly frustrating."

"Sounds discouraging. I realise the Great Recession's impact is wide and diverse, but to sound cynical, I think it provides companies, institutions and governments – especially conservative-leaning ones – an excuse to implement predetermined cuts. Just as you illustrated. Funny, but when the 'other woman' dropped the laundry list on why she wanted me gone, a top reason was that although interested in politics and current events, I never did anything about it. Never joined a group. Never demonstrated. It seemed—"

"Pardon me, Edward. At the risk of sounding rude, I don't want to know anything about your ex-wife. Not what she looked like. How she acted. Why she did what she did. Nothing. It's about my fear of comparisons. It will burden us… and I don't want that, no matter how long we enjoy being together. I don't want to find myself changing behaviour so as to be different from her. Is that okay?"

"Of course, certainly. I should have been more careful. Wasn't thinking, but you're right. Why should the past weigh us down? As French poet Guillaume Apollinaire wrote almost a hundred years ago, *You can't carry your father's corpse along with you wherever you go.* Easier to recite than follow, I think, but excellent advice for those who want to begin again."

"Thanks. From where do you pull these names? Honestly. Now, please continue the 'history lecture.'"

"Oh, it's a lecture now, I see. Anyway, both countries are in for dramatic change. I'm not certain but I doubt Obama will cut social programming. I'll go one step further and bet he'll make good on his promise for national healthcare. Had Bush, Cheney and company remained in office longer they would have used the economic downturn to sever social and environmental programmes, including the social security programme started by FDR during the Great Depression – something every American pays into and counts on in one form or another. Enough about politics and history. I've put the lecture notes into my portfolio. I won't refer to them again. Promise. I recommend we talk about us. Whatta ya say?"

"I would love to, but first things first. Where's the loo?"

Having never been to Lever House I was clueless where the restrooms were located. I flagged down the waiter. When Sara returned she was giggling.

"Lord, the toilets are so dark I couldn't see my own shortcomings! Wait till you go." We laughed as if reading a movie script.

I concurred with Sara's assessment about the toilets; however, not getting a clear view offered more relief than angst. With nature handled, we decided to relax and enjoy the remaining half bottle of Sancerre, having ravenously devoured what the menu described as a 'fresh winter green salad laden with candied pecans and pomegranate seeds and a freshly grilled sea bass languishing in light caviar cream sauce topped with a sprig of fennel'.

"You know, in the last three to four months we've talked and written a lot about ourselves, mostly about contemporary events, lots of politics, and enormous quantities of humorous and uplifting banter. And while I don't want to become maudlin, we've never touched on how we dealt with difficult challenges. Maybe you didn't have any. It's been a smooth road without potholes. But I—"

"Ah, I assure you, Edward, it hasn't been a comfortable ride. I'm willing to contribute, in fact, I was about to ask a similar question, but since you beat me to it, why don't you begin?"

"Okay, sure. Let's see... well, the divorce was crushing. Destroyed the foundation of everything I had believed. The death of my parents was difficult, of course, but everyone experiences one or both of these life-altering events. The feeling of loss lingers but the time spirit gains the upper hand eventually and we move forward. There are others, however, that aren't in the natural course of events yet wreak havoc long after the event has passed... I had to repeat the first grade."

"You remember being told by the school head you weren't advancing?"

"Oh, I remember it well. Couldn't forget it. But I wasn't told by what Americans call the principal. My mom told me. I recall her exact words: 'You haven't taken to school like you should so your father and I have decided you should repeat the first grade, Eddie. Repeat the first grade. Repeat the first grade. Repeat the...' I'll never forget the sympathetic tone of her voice. Apparently school officials had urged them not to. I had performed well enough to advance. I was only five when I entered first grade. Studies indicate nowadays that kids born in August and September do not perform as well as those born earlier in the year. The residue of this action created personal repercussions that lingered for thirty-five years – until 1999 actually. Self-doubt and self-worth semi-paralysed my actions and reactions to life's offerings."

"So what did you do? How'd you react?"

"I went to my room and pulled a white box from underneath the bed, opened it, and aligned the blue-uniformed lead soldiers on one side of the room and the grey-uniformed lead soldiers on the other. The American Civil War Centenary was in full swing in 1964, Sara. I retreated to the safe cocoon of history – something I've done repeatedly when life disappoints. Silly, really. Of course, the bitter irony – which I learned decades later – was the school system had pressured my parents to enrol me in first grade at age five. It seems the class I ended up graduating with in 1976 was the largest in the system's history. Fearful of not being able to handle the large influx of children, administrators had coaxed parents with under-aged children to enrol a year earlier so they would graduate in 1975. So what did we have? A bureaucracy using 'indisputable data' to manipulate the lives of scholastically immature children for no reason except administrative expediency. Fast forward a few years and it's similar to how the US government manipulated data to show the American people it was winning in Vietnam."

"That may be a bit of a stretch, don't you think?"

"No, I don't actually. You'll have to remember the World War II generation placed inordinate amounts of faith and trust in the government. The government manoeuvred the country through the Great Depression. The government won the war. The government secured the peace. The government afforded millions of veterans to attend university for free. And the government created a post-war economy that absorbed these freshly minted graduates and offered them genuine professions. So to veterans and their wives, authority was respected, trusted and seldom questioned. Therefore, it isn't difficult to understand why my parents, in that window of 1963 – 1964, supported the recommendation of school administrators. Why question a government that had provided so much? To their thinking, the school authorities had the child's interest at heart. It certainly wasn't complying with conclusions reached by a management consulting firm.

A similar reliance on manipulative data was used to justify government policies in Vietnam and its filthy conclusion. The manoeuvre backfired eventually, causing serious blowback, increasing the levels of distrust of government, the disrespect for authority and the continual questioning of almost every institution. It continues today."

"I see what you mean. And Bush's and Blair's unilateral invasion of Iraq only added to this distrust."

"Exactly. Compounded it astronomically, making wholesale, retail and personal integrity a scarce commodity."

"So what impact did repeating the first grade have on you?"

"Like I was covered in a green patina. The personal stigma endured outwardly throughout high school and inwardly until about ten years ago. Finally wore off in late 1999 after an unsolicited article I sent to an academic history journal in Australia was accepted for publication. Needed editing and expansion, of course, but it was reviewed favourably. I was, as you say, 'happy as Larry'. Sadly my mom had died nine months earlier so she couldn't share in the excitement; however, this event proved I was intellectually viable. Subsequent successes have washed away any remaining stench of repeating the first grade."

"So, what bumps in the road have you encountered?"

"It also had to do with education ironically. I really struggled at school. My social skills and English were always fine, but numbers, sequences and patterns presented challenges. It all seemed too baffling. People accepted I must be thick and eventually I did too sadly. My teachers couldn't consider something might be askew and, if not corrected, at least understood and managed sympathetically. Not to be egotistical, but after years of perseverance and persistence I developed a convoluted but workable solution. Experts wouldn't sanction it but I've made it work. My love-hate relationship with numbers remains as hot and heavy now as it did thirty-five years ago. Takes a bit longer to arrive at the answer or to recall a particular sequence but I get there in the end. I'm contented."

"Incredibly challenging. I can only imagine how you must have felt."

"As I said, difficulty with numbers caused teachers to ignore my overall academic development. I'm a voracious reader, love art and painting, and, if I say so myself, possess an almost innate affinity for throwing and turning clay."

"Interesting but tragic, really. Must have had repercussions throughout life."

"I've managed okay but had to work harder to prove myself. It hasn't been easy. Nothing ever has happened in life as I expected it to happen."

"Obviously you're intelligent. You couldn't have been a successful constable and detective for the last twenty years. That alone speaks volumes about your inner core, your tenacity and, yes, your stubbornness. Impressive. Other teenagers in similar circumstances may have resorted to drugs or crime or pregnancies. That you succeeded without the school's support is truly remarkable."

"How did the opportunity with the London police come about?"

"I responded to a newspaper advertisement. The Met was expanding and wanted to diversify the force so it recruited nationwide. I passed the written examination but failed the physical aptitude test due to weak upper-body strength. They gave me a three-week extension so after dutifully doing press-ups all hours of the day for twenty days I passed. Started the five-month training school at Hendon – in north London – six weeks after my twentieth birthday. I've never looked back. It got me on my own where I experienced a genuinely cosmopolitan environment. The discipline of Metropolitan Police and the diversity within London made me. I shall be forever grateful."

"Wonder how a psychologist would interrupt our stories?"

"I couldn't possibly say, Edward, but it seems both of us weren't interested in settling. We selfishly pursued what we needed, ignoring cries from detractors. Less stubborn people would have surrendered."

"You're probably correct. We substantiated our own self-worth… but not necessarily to prove others wrong. 'Revenge', it seems, wasn't in the recipe for our success. We may just have corroborated what I've thought for some time: life is about a lot of spillage that we try to clean up and conceal from others."

"You may have something there."

We glanced around to realise we were alone. Only our waiter remained, standing dutifully in a far back corner. Slightly embarrassed, we signalled our desire to leave. After bringing the bill we apologised.

"Not necessary, Sir. It is rare to find a couple engaged so intently with one another – at least at Lever House. Clientele this time of day are discussing acquisitions hot from the 'Street' or comparing purchases of the latest *au couture* from Bergdorf's. You fit neither of these."

"Well, thanks, but I only met this charming woman standing alone outside the restaurant so I asked if she'd like to join me. She said, 'Why not?'"

The waiter looked incredulous.

"Just kidding."

"I was going to say, I've heard of working quickly but that could've been a record. Thanks for clarifying."

Stepping onto Park Avenue we decided to walk. The crystal-clear sky made it frigidly cold. As we approached 79th Street from Park Avenue I realised we were exceedingly close to the Neue Galerie, one of my favourite museums in the world – well, as much of the world as I had seen. As we crossed Madison Avenue I asked Sara if she'd like to visit a boutique museum. While familiar with Klimt and having a vague understanding of the Vienna Secessionists, she didn't know specifics. I offered a *Cliff's Notes* summary before reaching the building's threshold.

Sara found Klimt's *Adele Bloch-Bauer* impressive, marvelling at the brightness and thickness of the gold. She liked the modernist aspects of Josef Hoffmann's furniture, especially the warmth and colour of the woods he chose. She thought Adolf Loos's designs, with their unobstructed linearism, almost contemporary. She drew a line that couldn't be crossed regarding the works of Egon Schiele, finding them perverse and ugly. She appreciated their artistic and historical significance, but the subject matter and the grotesque forms bordered on disturbing.

"I really couldn't see either one of these adorning my dining room wall."

I walked closer to find her pondering *Seated Male Nude* (1910) and *Reclining Female Nude on Red Cloth* (1914).

"Too many bits and bobs on display for my taste. It would put me off my Waldorf salad. Nothing is left to imagine what might be housed underneath."

I could not contain my laughter. Sara looked my way, smiled gently and sauntered into the adjoining room.

After another hour Sara had reached her limit absorbing early twentieth-century Austrian culture. By self-assessment she thought she'd recall about sixty per cent in the morning.

"If given a multiple-choice exam at breakfast tomorrow, I'd pass. An essay would be more challenging but I'd squeak through provided you didn't deduct for dangling participles and split infinitives. But honestly, don't you think we may pursue a less *intellectual* and more *emotional* activity tomorrow morning?"

"Alright, fine, I won't take off for dangling participles, but there is no excuse for split infinitives and wrong dates. I cannot abide in slovenly scholarship… what kind of emotional activity?"

We exited into the cold.

Prior to descending the steps Sara turned to me.

"Before we go further, Edward – and I realise it's pure conjecture – but kiss me the way you believe Gustav Klimt may have kissed his muse."

After turning left onto Fifth Avenue from East 86th Street we encountered a bone-stiffening headwind. We trekked to the hotel after wrapping our arms around the other. What a memorable afternoon.

We slept in Saturday. The sheer excitement, late evenings and time differences had caught us out. And we weren't fussed too much because dinner at the Carlyle Hotel and an intimate performance by Jane Monheit was on tap. After a small breakfast, Sara announced she needed to go shopping. Despite having packed a cornucopia of bras and knickers, she forgot evening shoes.

"I have only trainers and flat casuals which are totally inappropriate to wear with a frock. I need something a bit jazzier. Do you mind awfully if we visit the shops?"

"The evening shoes you have in mind… will they highlight the thinness of your ankle?"

"Don't be ridiculous. You're not a misogynist… are you? No, of course not. Where do you recommend?"

"To be truthful, although it's *the* place to shop in the States, I'm not familiar with women's shoe stores. Would a department store like Saks Fifth Avenue or Bloomingdales work or would you prefer someplace that only sells shoes?"

"The weather looks marvellous today, let's walk and see what we find."

Soon we found ourselves on Madison Avenue. We stopped momentarily to window shop at the Bally Store where Sara quickly spotted a pair of open-toed high heels; silver in colour with a whitish-silver ribbon tie.

"Oh, Edward, I fancy those. Let's do have a nose."

They looked nice. They looked expensive.

I had never been inside Bally's before. The deep pile, white carpet felt nice on my cold feet. The store smelled clean and fresh, like a purposeful rather than ad-hoc mixture of fine leather and Chanel No 5. I retreated to the safety of an oversized, black leather chair excited to watch Sara's English retail demeanour in action. I wasn't disappointed. Turns out the shoes were made of snakeskin and unsurprisingly the signature item promoting the new spring collection. Retail price: $800! Because of the fragile American economy the exchange rate massively favoured the pound, dropping the price to a mere $350.

"What do you think?"

"They look classy and—"

Suddenly the salesclerk interrupted.

"They highlight your lovely thin ankle wonderfully, Ma'am."

Sara grinned, quickly looking my way.

"What is it about Yanks and women's ankles?"

I reassured the clerk she hadn't overstepped her bounds.

"Glad you agree. I've told Sara for years she should emphasise the narrowness of her ankle. It's just one of many attributes."

"What a nice thing for a husband to say. You're very fortunate, Ma'am."

"Oh, yes, I agree. He's a definite 'one-off.'"

Neither of us caved. Since the clerk thought we were

husband and wife, the charade continued. I thought it impolite to disabuse her. Sara paid for the shoes and the clerk wrapped them in a cloth bag.

"You both have been a delight. Thank you. And Sir, for being supportive, I've enclosed a leather pocket secretary as a gift. It's a promotional item from the men's department. Enjoy New York."

As we left Bally's I looked at my watch: half two. Dinner reservations were half seven and Monheit's gig started at nine. Sara thought she wouldn't be rushed if we started sprucing up at five. With three hours to spare I asked if she'd like a drink from the Algonquin's Blue Bar. Knowing she was an avid cat lover, I explained how the hotel's resident cat, Bix Beiderbecke, may be comfortably stretched out in a booth, or perhaps sitting confidently on a bar stool scrutinising customers as they entered his living room.

"I'm as dry as a stick. That sounds brilliant. I want to meet this Bix. Sounds like my kind of critter."

The early afternoon hour happily meant privacy. Sara chose a table at the most concealed end of the bar. Only a recording of Ellington's rendition of Strayhorn's 'Blood Count' disturbed the silence. After ordering our drink – a gin and tonic for Sara and an extra dry gin martini with a twist for me – we had company. Bix Beiderbecke appeared from an undisclosed corner. Sitting himself atop the small table next to ours he pompously looked at us and yawned. He seemed a good sport despite us disturbing his afternoon nap. About twenty minutes later the bartender came over and asked if another round was in order.

"Yes, that would be wonderful. Thank you. Can you tell us anything about Mr Bix?"

"Well, not too much except – and if jazz aficionados you'll appreciate this – his mother's name was 'Lena', after Lena

Horne, while his father was called 'Duke' as in Ellington. I've never seen two cats dote so much over their offspring. And, of course, the hotel owners are huge cat lovers who really looked after Bix in his younger, more vulnerable years. Guess that's why he is so confidently friendly. I better get your drinks – an extra dry gin martini with a twist and a G-&-T."

Bix saw an opportunity after the barman left. He approached Sara, stealthily inching his way towards her lap. Experiencing not even token resistance, Bix sandwiched himself between the side of the chair and Sara's hip. He ended the escapade by turning completely around and placing his head self-deservingly on her lap.

"Well, hello Bix Beiderbecke. Aren't you a gorgeous boy? I understand you've descended from two original Jazz Cats?"

He took no notice of the conversation, opting instead for purring, followed by a deep sleep that transitioned quickly into heavy snoring.

"I've never seen a cat act so friendly to a stranger, Edward. Absolutely amazing. Honestly."

"Well, I've never experienced a cat exuding such friendliness either; however, there *was* a ginger in Chicago a few months back that—"

"Oh, I can't get my head around it. I had no idea what we're experiencing was possible. I simply can't."

"I'm dumbfounded. I'm excited. I'm scared. I'm ecstatic. I'm bewildered. I'm… well, Sara, I am absolutely unencumbered. I act and feel as I want. No rules. No expectations. No boundaries. I think I'm immersing myself without worrying about tomorrow or next week or next month. I don't look at us as doe-eyed romantics or cross-eyed cynics but as realistic-romantics. I've never been so comfortable. Age and maturity account for some of what I'm feeling, I'm sure, but your approach to life – your *joie de vivre* – is intoxicating. I've often thought that as we become older, life takes away more and gives us less. You certainly have upended that philosophy."

"My mind is stuffed with constantly changing scenarios. I can't describe them because they're always being messed about. When I think I've figured one to a viable conclusion, for one reason or another, it becomes unacceptable. All I can do is repeat what I wrote a few weeks ago: *The angels have been kind to us so far. Let's hope it continues.* We'll work it out – somehow, anyhow."

"I guess you're right. Our relationship will solidify or fall apart organically of its own accord. For one or both of us to steer it in a certain direction or another would cause irreparable damage. Do more harm than good."

As if on cue a recording of Julie London's 'It Never Entered My Mind' started playing. The ending lines made us pause.

"Hope it's not prophetic."

"So… do… I. It could be worse, I guess, if it had been Chet Baker's 'I Get Along Without You Very Well'. As you say, that would have 'put the tin hat on it'."

"Ahhhh, quick, good one. Your humour is getting there, My Disillusioned American."

"Where did that come from?"

"Oh, I've been mulling it around. Fits, I think. Like it?"

"Makes me self-conscious… but only a bit. God knows my ego is big enough to handle it. Consider it yours to use, Sara."

"Yes, darling, I'm confident God is well aware of your ego."

And with that, we thought it best to head back and prepare for our fabulous evening, the last hurrah, so to speak. Cat logistics presented a minor concern. Sara arose cautiously from the chair, trying not to disturb Bix Beiderbecke. He purred a little but seemed non-fussed by the disturbance; he snuggled his upper body and head onto the warm spot formerly occupied by Sara's bottom. After paying the bill and bundling up to embrace the weather the barman wished us a 'happy anniversary'. As we had done so often during this rendezvous, we smiled and simply said, "Thank you."

Sara looked elegant in her frock. A one-piece black number that kept my eyes working overtime. Dangling silver earrings accompanied by a thin silver necklace completed the look. Her new snake-skin shoes brought it all together. She was a knockout.

"Sara, I'm, ah, I'm, ah…"

"Have you gone wobbly on me? It's not polite to stare."

"Then you shouldn't look like that."

"Don't be ridiculous. But since you are, come here, MDA, and kiss me."

Even though the Carlyle was nearby we decided on a cab. I didn't want to jeopardise Sara's efforts. Entering the hotel we were taken aback by its splendour, its sophistication and its quietness. Highly polished marble floors reflected our every movement. Fresh flowers adorned corner nooks while perfectly thought out centrepiece arrangements sat atop glistening tables. Guests and hotel staff spoke in hushed tones, being careful not to call attention to themselves. We made our way to Café Carlyle and shown our seat by the solicitous maitre d'. It wasn't a seat at all, in fact, but a small, art deco design, soft-cushioned love-seat facing the tiny stage. The low ceiling and individual table lamps contributed mightily to enhancing an already intimate and lush setting. The walls consisted of the colourful and whimsical murals painted in 1955 by Hungarian expat Marcel Vertès. They wrapped around the entire room allowing dinner guests to enjoy differing music-themed images of ballerinas, minstrels, children playing instruments and dancing dogs. The ambiance couldn't be improved. Its innate refinement created a cosy elegance.

Our tastes in cuisine again reflected an uncanny similarity. We ordered the same items: lobster bisque soup, wild Alaskan king salmon with broccoli puree, red beets and sorrel sauce, and shared side orders of whipped Yukon potatoes and sautéed spinach. Since the evening was my personal treat I decided, with Sara's consent, to order an outstanding white Burgundy, a '06 Montrachet Grand Cru.

"I don't believe I've ever tasted such an expensive wine. It is delightful. Thank you."

"Yes, it is. And you're most welcome... neither have I. Not familiar with proper wine lingo so I can only describe it as 'exquisite.'"

"Oh, I taste a hint of grapefruit, a pinch of elderberry and cherry, and maybe, just maybe a little of the... gritty soil of Beaune. Yes, yes, I do. Gritty soil of Beaune."

"Wow, that's fabulous, Sara. I'm impressed."

"Oh, you're so easy to wind up. That was all gibbering nonsense. I am absolutely clueless about describing wine. But I certainly liked your reaction. I must have been convincing."

"Well, there's one thing you've learned on this trip: I am quite gullible. In my last year of high school one of the senior superlatives – when fellow students vote who is 'most likely to succeed', 'best-looking', 'best dancer', 'best legs', 'best actor', 'best laugh', 'best athlete' – was 'most gullible', and guess what, I won! I also won 'most studious' but that discussion is for another time."

"That is so typically American. We don't do such rubbish in England. Rating someone's looks and legs. God, how misogynistic! Makes my teeth itch."

"Don't know if they do it now. It probably originated in the 1950s during a more optimistic time in the nation's history. Not for everyone, of course. Prior to the whole gambit of self-inflicted horrors that defined the 1960s and 1970s."

"So Edward, tell me, we've chatted lots on this trip but I don't know what you want from life. You're only fifty-two. You talk a lot about the past – your personal past – but not about the future. Any thoughts?"

"Oh, yeah. After Bush was re-elected I kinda decided I didn't belong *in* or *to* America any more. That the nation could re-elect a man who unilaterally invaded another nation, lied to the United Nations, sanctioned torture at Abu Graib and had non-existent or, at best, inadequate plans for a post-war Iraq seemed incomprehensible… not to mention his appalling response after Hurricane Katrina was, well, a bridge too far. And with Dick 'Darth Vader' Cheney as VP and Donald 'Known Unknowns and Unknowns Unknowns' Rumsfeld as Secretary of Defence well… my 'Known Knowns' told me it wasn't going to change, only get worse. So I began thinking of retiring at fifty and getting the hell out. Thought I'd spend the year travelling, trying desperately to minimise time in America. Of course, last July that plan became infeasible. So I'm now living in the 'state of flux' located in the 'nation of limbo.'"

"It is early days, I suppose."

"It is, Sara, but my good friend in Seattle – Chris – the architect dying of cancer – chastises me for being too cautious. He told me over dinner a few months back to, *Be free for once in your overly disciplined and predetermined life.* He encouraged me to, how did he phrase it… *Take a bite out of the ass of life!*"

"Sounds like a character. Sad he is so ill. You'll going to miss him."

"Oh, I will definitely. He would have been a fabulous older brother. We can't choose our family, though. Anyway, he thinks I need to shrug off my deterministic lifestyle, jettison material possessions and become bohemian. I want to, believe me. Don't know if I can. I've fought this personal battle for years. As a compromise, I've developed some work goals I need to complete: finish writing a manuscript I've toiled over for a decade on early modernisms and secure an archives contract from a multinational corporation I've been trying desperately to win over for two years."

"Funny, but I don't see any 'bohemian' in your compromise. I understand working for a cause, but I can't see working for ambition. Maybe you should listen to Chris. I don't want to sound callous, but he is dying and the terminally ill often redefine the meaning of life for the living. Just a thought."

Sara always espoused kernels of wisdom at the most appropriate times. She had a knack for cutting through and defining what was important. It gave me pause.

"Well, I *have* been mulling over what he said. In fact, I've booked a trip in June to a remote island in Greece where my grandfather travelled with a fellow soldier for R-&-R in summer 1919. Thought it might be interesting. Might test some of Chris's other 'progressive' ideas, too. The real question is whether a middle-aged man can alter a philosophy of life that churned and moulded his identity."

"At the risk of sounding cliché, MDA, I believe one can do whatever they want if they want to badly enough. I've seen no evidence you're possessed by possessions. And you certainly aren't some *nouveau riche* man showing off bountiful material goods to appear cultivated. You've got a fit mind in a fit body. Don't be constrained by your past. Perhaps you should try and loosen up, explore and see what happens. Bet you'll be surprised. When do you think our dinner will arrive? I'm famished."

"Ahhhh, that segue was a *liiittle* too abrupt, Miss Hawes. I'm not the only one in a life raft navigating rough seas. What about your future?"

"I've got ten years before I retire. I hope to move to a small cottage surrounded by dry-stone walls in the Yorkshire

Dales National Park and rekindle my love of pottery – handbuilding, throwing, turning, glazing and kiln-firing. I don't want to found a business necessarily. As I said in Chicago, if I evolve only into a struggling artist that would be splendid. After my experiences in the smoke – what we call London – I desire a simple, rural life void of extravagances, sudden movements, loud noises and sullen people. I want to share a oneness with nature, including healthy food, lots of vegetables, fine wines and copious amounts of gin with a bit of tonic and a hint of lemon or lime. What's that design/architectural philosophy… 'less is more'? *That* will be my mantra."

"Why would I have thought – even for a mere thirty seconds – that Detective Sara Hawes wouldn't have it all going on and all figured out! Let's see you do it."

"I will, Edward. I will."

"You know what… I *know* you will. You're tenacious with a capital 'T', that's for certain. Well done. You realise that artistic obsession can lead to brilliance so you may never 'achieve' struggling potter status."

Whereupon I leaned over and gently kissed her lips.

As I regained composure and straightened my back Sara moved closer and whispered in my ear.

"I'm in like. I'm in deep like."

I felt my temperature rise and my face turn red.

"Wonder how our play's going to end, Sara?"

"There's no final act in my *Playbill*."

Soon dinner arrived, enabling us unconsciously to lighten the conversation. We talked endlessly about the meal's quality, the lush atmosphere and the attentive but non-bothersome waiters. We received our perfectly raised chocolate-raspberry soufflé as members of the quartet began tuning their instruments. Prior to the performance starting, and in an effort to settle into the small sofa more comfortably,

I ordered two cognacs. Sara cuddled in closer as Jane Monheit approached the stage. We anticipated a fabulous evening. She didn't disappoint. Her interpretation of American standards was winsome but poignant, adding the requisite amounts of emotion. Whatever Monheit sang, from 'More Than You Know' and 'My Foolish Heart' to 'In the Still of the Night' and 'Embraceable You', she seemed iron-focused on us. It may have been her disciplined manner but to us, it seemed intimately personal, as if we were alone together. Ninety minutes seemed like fifteen. After completing an a cappella arrangement of 'Over the Rainbow' the gig ended, but the lights remained low, permitting a comfortable transition to reality. Without having to ask, our waiter took a picture of us on the sofa – the capstone of an indescribable three days.

As we left the Carlyle the cold temperature and fresh air spurned us on to walk to the hotel. Our departures the following day ironically were within twenty minutes of the other. Sara's was 1520 while mine was 1540. Although our whirlwind was nearing its end we still had the next morning to enjoy one another's company.

"I think there is something here, Edward, between us, I mean. I'd like to keep exploring, see if it has legs. Any thoughts?"

Just then we stopped at a crosswalk waiting for the light to turn. I pulled her close and kissed her right cheek.

"To do anything less would be a sin, Sara. We couldn't possibly waste the toil of your providential angles, now, could we?"

"I could arrange time in early May to fly to Seattle for a six-or-seven-day visit if that would fit your schedule."

"My schedule be damned. I'll make it work. It would be fabulous to see you romping around the condo, running through Queen Anne, shopping at Pike Place Market and, of course… meeting Chris. Fantastic. My God, though, that's like seven weeks away."

"Seven weeks… that's nothing."

Like we had done throughout the trip, we laughed in unison.

We slept in the next morning, relying on room service for a light breakfast. I didn't ask Sara, but my nerves could not have tolerated a meaningful intake of food. After enjoying two pots of coffee into the late morning Sara grabbed her diary and, corroborating what she said last night about 'having legs', rattled off possible dates when we could visit on an alternating basis.

"Let's see, I'm coming to Seattle in early May and, if I can secure leave, I'll fly over in August and October. Could you visit in June/July – I know you've planned to be on some Greek island in June – September, and… what do you think about having an English Christmas?"

"Now that's what I call military precision. Sounds fine to me. I'll look at the logistics regarding June. I may visit immediately after my Greek experience. That would save a lot of wasteful travel time. I think the UK is three hours or so from Greece. I should be oiled-up and well-tanned by then."

"And a sight for my sore eyes."

Soon we started the unfortunate task of packing. I put on the *Brideshead Revisited* soundtrack to ease the tension. Sara recreated her cottage atmosphere as she opened the dresser drawer containing her knickers and bras, re-releasing the pungent smell of smoke. It filled the room.

"I'm concerned you may set off the fire alarm, Sara. That would upset the other hotel guests."

"Oh, don't be ridiculous, Edward. But I can't help it. It's a fifteenth-century building with limited ventilation, especially in the dead of winter. What am I going to do?"

"Heavily douse the clothes with a favourite perfume?"

"No, then I'd smell like a tart. I'll just have to go around smelling of a chimney sweep."

"That's a noble profession. Especially in London. It worked wonders for Dick Van Dyke in *Mary Poppins*."

"You do talk rubbish sometimes, Edward. Honestly. And, by the way, his portrayal of a London cockney was awful, bloody awful. The worst ever."

"Just nervous, I guess. Trying to ignore, as you'd say, 'the bleeding obvious.'"

Packing completed, we approached the check-out desk to settle the bill. We divided the cost evenly. The clerk who checked us in handled the transaction. He wasn't bothered by halving the bill, appearing as if he had done something similar numerous times before – especially for those engaged in a clandestine affair.

"Hope you enjoyed New York. Look forward to seeing you both again soon."

"Thank you. We've had an absolutely stupendous time, but unfortunately our trans-Atlantic affair has come to an end. I must emphasise, however, Anglo-American relations never have been better. We've accomplished a great deal and made plans that may bear fruit."

"That's good to hear, Mr Lee. I think both nations need some positive news in times like these. Safe trip home."

As I loaded our luggage into the cab Sara leaned towards me.

"Honestly, your American hyperbole is out of control… 'trans-Atlantic affair', 'Anglo-American relations never better', 'plans that may bear fruit'. Now everyone in New York knows our business."

"Don't worry, Sara. He's assisted me before. He'll be discreet."

She looked at me questioningly but soon realised I was kidding. As she scooted across the seat and before I closed the cab door we giggled. Our conversation was restrained during the ride to LaGuardia. The casual touch of one another's hand seemed the most effective way to communicate. What normally is a tediously long journey went too quickly. Secretly I had hoped for a traffic jam or at minimum a meandering ride. Neither occurred. While checking our luggage we discovered our flights departed not only from the same terminal but the gates were next to each other! We enjoyed each other's company for another hour but the clock was ticking inexorably towards departure time. The flight attendant announced boarding for Sara's flight. Neither of us moved. Intense, uncontrollable emotion consumed me: my legs grew weak, my hands shook and my eyes welled-up. I looked down, trying to conceal my wimpiest self. Sara raised my chin with her hand. When our eyes met I saw remnants of her tears.

"Don't, Edward. You'll only making it worse."

"Do you see us following through with these visits? I fear I'll never see you again. We're just deluding ourselves… the distance, our jobs, our ages, well, at least my age… everything."

"No, we're not. Maybe you are… I'm not. You'll see. I'll send a message as soon as I return to Plough Cottage."

The attendant announced final boarding. I brought Sara close and, hoping to convey reassurance that actually was meant more for me, kissed her as if it were the last time. And with this act, Sara turned, walked a few steps and presented her ticket to the attendant. My whimsical – seat-of-my-pants – event of a lifetime had ended.

I collected my carry-on items and boarded the plane. The attendants commenced cabin service after the aircraft reached level flight. To my surprise the lady who attended my Scotch needs travelling to New York was reprising her role.

"Good afternoon, Mr Lee. Nice to see you again. I seem to recall an exciting visit was planned with a young lady in New York. Is a glass of champagne in order or would you—"

"No, you are spot on, thank you. And, yes, a glass of champagne would be exquisite. The perfect way to cap a memorable few days."

"Wonderful to hear. Would you prefer Veuve Clicquot or Moet & Chandon?"

"Clicquot, please."

The plane landed at five. By half six I was in my condo unit sorting personal mail and reviewing back issues of *The Wall Street Journal* and *The Financial Times* – a pathetic anti-climax to four luscious days. A few hours passed and city lights appeared outside the window. I poured a double neat Scotch, slouched into my favourite chair, put on Shirley Horn's 'Do It Again' from her stellar album *I Love You, Paris* and began thinking.

If I wanted a different lifestyle – for however long – than I was 'on course, on glide path'. Who would baulk at the sheer classical romance of a relationship with a woman living abroad? That alone has provided ample copy for theatre plays, film scripts and romance novels. Something like this never happens, except perhaps during wartime. There was no denying, 'We gelled'. 'We were made for each other'. 'We were two peas in a pod'. 'We were simpatico'. Any number of relationship clichés described us. My difficulty, and the struggle I'd have if I continued seeing her, was predicting or being consumed by how long it would last and how it would conclude. If I went along for the bohemianism of it but that fizzled after six or eight months or even a year, at least I would have done something unique. Maybe it didn't end successfully – however we defined success – but I could be contented. Most importantly, from a selfish standpoint, I would have broken the impenetrable mould I had crafted at university and reforged intermittently throughout adulthood. But the opposite also could happen. I could revert to type. I always liked to plan ahead, see what's in front, anticipate pitfalls and manoeuvre through, over or around obstacles while focusing on the success that surely awaited me. Any toil needed predetermined confirmation the task was worth it. If I followed this formula, as I had done throughout life, the mould would remain unbroken. Nothing would have changed. I would have accomplished nothing. I would have learned nothing. If the desire to break from the past, to achieve unconventionality and live unencumbered by past formulae was cast aside and ignored, then I would return to 'living the way one ought to', deterministically bored… but safe.

FIVE

SEATTLE

I TRIED FALLING ASLEEP but remained restless. Giving up, I turned on the computer to find Sara had composed a melancholy message. *Mr Lee, I can't believe a very short while ago we were running together. I wish we could do it again soon... Do you know I have no funny thoughts at all today and that never happens? I am flat. Back to work in the morning and I will book my leave for May and then sort the flight times, etc. with you. Sorry I am a wet blanket today, I miss you. Will cuddle you soon. Sara XXX*

I, too, felt deflated, unsure whether I should contribute to the downheartedness or sound positive. I opted for the latter. *Miss Sara, I'm trying to be optimistic. When that proves difficult I think about you prancing around the condo unit in about six weeks. If we enjoyed ourselves in NYC wait until Seattle. Make sure you bring some clothes and shoes you can leave. You could even bring plentiful amounts of bras and knickers imbued with a hint of smoke. I've got plenty of drawer space for storage and airing!* It will keep your memory alive with me and work towards lightening your load luggage-wise during future visits. Notice my sense of optimism? Cannot wait to see you. Your MDA.

Late that afternoon I received a message from Fritzy. He asked to visit, share a bottle of Chateauneuf-du-Pape and hear details of the NYC adventure. Submerged in a funk, I agreed nonetheless to hold the seminar Friday evening. Discussing Sara would diminish the anxiety of her absence. He sauntered up to my place after dinner. Always prompt, the intercom rang exactly at half eight.

"RESPECT."

Per agreed procedure from long ago I didn't reply. I buzzed for the building's main entry door to be unlocked. Minutes later I heard a knock. Having not seen him for over a month he looked damn good.

"Buttons, you're a sight for sore eyes. You certainly look, well, worked over, refreshed and fit. Looks like you worked things out."

Knowing Chris like I did, I understood his propensity for the double-entendre so I acted as if went over my head. He offered his characteristic hug before crossing the threshold.

"Come in, Fritzy, take off your coat, sit down in your favourite chair so I can tell you all about it. The wine is ready to be enjoyed. Prefer a bit of Miles during his 'acid days'?"

"I think so, Buttons. And with this wonderful wine… no telling where we'll end up."

I put on *In a Silent Way*, settled into my club chair and poured us each a glass. I recounted everything Sara and I did during our time together, from her hiding behind the column at the airport and the Central Park run to our dinners, intimate conversations and, most of all, her classy demeanour.

"Sounds made up, Chris, but we have much in common, seriously – music, food, wine, fitness, movies, critiquing the human condition and body politic, and most importantly... humour. My, God, did we laugh. It wasn't forced or faked but genuine. Never has a trip been so beneficial."

"Interesting use of the word 'beneficial' to describe your escapade. Was it mutual?"

"Hope so. She enjoyed my company, I think. Became emotional at the airport before leaving. I did as well."

"Buttons, please, I'm asking if you connected—"

"If you're asking about sex, no. Sara and I decided not to proceed down that ticklish path at this point. That's not to say we weren't intimate. We were but in a more loquacious manner. No one applied pressure. She knew about my issue already. And in Sara's inimitable way she put me at ease early. How did she say it... *If our relationship reaches that level, we will work it out. Could be kind of interesting, you know, half the equipment twice the entertainment. But until then, let's enjoy the idea of us.*"

"Wellllll, yessssssss, Buttons. An interesting turn of phrase. Not what I expected. Seems Sara's worth pursuing. Could be invaluable in tossing out that predetermined lifestyle of yours. Excellent."

"Yeah, I agree, Fritzy, but the onus is on me, really, no one else. Sara can serve as a conduit – an excellent one, I might add – but only I can alter the taxonomy. She certainly can help. Sara believes a life of unencumbered freedom is preferable to achieving status and owning things; simplicity creates contentedness while genuineness elicits security. It's a life recipe worthy of consideration, I think."

"I agree. Only you can alter the course but she may be the reason you do it. One cannot underestimate the innate ability of women to influence men in profound ways. I know the women with whom I've been associated left an indelible imprint. You are a richer man if you absorb their message."

"Wait a minute, Fritzy, months ago you chastised me for contacting Sara at Christmas. What did you say? *I was vulnerable... and if I entered into a relationship pain will be my best friend.* So which is it, my friend?"

"Edward, Edward, Edward..."

What followed would be damn serious. Fritzy never addressed me using my proper name unless irritated. Now he had used it three times consecutively. I'd soon find myself alone in the doghouse, cowed in the corner, licking my wounds.

"I was afraid you'd only be used. Sara would take what she needed – whatever that may have been – and departed, leaving you peering over the precipice of frazzled disillusionment. Then a second scenario came to mind. You could use her, not in a malicious or sexual way, but as an aid in transitioning from your deterministic lifestyle. She would be one of several temporary women who would deconstruct your life. My prescription has been upended after hearing about the NYC trip and your description of Sara's personality and approach to life. I'm kinda thinking now it could be, well, a symbiotic relationship – both might derive meaning. When it doesn't work out long-term at least you will have absorbed her message and she yours. Separation without rancour or malice, now that's unique. Sadness, perhaps, but both will have developed a heightened level of emotional intelligence that will be put to good use in the future. Neither will have suffered the bitter pleasure of ingratitude. Pretty lucky, I'd say."

"Hold on. What is it you tell me: *Luck is the residue from thoughtful planning and good design?* Well then, if Sara and I continue long-term it won't be due to luck."

"Buttons, I must say, your memory is a wonderment. Glad you chew on my philosophies before digesting. I'm flattered actually. But you're correct – Architecture 101 – everything under one roof. Luck can play a surprising part but only through thoughtful planning. Architects approach each structure with the best intentions. They conceive a style and form that functions, develop detailed plans, construct a prototype model and build the structure. It is during this last phase that luck comes into its own. Despite all the prior planning, in the end, artistic creations evolve into something unique that was unpredicted. The structure takes on a life of its own. I cannot recount how often while in the throes of building that the structure has spoken to me, in effect, told me how it wants to be completed. But the building's intuitiveness, its ability to convey this desire, comes only from prior planning and superior design."

"Okay, I understand the concept, Fritzy, but how does it apply to human relationships, to me and Sara?"

"Well, most relationships evolve in a similar fashion… but in reverse. Luck is what brought you and Sara together. She asked you to sit at her table. There was no prior planning, no forethought, no design. Your personal life was broken enough to be receptive. Again, luck played its part well. Now comes the challenging part, so listen carefully. After luck brings people together they start planning and begin designing an emotional structure that will support a life together. Both of you need different things from this relationship. It's hardly a secret the problem throughout your life has been too much planning, too much anticipating, too much expectation and too much control. So the last thing you can afford to do is any of these things. You must break free from determinism. Sara, however, may want to begin planning and designing, something, it appears, she hasn't attempted as an adult. She may be exploring the potentiality for an emotional structure. Because you both need or want something different the relationship is doomed to fail; however, what is achieved in the interim will benefit each separately in the future. So that's why I said earlier, *without rancour or malice… nor the bitter pleasure of ingratitude.* Perhaps someday you'll look upon my theory favourably. The other reasons, of course, are the common sense, impracticality of the whole thing: the distance of separation; the twelve-year age difference; the subtle differences between two cultures; and, your physical disquietude."

"Of course… the uninvited guest."

"Two additional things you may want to consider. While we sit here enjoying this fine wine I'm struck – not this evening so much – but often when we hold seminars – by your alcohol intake. God knows I'm no moralist but I'm thinking if you engage Sara towards something more intimate, I recommend cutting back. I'm the first to admit consciousness is highly overrated, but nothing is more off-putting than a booze-swilling man. Just an observation. Think it over. Secondly, when Sara visits in May, may I extend the use of the San Juan Island house for a few days? You've been there. You know what it's like. She might enjoy its natural setting and isolation."

"Thanks for the alcohol comment. I'll take it on board. Months ago when I told an old university history professor and friend what had occurred he encouraged me to drink all I wanted, arguing I didn't have an addictive personality and soon would tire of it. But, yes, I'll cut back. You are correct. It can be a bad scene. Regarding San Juan Island… I would love to stay two or three days, if possible. I think Sara would absolutely love it. That it's your design makes it extra special."

"I'm off to the Big Island for the next month but return to Seattle right before Sara arrives. I trust you find me palatable enough to be introduced. I would love to meet this confident and fascinating woman."

"She's heard all about you, Fritzy, and looks forward to meeting the man who addresses my foibles, reigns me in and points me towards untrodden paths. Sara would think it an unfulfilled trip if she didn't meet the 'Architectural Sage of Seattle.'"

"Buttons, you've got more shit in your cavity than a Christmas turkey... but I appreciate the underlined sentiment. Thank you,"

And with that final barb, Fritzy was gone. I wished him well in Hawaii as he worked towards completing his home. A task that had morphed suddenly into a competition between architectural skill and personal longevity.

Fritzy's plan of five months ago had become unsaleable. An intense, albeit temporary romp with Sara, seemed inappropriate. We were at places in life where thoughtless posturing could have long-lasting consequences, doing neither one any good. But when the relationship fizzled – something Fritzy ironically believed necessary to alter my taxonomy – Sara and I will have developed a heightened level of emotional intelligence. Something, he felt, could be used in another time with another person. That alone provided enough benefit to continue the affair. I wasn't convinced immediately but after hardened reflection I began slowly to absorb his complicated message.

As the weeks unfolded our emails and phone conversations reflected restrained excitement. Sara said I made her calm and brought out the best in her. *I can make my little jokes and now I have someone who finds me funny. Remarkable. I was the only one who laughed at my jokes until I met you. I've been searching for thirty-eight years. We have a total meeting of the minds. Two people who should have nothing in common, have everything in common.*

I ruminated on how distance would make our visits special and ticklish than if we lived nearby. *My fear, Sara, is that we won't be authentic, that is to say, we'll be on our best behaviours... We cannot be overly cautious or guarded. We must present our genuine selves. If we do our relationship could reach a height experienced by only a few. And believe you me, I'd like to reach that level! Cannot wait to lie beside you, talking, laughing and loving you up like we do. May can't come soon enough.*

Email chatter consumed my mornings and occupied her evenings. We could not have sustained the intensity had email not existed. Relying on the post would have delayed spontaneity. We also looked forward to weekend phone conversations: no rush, no interruption, no fiddling – all in the comfort of our homes. While Sara provided the comedy, I furnished the earnestness, focusing too often on whether what we *thought* we had could endure. Sara's humour and timing were so perfect I chronicled the more memorable lines. Regarding my ignorant ways of not understanding 'British' English: *I look forward to the day you feel confident enough to adopt English as your first language. Until then I will, of course, do my best to teach you everything you need to know (sorry, very cheeky).* Her attempt to touch-up her hair with natural henna proved disastrous: *My hair turned shockingly Celtic to say the least, darling. But please don't worry. There is a way of toning it down. I will sort it tomorrow night. I have the humiliation of a day at work like this. It serves me right for being vain. Well, we must say goodbye for I'm tired and desperate for my bed. Just hope my hair does not light up the room and keep me awake.*

Despite concerted efforts to let events proceed naturally, I obsessed asking myself rhetorical questions, unable to shake the determinism that controlled my life. How long it would last? When will it fall apart? Why would it end? Who would end the relationship? I couldn't answer the unanswerable but Sara tried her best: *Nobody knows why people are attracted to each other and then stick together. It's physical, mental and a bit that we will never understand. Let's just enjoy… We are strong, lucky people and we can do anything we want. As I've said before, the angles have been kind to us so far. Let's just enjoy each other. Try not to write the ending when we're only on Chapter 2.*

The most difficult questions dealt with the matter-of-fact reality of a trans-Atlantic relationship. Who would forego their job? Would I leave America or would Sara leave Britain? How would I occupy my time in London if I 'retired' early? What impact would leaving the police have on Sara's pension? Would I need a larger condo unit if Sara moved to the States? Would the unit be in my current building or one of the other condos proliferating throughout downtown? I held these questions close, choosing not to burden Sara. Her innate perceptiveness, however, brought about an insightful comment: *You know if you wanted to remain in the US due to having greater opportunity we can find a way to live there. Let's talk about it next week during my visit. Please don't worry. I have only a few evenings at home alone now before we meet. Can't wait to see you; only seven days to go. That's nothing! Can you believe it?*

Not knowing whether Sara was a stickler for cleanliness, I erred on the side of caution and gave the condo an old-fashioned GI clean. Every nook, every corner, every crevice, every appliance thoroughly gone over and then gone over again. It would have passed any military inspection I ever stood. I made reservations at two favourite restaurants I thought Sara would enjoy. I booked an evening at Jazz Alley to hear Terrance Blanchard. Most importantly, however, I left most days unplanned so we could do whatever we wanted whenever we wanted unburdened by obligations.

Her emails sent days before arriving conveyed a genuine sense of anticipation.

I hope you won't feel smothered when I visit. I need six weeks of love in seven days.

You are wonderful and I am happy and content with life for the first time. Thanks for being free when I found you.

Totally absorbed in the time we'll have together on Friday and all our tomorrows.

I am thinking about Seattle all the time now. It is my little escape more and more to dream about the things we will do.

I'm full to the brim with anticipation of chatting and being together.

Kisses to you, My Disillusioned American.

I poured another Scotch, keyed up June Christy's sensual rendition of 'Soothe Me' backed by the powerful Stan Kenton orchestra and thought about Sara. Could I replicate her fervency? I possessed the emotion but communicated it inadequately. All I hoped for was not to disappoint.

SIX

SEATTLE

THE DAY SARA arrived I wore a black suit, a starched white shirt, a conservative tie and... held a twelve inch-by-five inch sign with 'Lady Sara Hawes' in large, bold print. Although the flight arrived on time she was slow to clear immigration. While standing around waiting, a professional limousine driver approached and asked my geographic range. I told him I had a few select customers but only worked the central downtown area. No need to venture east of Lake Washington, north of Queen Anne or anywhere near SODO – south of downtown. I held a captive market as my customers travelled frequently, tipped well and desired anonymity. I must have been somewhat credible. He seemed impressed but lamented his difficulty developing a loyal client base. I encouraged him to stock his vehicle with French champagne, Rainier sparkling water and European chocolates. Customers appreciated the extra effort. Suddenly I received a text from Sara: *Long queues through immigration.*

Probably will be at least another thirty minutes. Oh, I can't wait to hug my MDA.

I relayed the relevant information to my 'colleague'.

"Was that from your client?"

I confirmed it was.

"My God, my clients don't treat me with any kind of respect. They'd never do anything like that. That's first class! You're certainly lucky, Dude. Ever think about expanding the operation, you know, increasing the geography and hiring new people?"

I told him I didn't want or need to expand the operation. Ten minutes passed. Another text from Sara: *They've opened a fourth desk. Should be only five minutes more.*

I relayed the information.

"Christ, your customer is… I mean, who is she? Someone famous?"

I told him she was a well-mannered British woman who anticipates travelling frequently to Seattle in the coming years.

Passengers soon began emerging from the escalator. I moved forward to ensure Sara could see the sign. My 'colleague' did likewise. Two or three minutes passed. A mist of nervous perspiration dotted my forehead. I saw Sara visually scouring the luggage area as she stepped off the escalator. I held the sign aloft. Our eyes met. As she got closer she read the sign.

"Oh, Edward, that *is* ridiculous."

As I lowered the sign she dropped her carry-on baggage. A lengthy hug initiated a long kiss.

"You look fabulous, darling."

"I cannot believe you're here. God, you look… well, beautiful and feel wonderful."

Picking up her bags I looked at my 'colleague' shaking his head in disbelief. As we walked away I wondered uncaringly what he thought. Sara had arrived in Seattle and nothing else mattered – nothing – except her presence.

Sara liked the condo unit. Thought it looked masculine but not boorish.

"As you may notice, Sara, I'm not too interested in contemporary design. Classic modernism, yes, but nothing after 1955."

"I must say in my mind I visualised it as a hive of intellectual activity. With all these books, antiques and fine art I wasn't far off. Reminds me of the library in an upscale British men's club located in Pall Mall where I arrested a man once for conducting unsavoury acts. Anyway, I like it. It's you. And it's got warmth."

She walked towards the large windows, opened the sliding door and stepped onto a deck that offered panoramic views of Seattle's downtown.

"Fab view, Edward."

"Yes, but the 360-degree one from the roof-top is – with no allowance for American hyperbole – truly fantastic. Wait till you see it. Depending on the weather the sunsets over Elliott Bay can be memorable."

"Can't wait. Sounds wonderful. But would you mind awfully if I have a shower? I need to wash away the travel grunge."

"Absolutely. Certainly. I've laid out fresh towels already. Feel free to use my shampoo and anything else, but I'm guessing you brought special toiletries."

"You are perceptive, MDA."

I prepared the champagne as Sara showered. Since Chet Baker had 'brought us together' I thought it appropriate to play one of his CDs. It didn't take long to embrace the disquiet of Sara's presence. Her soft humming, the sound of the hair dryer and the smell of her shampoo, soap and perfume gradually filled the unit – competing ever so slightly with 'You and the Night and the Music' and 'Let's Get Lost'. I liked the atmosphere. A bachelor's pad had transitioned into a couple's nest for a few days. After pouring the Veuve Clicquot I toasted to the sheer incredulousness of us meeting, to coming together and to sharing time together. Sara offered a similar sentiment: "Let's just do whatever feels right." An idea that conformed perfectly to my aspirations for a new life.

I gave Sara a brief tour of Pike Place Market while en route to Campagne Restaurant, a secluded French brasserie set amongst the bustling array of fish, produce and flower vendors. Its soft lighting, honey-coloured wood panelling and amber hues complemented the vintage recordings of French and American jazz artists from the '20s and '30s – Lucienne Boyer's 'Parlez-Moi D'Amour', Charles Trenet's 'Boum' and, of course, Josephine Baker's 'J'ai Deux Amours' and Sidney Bechet's 'Si Tu Vois Ma Mere'.

"Hard to fathom but it will be six months tomorrow since we met at Jilly's."

"You know I'm horrible with numbers. Glad you're the historian so I can be kept abreast of important dates."

"Are you trying to be sarcastic or sweet?"

"Sarcastically sweet?"

She scooted closer and kissed my cheek.

"I'll never complain if your sarcasms finish with a kiss."

"You have my solemn promise."

Ordering dinner proved easy: salade verte with Roquefort cheese and pan-roasted Copper River salmon with celeriac remoulade for two. Only our side orders differed. Where Sara requested roasted seasonal vegetables I asked for sautéed champignons. We opted out of dessert to savour the 2004 Saint Emilion Grand Cru Chateau Fombrauge ordered earlier. Not a couple to stand on pretension, we found little difficulty pairing fish with red wine, especially a meaty Copper River.

"I made a career decision, Sara, which I didn't tell you about. Thought it should be done in person."

"What is it and, more importantly, are you fine with it?"

"My boss in New York asked if I'd accept a position on the company's board of directors. She assured me I could remain in Seattle but I'm a realist. It will require relocation eventually."

"So… when would you move? A year, two years… ?"

"That's rather presumptuous. Actually…"

"I know how you value a career."

"I said, *No*. I desire freedom and independence more. My salary and benefit perks would increase substantially but I'd also be adding another room – a couple rooms actually – to that 'tiresome house of life' of mine. I'd be a fly stuck to flypaper. Never be able to experiment with life. It would be easier travel for us both but I'd probably see you less. Too big a commitment at this juncture. I'm more interested in what occurs between us and reforging my life than hanging from a higher rung on the corporate ladder. She even enticed me with coordinating, processing and managing the archives of Debbie Harry of Blondie."

"I can't believe it…"

"It's true. I didn't accept."

"No, no. I did something similar. My supervisor asked me to study for the sergeant's exam. He lauded me with praise – something incredibly uncharacteristic of him – but I turned him down. I like being a detective and have no desire supervising others. It's not even a skill I want to develop, to be honest. Like you, I knew I'd lose more than I'd gain."

"Is it merely a coincidence or did our hearts make a decision reserved usually for the head?"

"I suppose it will be revealed separately to us in the future."

"Your thoughts are so pithy, so matter-of-fact, Sara. Christ, my response would have been so verbose it probably wouldn't have been worth listening to."

"Must come from the reports I submit. You can take time to develop a narrative. I can't. The correct words ensure justice prevails."

"See, you did it again!"

Sara started fading fast around 11-pm but never asked to leave even though it was 7-am her body time. Feeling guilty I floated the question about returning to the unit. She offered little pushback. As we left the restaurant Edith Piaf's 'La Vie en Rose' started playing. Crossing First Avenue at Virginia and turning left towards the condo, Sara let out a barely audible sigh:

"I want my bed but I need you beside me. That would make everything perfectly… pink."

We spent the days before departing for San Juan Island getting comfortable and settling in. Sara filled a couple drawers and half a closet with clothes she planned to leave behind. We stocked-up on fresh produce, fruit, berries, wine, champagne, fish, northwest cheeses – everything and anything we could think of to make the trip memorable. I introduced her to one of the more difficult running routes that included the steep incline of Queen Anne Hill, a challenge made worthy only for the expansive views it offered of downtown, Mt Rainier, Elliott Bay and the Cascades. Sara thought Queen Anne too posh a name. After regaining her breathe she decided it should be called what it truly was: 'Bastard Hill'. I suggested she present the idea formally to the city council before returning to England.

The next evening Fritzy stopped by to meet Sara, drop off the key to the San Juan house and discuss any special procedures we needed to follow. Moments before Fritzy arrived Sara was on her knees, leaning far forward to change the disc in the CD player located on the floor in the far corner of the room. Her contorted position accentuated her feminine figure. Upon entering the unit Fritzy hugged me but withdrew quickly, looking for Sara.

"In the far corner of the room, Fritzy, is Miss Sara Hawes."

"Well, yessssss, I like what I see so far."

Sara burst out giggling. I laughed too… at Sara's expense.

"I'm sorry, Chris, I was changing the CD. Not the most gracious way to meet someone the first time."

"Oh, I don't know, it's a beautiful way to keep the mystery alive a few more seconds."

"Edward did warn me well in advance about you. Honestly."

"Edward told me of your wit and beauty but I think he held back."

After this simple exchange they hugged one another. I knew each well enough to know they would like the other. A wonderful evening was in the offing.

As Sara prepared the snacks I opened the wine – two bottles of 2005 Vacqueyras, Les Clos, Domaine Montirius – a personal favourite. Fritzy contributed a large tin of fresh macadamia nuts and a pound of coffee beans harvested from his plantation. He also included a CD of him and Eleanor performing at a local arts centre on the Big Island: Eleanor, the professional harpist, and Fritzy, the musical bon vivant playing ukulele. While the combination seemed strange and discordant, it worked wonderfully well each time they had performed at cocktail parties in their Seattle condo. And, of course, the serious intensity on Fritzy's face as he plucked the strings only increased my enjoyment.

Fritzy gave me the house key before we forgot and prior to him getting pissed. An instruction sheet was in the right-hand drawer of the fireplace mantel that he hoped we'd follow.

"I'm not worried about you adhering to instructions, Buttons. The house will be in responsible hands. Knowing your overly frugal nature I'm guessing you won't use any heat and, not to waste electricity, will walk through the house at night using a flashlight. Are you familiar with his miserliness, Sara?"

"Ahhhh, no. He's been generous really. I must say, I respect a man who isn't wasteful and lives within his means but also not constrained by boundaries or convention. To be honest, Chris, I've kinda burned it at both ends, too. It demonstrates what could be if money became plentiful."

"You'll never have enough. One should aim for a life philosophy that is expansive, not restrictive – vary experiences and expand emotions, forego crass materialism and limit possessions. Don't know what it's like in Britain, Sara, but in America I think people are so busy consuming they're absent from their own lives."

"I told you he's insightful, Sara."

"Buttons, please, don't blow smoke up my ass, you'll ruin my autopsy."

"Come on, Fritzy, you know I reflect on your ideas for hours when alone. You've even thanked me in the past for, what'd you say, *chewing on my philosophies before digesting.*"

"Yes, Buttons, I realise that. Thank you. You excel at elevating my sense of importance. So, Sara, what's it like in the UK?"

"There are similarities for sure – especially for those working in the City and Canary Wharf – but if I generalised, I'd say we are not identified or consumed by our jobs like Americans. Because England is imbued with an inquisitive, cultural wanderlust we place tremendous value on holidays, evenings after work and weekends. The mere fact we aren't chastised for taking more than a week's holiday at a time reflects, perhaps in some small way, the value society places on individual freedom."

"I've always been envious of Britain's liberal vacation policies and healthcare system. I dated a Brit a few years at the U of O architecture school – Briony – can't recall her last name, but she was a—"

"Stay on course, Fritzy."

"Sorry, yes, I digressed. Seriously – and this isn't claptrap absorbed in '67 during the Summer of Love – most people's lives lack emotional intelligence. By having plenty of drive and ambition they think they know where they're going, why they're going there, who they're going there with and what they'll going to do when they get there. Possessing emotional intelligence isn't important. They're comforted by the fact their life is planned out. The bigger home, the fancier car, the ritzier vacation and the latest technologies all await. Everything is within reach. Failing this, which most do quite early, they beget children and wear the laurel crown of virtue to which they feel entitled. Over time their lives become so unrealised they lay together in bed totally alone."

"That's why I'm developing a new taxonomy, Fritzy. You know that."

"How do you feel, Sara?"

"I've thought for donkey's years that simplicity and unencumbered freedom create a level of contentedness I enjoy. I prefer it over status… at least I think I do, having little chance of actually achieving it."

"I don't understand what a donkey's ear has to do with it?"

"Don't be ridiculous, Lorrrrrrd. It's 'years' not 'ears', 'donkey's years'. It's a British term, means a very long time. Will I have to teach *both* of you proper English?"

Fritzy and I looked at each another and laughed.

"Do you offer a correspondence course, Sara?"

"Hopefully being in your pocket and visiting England will broaden my understanding."

"Chris, sign-up for an online BESL Course – British English as a Second Language. And Edward, don't be rude."

We filled the remainder of the evening discussing Chris's illness and his newest architectural project, the unsavoury parts of Sara's job, and my upcoming trip to Greece prior to visiting Sara on her home turf. In between sips of a double, neat Lagavulin, Chris suggested things we might do on San Juan Island but encouraged us to embrace the natural beauty and enjoy one another. He knew of few places – to include the plantation house on the Big Island – where a couple could experience the peacefulness of being alone together. "The world has ended," he remarked. "It is up to you to make it new." As he hugged Sara goodbye he glanced my way and smiled. His eyes twinkled. These gestures communicated approval. Sara had become integral to tearing down that 'tiresome house of life' where I had resided for far too long.

Following Fritzy's advice Sara and I arrived at the ferry terminal at half three in the morning. Only an early arrival would guarantee a place for the five-thirty departure. His strategy worked: we were first in line and remained the sole car for forty-five minutes. Not fussed either way, we dozed off and enjoyed the warmth of a Pendleton blanket until a ferry worker motioned me to drive onto the boat. Except for spotting a boisterous whale pod and frolicking seals prior to arriving Friday Harbor the ninety-minute sailing was smooth and uneventful.

Turning off the paved road onto a dirt track began our journey to a less harried era. The morning fog had not lifted, partially obscuring the thick fir and cedar forest we had entered. After negotiating a steep decline about a mile in, we arrived at the house positioned a mere fifty feet from the water's edge. The only audible sound was the lapping water against the craggy coast and the squawks of passing crows. The house's exterior design was Fritzy's reverent homage to the Jugendstil movement, reflective of Josef Hoffmann and Otto Wagner. The interior evoked the refined style of Charles Rennie Mackintosh and the ornamental minimalism of Adolf Loos. The huge, sliding glass door served as a supporting wall and an access point directly to the patio and the water.

"Do you like it? Will you be comfortable?"

"Darling... don't be ridiculous. Why wouldn't we? I've never experienced anything like it. It's enchanting. So... so romantic... so isolated. Fab! How fortunate are we?"

"Damn fortunate, I'd say. To have a close confidant like Chris and a charming woman such as yourself – and all because you liked Chet Baker."

Suddenly the sun pierced the trees, targeting a small grassy area. I grabbed the Pendleton and spread it on the sun-filled spot. Our early departure had taken its toll.

"Any suggestions on how to implement Chris's mantra to 'make it new'?"

"All I can offer is what I said earlier: *Let's just do whatever feels right.*"

I don't know how long we slept – thirty minutes, maybe two hours – but we were startled by the screeching of a bald eagle plucking a huge salmon from the water. He flew a few hundred yards onto the shoreline to the left of where we sat. Neither of us ever had seen anything like it.

"Of course, you know what Theodore Roosevelt thought about the eagle?"

"No, but I'm sure you're about to tell me."

"He didn't like it being the symbol of America. He considered it nothing but a dandified vulture, believing only the grizzly bear symbolised the real America. Of course, in light of Bush, Cheney and company, I think 'dandified vulture' is probably appropriate."

"Tell me another story about TR."

"I believe I've just been made a figure of fun."

"Not at all, MDA. Snuggle closer and kiss me please. Let the eagle enjoy his sushi in peace."

Our time on the island was well spent. We managed doing a few things Fritzy had recommended: visiting the lavender farm and touring British Camp and American Camp, sites of mid-nineteenth-century imperial overreach and international arbitration. But what we relished most was also what Fritzy had emphasised: being alone together. The ever-independent, free-thinking Sara found morning swims in the 50 degree Fahrenheit water temperatures delightful. I didn't and wouldn't. Twice we ran a respectable six miles in high heat at American Camp on the island's west side. The views of Mt Rainier to the south and the blue sea on our horizon made it memorable. We grilled fresh fish over an open fire each evening and sipped champagne as day transitioned to night. Once darkness dominated the sky I would place another hefty log on the outside fire, open the sliding door and play Aldo Romano Quartet's 'Non Dimenticar', Sinatra's 'All Alone' or Stan Kenton's 'Standards in Silhouette'. The music was soft and the water so smooth it resembled glass. As the sounds bounced off the water and crossed the channel, we jokingly hoped that Orcas islanders appreciated jazz standards.

On the final evening we shared ideas on whether it possible to find someplace similar, where isolation, solitude and simplicity would ennoble one's life.

"Why the wistful smile?"

"Because I've asked myself this question for twenty-five years. Always answering, *Yes*, but consistently failing to act. Coming away empty. Came damn close to leaving for the wilds of Canada after 'W' was re-elected in '04 but couldn't act unilaterally. So even now, with no strings, no obligations, no responsibility except to myself, I remain too cautious."

"I understand. It is early days but, if keeping score, look at the changes you've made already. You turned down a position on the board. Said no to New York. You're enjoying me – which surely increases the tally. Don't believe you've encountered many gingers in America with a mellifluous British accent. And who knows, you may soon be approaching that proverbial fork in the road, taking the path that will substantiate your desires."

"Possibly. Yes. So what about you, Sara Hawes, will you ever find isolation and solitude?"

"As discussed in New York, an artist's pottery in the windswept Yorkshire Dales would do me nicely. Some areas are incredibly remote. But of course, we're not talking mere physical isolation, are we? We're aspiring to a state of mind, achieving that level of emotional intelligence Chris talked about earlier. To me, self-awareness develops simplicity. And if the self-awareness is true and honest, it creates contentedness which evolves into meaningful happiness. I haven't found it either, Edward, but I'm still searching. Still desirous of discovering what most consider an elusive dream."

"It isn't elusive if you know what it is. You just have to find it."

"I suppose you're correct."

Sara repositioned nearer the fire, the flames almost reaching her waist. Its yellow-orange colour accentuated her hair, melding perfectly with a newly acquired tan. She never looked better.

"I propose a toast, darling, on this our last evening on the island. *My heart is laden for the American I have. This rose-lipped maiden adores her light-footed lad.*"

She placed her glass on the ground, walked towards me and kissed my lips. Nothing was said. She took my hand and we walked into the house together. I turned and locked the sliding door.

The following morning we took the first ferry departing Friday Harbor. To avoid rush hour traffic into Seattle we stopped at a roadside café for a light breakfast. Two hours later we arrived at the condo with ease, deciding along the way that during Sara's remaining three days we would follow a truncated form of domestic bliss. This consisted mainly of running, food-shopping, reading, cooking, cocktail-making and talking – the latter being one activity in which we both excelled.

Our blissfulness was marred after reading about a scandal consuming MPs that unexpectantly had become public: expense-fiddling. Their malfeasance far exceeded two martini lunches at Michelin-starred restaurants in Mayfair and Chelsea or other hedonistic adventures. This scandal reached deep into the psyche of the British electorate, mocking the essence of representative government. We were beyond shocked as Sara read aloud a few specifics: switching the designation of second homes; inflating council tax on the second home; renting the second home to a third party and collecting revenue; evading capital gains when the second home was sold; filing claims for furniture and other home furnishings for the second home when the items were delivered to the MP's permanent residence; inflating monthly food bills even when Parliament wasn't in session; and finally, filing monthly claims slightly below the £250 threshold so no written receipt was required for reimbursement.

"So... here's Britain, reeling from a severe economic recession caused in no small way by the financial godfathers of Wall Street and the City, now having to deal with the sanctimonious hypocrisy of their leaders. This is rich, really rich. Poorly written fiction if I read it in a book. Couldn't happen."

"Bastards. They froze our wages as soon as the recession hit and then strong-armed us into paying more for public transport. Soldiers are still getting killed in Iraq and Afghanistan, and the 'posh boys', who don't know the price of milk and with their sense of privileged entitlement, are gallivanting around fleecing the public... unburdened by a damn thing. Happy as Larry. Sorry, but this government and the one after are banjaxed. An absolute mess. Will take me years to get over this."

After digesting additional articles concerning MPs, Sara and I spent the afternoon ruminating about events in both countries, aided and abetted by full octane: gin martinis. The General Motors and Chrysler bailout Obama initiated chapped my ass, as did TARP – the Troubled Asset Relief Program – created in the waning days of 'W's' administration. Obama had the moral courage at least to demand the CEOs of both auto companies resign. This ultimatum, of course, didn't prevent them from floating comfortably to the ground in several gold-laden parachutes. And while TARP didn't cost the US taxpayer money, it didn't rid the eight mega banks of their respective chairmen. The heads of Bank of America/Merrill Lynch, Bank of New York Mellon, Citigroup, Goldman Sachs, JP Morgan, Morgan Stanley, State Street and Wells Fargo all survived, unembarrassingly lapping up the money offered by the federal government. An entity for the many that these powerful few never respected. Like it or not, we concluded the banks had to be bailed out to salvage not only the US financial system but the global financial network that depended on it. To do otherwise would have had dire consequences for several nations including Britain.

But it seemed reprehensible for the fat cats to remain at the helm after devouring all the canaries.

"If I tampered with evidence or failed to follow procedures, not only would I spend time in the clink, I'd lose my job and my pension. Once released and if lucky, I'd scrape out an existence behind the bar serving drinks in an isolated country pub in the Outer Hebrides!"

"I'm sure your government would show zero mercy. An archivist stealing, defacing or selling documents would suffer stiff penalties – incarceration and financial restitution. They'd never work in the field again. Ever. And I'd be fired immediately if I fiddled expenses of either a client or the company.

"Our responses sound juvenile, don't they, Edward?"

"Maybe, but like so many, many others society depended on the money boys. There was an understanding. Earning a decent return on investment is their mantra. Fine. But at what cost? Achieving financial insolvency and throwing millions of unsuspecting citizens into financial panic and possible insolvency? I didn't agree to that and neither did you."

"We both know life isn't and will never be fair, but the blatant disregard... the sheer arrogance of those in charge... gives me serious pause. As I've done so often before, it will force me to tally up and inventory how I should live life."

"I've tallied my total, Sara, and I'm trying my damnedest to follow through. Tallies don't lie. About four or five years ago, while surveying the records of a global management consulting firm, I reviewed a speech delivered by some kahuna at someplace where 'big heads' verbally fondle one another. Can't remember where exactly, maybe Davos. Anyway, he warned that a huge crisis was brewing. The public would turn against globalisation, a credit and monetary downturn would weaken financial institutions with several going out of business or forced to merge. He predicted also that people would turn against big business, desiring instead to concentrate on social equity, social services and the environment. Even hinted that if the downturn festered more than two years it could give rise to populist-led, reactionary governments. It piqued my interest at the time and now look..."

"Lorrrrd. Doesn't look promising, does it?"

"It doesn't. It certainly doesn't. And so it goes..."

I couldn't allow the seriousness of events nor our reaction mar the time remaining. Sara demonstrated her culinary skills with several decidedly British delicacies. Her apple crumble bourgeoning with cinnamon and a crunchy top was superb, as were the savoury cheese scones we devoured at mid-afternoon on the rooftop overlooking Elliott Bay. Her raspberry fool, of course, not only was characteristically good but criminally fattening. After completing a side-splitting run up Bastard Hill one morning we spent extra time in the steam room afterward hoping to sweat out the additional calories. As intense heat invaded my nasal passages and salt irritated my eyes, I began to understand why author Lawrence Durrell referred to Britain sarcastically as 'Pudding Island'. I never had appreciated the country's proclivity for such diverse, devilishly sweet tarts.

"Don't worry about the extra calories. A bit extra won't do any harm. You're too young to develop 'old man's bottom.'"

"What *are* you talking about?"

"I'm sure it's not restricted to the British male population. Haven't you noticed as men age many lose all pretence of owning a bottom? Their bum simply vanishes... gone... perished. They have a back with a hole. Yours is teetering on obscurity so please don't worry. Think of my tarts as medicinal."

"Well, I'll be damned. An excuse for culinary hedonism. I'm off with it."

"Careful now. You can't morph into a fatty who scuffs about only watching telly. I won't abide by that."

"Don't worry, Sara, I'm much too vain to emerge suddenly or even gradually into a manatee. I won't embarrass you to friends in June."

"I'm not the least bit worried. I know your constitution. And besides, after three weeks on that Greek island you'll look bloody marvellous."

"You'll be disappointed if you think I could possibly resemble a Greek cabin boy."

"Oh, I don't expect that. I'm thinking instead you might regale me with stories from Herodotus."

"*Brideshead*, Chet Baker and now Herodotus… what am I going to do with you?"

"As I said earlier, *Just do whatever feels right*."

The atmosphere on the morning of Sara's departure couldn't help being melancholy. But we shared an optimism now, a confidence that had been lacking in New York. Seattle solidified the relationship. What initially had been a wobbly, one-legged stool turned on the lathe named 'curiosity' had developed into three, well-balanced legs that supported our intellectual requirements, emotional needs and physical desires. It had been a good visit.

The long line at passport control enable us to engage in our favourite pastime: talking. The emotional insecurity displayed in New York had disappeared, replaced by the certainty we'd follow our pre-planned visiting schedule. She cautioned me about Greece – limit the Vespers, drink plenty of water and don't swim alone. Her concern produced a comforting and all-consuming warmth. I hugged and kissed her one last time.

"I won't do anything that would keep me from seeing you."

"It's taken a lifetime to feel in sync with a man, to be respected and to feel valued. I'm just a bit selfish right now, MDA."

"I understand better than you think."

***

Her email upon returning to Plough Cottage from work the next day had the hallmarks of a secure but passionate woman: *I have to say I find this much harder than I thought I would. I have managed my life alone with few problems. Now I feel I finally have someone on my side. I feel frustrated that we cannot be there for each other more. I would have loved to come home tonight and been able to talk about my day, and I am sure you feel the same sometimes. I find I envy people who are able to do the simplest things, like go home and have dinner together. But the great thing is we'll be together at the end of June and you'll be tanned and buff from your island visit. It's only seven weeks… that's nothing! I am filled to the brim with anticipation of chatting and being together. Yee Ha! Love you, My Disillusioned American (Englishman at Heart) PS You need to promise me one thing: you will live to be one hundred otherwise I will have to spend too much time without you.*

I responded with reassuring words that hopefully put our minds to rest.

SEVEN

FISKARDO

───

After a series of exhaustive flights I reached Argostoli, the largest city on Cephalonia. I had difficulty finding a cab but finally found a driver willing to take me – for €100 – to the far north of the island and my final destination, Fiskardo, a village I chose based solely on two sepia-coloured postcards my grandfather had sent my grandmother ninety years earlier. Tired and cramped, I climbed once more into an uncomfortable seat and prepared for a ninety-minute journey. The driver warned mobile reception was unreliable so if I needed to send a message or make a call it should be done before leaving the airport area. I wanted desperately to talk with Sara but, knowing she was in the throes of a double child murder investigation, I sent an unobtrusive text instead: *Arrived safely. Extremely hot – just the way I like it. Mobile reception unreliable so this may be my only message until I arrive at Heathrow brown as a shelled walnut. Will send postcards as events unfold. Miss you terribly (not American hyperbole). Your MDA.*

As we made our way northward the mountainous landscape wrapped itself around the car. The serviceable road hugged the steep cliffs on one side as the turquoise blue Ionia Sea emerged unconventionally on the horizon. The bluest sea I'd ever seen. Suddenly we came upon a herd of goats far above the fortress village of Asos. They had worked their way down the steep mountainside and congregated on the road oblivious to speeding vehicles. One goat in particular looked straight at me as if to say, *Yeah, you don't look like the kind who would hurt me. Probably won't even toot your horn.* The goat was correct. The driver silenced the engine and we waited for the herd to proceed cautiously further down the cliff. Replete with goatees and antique collar bells, these kindly animals looked happy and satisfied despite a parched terrain that offered what I assumed was limited nutrition.

We continued cautiously towards Fiskardo. Descending a steep hill revealed a small cove with a few buildings hugging the water's edge. The port housed a variety of modest sailing ships and attention-seeking yachts. The ruinous resorts of American capitalism seemed at first glance to have bypassed Fiskardo. It appeared only native Greeks or Greeks with Italian heritage – reflecting Cephalonia's history – owned or managed local establishments. The driver dropped me in the central car park and pointed towards the general direction of the waterfront apartments.

After navigating a steep set of white-painted steps, I found myself in the centre of a quaint village. A crudely constructed sign provided directions to a number of apartments. I turned right and walked alongside the waterfront. The smell of grilled fish permeated the air while the banter of well-tanned boaters relaxing on their vessels drinking, laughing and speaking an array of languages provided the international element. Seeing the sign for the flat, I realised it was the building that had figured so prominently in my grandfather's postcard. Obviously not used as flats in 1919, I nonetheless quivered to think he and fellow soldier, Stavros, had seen the identical structure. I accessed my unit from the rear of the building. Per prior arrangement the key was dangling from the door lock. I turned it and walked in. Bedroom on the left, toilet and shower on the right. A long corridor brought me to the open-plan kitchen-living area. Two large French doors opened onto a small deck equipped with a bistro table and two wicker chairs. From this vantage point I could absorb the sounds and smells from restaurants and hear the tall-tales of experienced sailors and novice boaters. It also offered a panoramic view of the harbour. I liked it. It fit my needs. It fit my needs nicely. I found little difficulty accepting the space as home for the next three weeks.

After unpacking and showering I walked about. The village contained several shops, some more high-end than others but appealing nonetheless to itinerant travellers. Others addressed the practical needs of boaters and residents. Restaurants looked considered with a bit of homespun thrown in. Each offered a varietal of furnishings reflecting the blue and white colours of the Greek flag. Some eateries had blue-painted chairs, white tablecloths and blue china. Others had the opposite, white-painted chairs, blue tablecloths and white china. A few even alternated glassware, evenly dividing table settings between blue and white. All had a welcoming if kitsch appeal. Numerous establishments displayed fresh fish offerings in refrigerated trollies sitting on the pavement to entice the passers-by. I chose a restaurant offering none of this. Located in an imposing building in the village centre that probably functioned earlier as a bank or government office was Tselenti's. It had been owned and operated by the same family since 1893. What attracted my attention was the music emanating from inside as well as the older man deep in thought, sitting outside on the left side of the building. A well-worn, wooden chess set made of olive wood sat atop his table and a bouzouki, a Greek-styled mandolin, leaned gently against the back of the facing chair. Physically he resembled the actor Robert Duvall. I assumed he must be *the* Mr Tselenti.

I thought eight in the evening a respectable time for dinner but I didn't know. All the tables were empty. Perhaps this was an awful place despite its pleasant surroundings. I asked an older lady with dyed blonde hair, strong legs and a pleasing smile if I was too early.

"No, no. Please sit here. Lovely table."

Not wishing to be impolite, I sat down. I learned later she was Mrs Tselenti. It *was* a lovely table. She had seated me on the far-right side of the building, facing about twenty-five tables in the courtyard, each equipped with extra-wide cloth umbrellas. I learned later that these protected guests from infrequent rainstorms and mulberries that dropped indiscriminately from the century-old trees growing in the square.

I ordered a bottle of local white Robola wine and pulled a book from my leather backpack. In between chapter endings I looked up to see tables filling. I felt pleased with myself. It appeared Tselenti's was *the* restaurant in Fiskardo. I watched the reaction of visitors walking on the pavement separating umbrella-covered guests from the tables aligning the front of the building where I sat. To those speaking English the response was the same: *What lovely smells. I haven't heard this song in years. Look at the size of that fish. Ahhhh, we ate at the wrong place, darling.*

My captive position also enabled me to view T-shirts worn by young and middle-aged women and the occasional man as they walked by, gawking at the restaurant's interior. I thought initially the more bizarre sayings were 'one-offs' but soon realised they weren't. Knowing I'd never remember them exactly I copied them into my moleskin: Bang, Bang, Bang, I'm Good in Bed, I'm Young and I'm Fertile, I Belong to the Night, Seriously, I Can't, I'm an Evil Girl, You Want a Piece of Me?, Less Talk More Action, I Know You Want This – strategically located across a fat woman's enormous breasts. A late middle-aged woman's shirt had 'GAY' in bold, capital letters. Didn't know if it was a corporate logo or her sexual preference. Another fashion marque was worn by an out-of-shape man whose meaning was lost on me: 'It's Miami, Bitch.' But it was an eight – or nine-year-old boy who, I believed, personified the tumescent state of contemporary fashion. Sporting an attitude, Ray-Ban aviator glasses, a gangster ball cap warn backwards and an oversized T-shirt with, 'Go Ahead, Make My Day, Punk' worn proudly as he sauntered by with parents in tow. I doubted whether they were alive in 1983 when *Sudden Impact* was released. *So*, I muttered to myself, *this is what crass merchandisers in America and Europe promote as fashion.*

I rose early the next morning and made my way through the village until I saw a directional trail sign to the sixth-century Christian Basilica, the ruin that had captivated my grandfather. A thick covering of pine needles blanketed the ginger-coloured footpath. Course rock protruding from the earth made me appreciate I'd worn hiking boots. In some spots, however, the needle coverings were layered so thickly it cushioned my step. The smell of dried pine filled the air. Chirping crickets muffled the idling engines of boats waiting entry into the harbour. I continued for about a mile on the winding path that cut through dense shrubs and prickly undergrowth, eventually arriving at the Basilica. The roof had collapsed centuries earlier. Only a few crumbled walls remained of what I perceived, based on the outlining perimeter, to have been a large structure. I sat on a pile of rocks where the altar may have been situated and pulled a canteen from my backpack and drank the iced water. The dry silence was interrupted by the scurrying of camouflaged geckos. As I enjoyed my water, I wondered if the ruin had been in a similar decrepit state when my grandfather had visited, or had it been pillaged during the difficulties Greece had experienced throughout much of the twentieth-century?

On the east side of the ruin towards Ithaca I saw a path that paralleled the water's edge. It ended abruptly but a small clearing about ten feet wide opened onto the sea. As I walked closer, jagged rocks bleached white by salt and sun buffeted the dry terrain from the sea. I made my way downward, balancing the weight of my backpack against the twenty per cent grade dropping towards the sea. About halfway down the slope I saw some flat rocks bordering the water that had been obscured by trees, perfect for lying on and absorbing the warmth of the sun. There was also a natural cut into the rocky shoreline that resembled an empty bread loaf pan. Just deep enough to lower myself into and, after navigating what assuredly would be slippery rocks underneath the water's surface, I could reach the end and launch myself into the Ionian. I sat on the flat rocks and, in between reading and thinking about the future, listened to the metronomic crash of waves against the shoreline. After the sun hovered over me for nearly two hours I became hot. I had pitted-out my cotton shirt long before and could feel droplets of sweat running down my legs into my socks so... I stripped naked and tested my hypothesis. I thought it merely a whim initially, but as I navigated the 'bread loaf pan', I realised subconsciously I was following Chris's advice proffered months earlier at table eleven: *Be free for once in your God-damn, overly disciplined and predetermined life.* I never had experienced such a semi-angelic act. As I treaded water and looked towards the salmon-coloured mountains of Ithaca, I asked myself, *What's next?*

After almost three weeks of skulking about Fiskardo intermixed with countless hours reading, running, swimming naked and sunning myself on the rocks, I ventured out on a three-mile hike to Antipata. The first two miles were uphill along a rugged, unpaved road. The overgrowth was dense, indicating a lack of use by locals and visitors. Before ascending the hill I came upon an ancient ruin called the Throne of Queen Fiskardo. Hewn from solid rock thousands of years earlier, it was thought by locals and academics to be where a powerful, ancient queen had held court. True or not it looked imposing. As the path levelled out I noticed signs pointing to the abandoned village of Psilithrias. I took the narrow dirt path, curious what I'd find. The several houses that lined the path had collapsed roofs, non-existent doors, decrepit windows lacking glass and elevated steps leading nowhere. The only occupants were bushes, scrub plants and, in many cases, fully grown trees. No explanation was provided as to why it was abandoned and no personal items, furniture or relics remained. The original inhabitants had taken them during the exodus, or they had been pillaged by other locals. One home appeared to be reclaimed, indicating a possible rebirth.

As I left the village, I turned and looked behind at the hill I had climbed. It resembled a green paint pallet card found in decorative stores. The olive trees exhibited a light, silvery green colour. The small-leaf holly trees exuded a richer green colour, while the towering cypress trees were almost a black/green colour that resembled candles on a cake. A magical site that probably hadn't changed for centuries.

Sara had not heard from me since I arrived. I had mailed two postcards but figured both might not arrive until after I did. My slightly higher altitude, I thought, could permit a text but again, no reception. I started questioning my fondness for remoteness. Having no contact with Sara was frustrating. Even worse, what would she think of me? I only could imagine what sarcastic snippet she'd throw my way... deservedly, of course.

I continued walking and soon reached Antipata. My shirt was soaked through and sweat dripped down my legs, tickling my shinbones. The Old Stone House Taverna looked hospitable so I sat at the outside porch, ordered a frosty Mythos and enjoyed the refreshing breeze. While reading my book, a plump tabby cat joined me on the opposite chair. She perceived I wasn't threatening and soon dozed off, snoring and twitching her paws in unison. A second Mythos cooled me to the bone.

The downhill grade made returning to Fiskardo quick and easy. I had canvassed the village for an internet café after first arriving but now after almost three weeks, I thought perhaps a more thorough reconnaissance was needed. It didn't take long to survey the village and, despite finding another bakery and a secluded high-end cocktail lounge, an internet connection remained elusive. After meandering alongside the harbour gawking at an enormous moored yacht surely modelled after that owned by Emilio Largo of SPECTRE, I visited a shop called Porto Panormos. The storefront looked inviting, with a whimsical display of artistic ceramics, silk gowns and cotton shirts, and fine art. A further enticement was hearing the vintage jazz recordings of a mournful 'Lady Day' – Billie Holiday – in the background, as well as the smell of what I imagined to be an ancient Greek oil. Far removed from the patchouli oil of Haight-Ashbury, this fragrance conjured images of aquatic Greek nymphs frolicking effortlessly in the sea, penetratingly strong but not overly aggressive. Behind the oversized desk immediately inside the door on the right sat an older lady with dyed red hair whom I learned later was the owner, Alexandria Tsoussis. It didn't matter that she spoke with a falsetto pitch; it exuded warmth and friendliness. Her smile was genuine. Her knowledge of the represented artists was encyclopaedic. She asked the typical questions: nationality, vocation and length of visit. After browsing a bit I asked about an ancient-looking copper totem displayed at the far end of the shop.

"I know it's not original but what is it exactly? What does it mean?"

"This is an exact reproduction of an ancient Cycladic goddess from the Aegean Sea side of the country, where I'm from. Solid copper. My artist friend, Theodora, in Athens, cast it for me many years ago, thus the greenish patina. The original dates from between 3300 – 1100 BC. This refined Aegean lady, in particular, shields and protects those harbouring medical maladies from further suffering."

"Don't know exactly if I believe in such hocus-pocus but maybe I should cover my bases. I have an erratic heart-beat, but if this diaphanous lady can help maintain a steady rhythm, perhaps I should suspend her around my neck to accompany the medical alert badge."

"It could offer great assistance. Provide comfort in time of stress. It's both masculine and beautiful and will age well with the furtherance of time. You'll see. Your heart will mend."

I succumbed to her persuasive salesmanship and bought the 'relic'. I never liked wearing neckwear, even bothersome army dog tags, but the Aegean goddess fit nicely on the chain. She seemed content riding shotgun next to the medical alert badge.

Ms Tsoussis's friendliness inspired me to enquire about my grandfather's postcards from the Great War. I had brought copies of the originals hoping an opportunity might arise where someone could offer insight into who Stavros was and whether family relatives remained on the island. Unsurprisingly she appeared interested and willing to help.

"Although from Athens, I have lived in Fiskardo over sixty years so I'm familiar with many families who lived and worked here before it became a centre for tourism – first the Italians, then the Germans and, in the early '90s, the British invaded our shores. But all beneficial. You are an American, no… seldom see Americans here."

I pulled the wrinkled copies from my backpack. She unfolded them, paused a bit and placed them under the desk lamp to take full advantage of the light. I heard some plaintive 'ummms', 'ohhhhs', 'yes', and some indecipherable Greek. As she turned over the card I asked, as a young girl, whether she or perhaps her parents or even grandparents had known a man named Stavros, who apparently served in the French army as a pharmacist during the Great War.

"Well, Edouardos, a family named Seferis, operated the village pharmacy for decades, really since the 1880s. They lived on the first and second floors with the shop – the pharmacy – located on the ground floor. As a little girl in the late-1940s – after the war – my mother often sent me there to purchase medicine. Greeks had manners and courtesies back then so I always named him Mr Seferis, but I think I'm correct in remembering adults naming him Stavros. If him, he died in the late 1950s. His son, Pello, managed the business until he died sometime in the '90s – that's when I spent years in Athens assisting my mother. About ten years ago the Seferis family sold the business, perhaps because of the village's increasing popularity. I don't know but they moved. They left the island, I believe, but don't know where they went."

"The current pharmacy is a narrow building next to the bakery. Was that its location when you were a little girl?"

"Oh, yes, yes. That's been the location forever. That's where I purchased mother's medicine. The inside is different, of course, modern but it's the same. The old grandfather's clock remains surprisingly. It still bongs loudly on the hour. I used to love seeing the tall, dark, wooden cabinets filled with various-sized glass bottles, the smell of camphor, of peppermint, of grain alcohol. Oh... so medicinal and clean! Mr Seferis loved opera. He had a phonograph against the wall on the right-hand side as you entered the store. One of the duties of the clerk when a record had run its course was to change it and put on another. Always opera. Nothing else was permitted or ever heard! Music filled the square on sweltering summer days. I thought it lovely. My friends and I swooned to the music, especially the arias."

"Well, Ms Tsoussis, *efkharisto*. You've been kind and I am incredibly appreciative for you assisting me in tying together loose ends of my grandfather's experience. To think he stayed on the first or second floor of the pharmacy with the Seferis family in June 1919. Wonderful to imagine."

Before returning to the flat I visited the pharmacy, even walking in, imagining how it had appeared and had smelled years earlier as described by Ms Tsoussis. I couldn't miss the enormous clock positioned in the rear near the pharmacist's compounding bench, its pendulum moving in what appeared perfect timing. I stared incomprehensively at a bar of Greek olive oil soap on a shelf in an attempt not to bring attention to myself. It failed. The pharmacist looked up occasionally, wondering whether I really wanted a bar of soap or, as an upper middle-aged man, was in desperate need of laxatives or in hot pursuit of prophylactics but too embarrassed to ask. Feeling a bit uncomfortable, I moved on. But as I left the store I realised that in ten days – 28 June 2009 – it would be exactly ninety years since my grandfather wrote the first Greek postcard.

I returned to my flat to enjoy the view from the deck while reading the last of what had been a sizeable cache of books while simultaneously pondering my grandfather's visit with Stavros and his family. Naturally I took full advantage of the sun and, per Sara's admonition, drank plenty of water. After two hours, and with storm clouds brewing to the west, I went inside and took a shower followed by a brief nap. I had an inkling the questionable weather foreshadowed a wild night was on tap at Tselenti's. I needed rest.

Although not raining, I did compete with a fierce wind walking to the post office to mail Sara's final postcard and onwards towards the restaurant. The wind's coolness highlighted the natural porousness of my linen and cotton clothes. And my skin, warmed and browned by the sun after almost three weeks, felt cold. The storm's imminent arrival did not deter Tselenti's from seating people outside surprisingly. Being my predictable self who always anticipated what might, could or will go wrong, I dined inside. Minutes after ordering my meal the clouds dumped their contents with revengeful pleasure. Soon a crowd of dinner guests infiltrated the area, disturbing all pre-existing table and seating arrangements. Instead of someone joining my table for two, a young lady in a group of ten thankfully only asked if she could borrow the extra chair. I remained on my own, free to watch, to hear and to enjoy the antics of fellow tourists as they transitioned from well-mannered diners to pseudo-inebriants.

When most guests had finished their dinners two confident British ladies asked for special music. Mr Tselenti happily complied. This request was followed by others: moving tables to the sides to create a wide-open dance floor as well as canvassing the remaining thirty guests to compile a list of their five favourite songs. Mr Tselenti wasn't bothered by the rearrangement and embraced his new DJ assignment with fervid aplomb. People began dancing within minutes of the music starting. The speaker volume grew progressively louder as the music became more diverse: Tom Jones, The Doors, Pretenders, Duke Ellington, Frank Sinatra, Coldplay, Shirley Bassey, Supertramp, Blondie, Jack Jones, Duran Duran, even Benny Goodman and, unbelievably, Demis Roussos! The summer bar attendant, a young, middle-aged Russian lady from Moscow with short blonde hair and a whippet-like figure named Lara, prepared drinks as fast as possible. The demand increased steadily with each new song. Fortunately I never moved from my original location. I remained tucked in the far back corner... observing. Having waited on me most proficiently throughout my sojourn, Lara seemed concerned whether I had enough Scotch. After asking for a double she brought the entire bottle to the table.

"I doooo not know what 'doooouble' means. Pour what you want."

"Well, that's very kind, Lara, but do you have a jigger so I can measure the correct amount?"

"We have nothing like that, sorry. I pour then for you."

Whereupon she filled what appeared to be a small water glass to the brim. An equivalency, I imagined, of eight measures.

"Wow, I'll be here all night, Lara, and I'll feel it all day tomorrow."

"You are good customer. Mrs Tselenti told me with all these people here not to ignore Edouardos tonight."

"I couldn't possibly feel ignored, and in about thirty minutes I probably won't *feel* a thing, but thank you."

Soon thereafter one of the determined British ladies, responsible for making the evening happen, used every coquettish cliché in her repertoire to pluck me from my seat and join the dancing. My stubborn self never wavered. I emphasised, as politely as possible, the enjoyment I received from watching others. My amusement increased in direct proportion to my Scotch intake. It was similar to sitting in a cinema, I explained, watching a picture in technicolour equipped with surround sound. Everything – facial expressions, fashion, lack of fashion, good dance moves, bad dance moves, eaves-dropping on personal conversations – could be appreciated in a comfortable seat provided by Tselenti's. She finally accepted my obstinacy.

"Well, I'm damned, it's wonderful at least one person knows what the hell they like. Bloody marvellous."

And with that parting comment she turned around, and around and around… and ordered another dry martini from Lara.

Soon after convincing 'Miss Coquette' of my contentedness three police officers entered Tselenti's. The music softened and the room, which only a moment earlier had reverberated with laughter, talk and fun, became hushed. Mr Tselenti appeared from behind his stereo apparatus to greet the officers. Mrs Tselenti accompanied him. To my provincial mind it seemed an arrest was imminent. I was wrong. All the guests stopped talking and listened incomprehensibly to what many imagined was a heated discussion in Greek. Bits and pieces slowly emerged. A rather seedy bar/restaurant around the corner had become piqued at the noise level. It was ruining their customers' dining experience. Although way past midnight, few believed anyone would be eating dinner at such an hour or that a kitchen still would be preparing food. 'Miss Coquette' emerged from a darkened corner, took one of the officer's hands and pleaded with him to dance. She even ran her fingers through his curly hair. Everyone viewing her escapade doubled over laughing. She either was clueless to events or strategically trying to change their minds. Her allure failed. After the police left Mrs Tselenti told us the event was caused by pure jealousy. It happens regularly anytime the competing restaurant/bar lacked customers simply because… everyone was riffing at Tselenti's. She apologised and hoped we'd remain but lamented the music must be lowered. The damage had been done. Those who had drinks slowly finished them while talking softly to friends. Others paid their tab and departed. I remained, enjoying the large glass of Scotch Lara had served earlier. To alter what had morphed into a somewhat tense atmosphere, Mr Tselenti keyed up Sinatra's album *Nice 'n' Easy*, starting not with the lead song but with 'Mam'selle'. Mrs Tselenti immediately placed candles on several tables and dimmed the lights. The remaining diehards eagerly embraced the new environ. I… ordered another Scotch and thought of Sara. We'd be together tomorrow evening.

Everyone has opinions based on personal experiences, but as the cab made its way up the steep incline from Fiskardo, through Antipata, Maganos and all points south, I reflected on my three-week sojourn: it had served as a reaffirmation of life, a place for renewal. There is an unadorned simplicity in Greece. The rugged terrain is softened by the friendliness of the people. The natural healthiness of the food compensates for its simplicity. The inefficiency of abundant bureaucracies provides opportunities for expressive individualism. And the country's spirit is never static. Whether the movement is forward or backward it remains in perpetual motion. I looked towards the blue Ionian as the cab navigated the coastal road. I vowed to myself to return. I must come back. To enrich my soul and, as Chris advised, *Take a bite out of the ass of life.*

EIGHT

LONDON

Arriving at Argostoli with over two hours before my departure, I walked to a nearby taverna for one last Mythos and a Greek salad. A strong mobile connection enabled me to access messages. Sara had sent a slew of texts spread over three weeks. She voiced initial concern something may have happened, but soon realised a connection simply wasn't possible. Fortunately she received the first postcard within four days, allowing her to grasp early on that I was well and having a fabulous time. After a third text she decided to indulge in stream-of-consciousness messages whenever the mood struck her. She wasn't bothered I might not read them for weeks. They made for pleasant and distracting reading amidst the sounds of arriving and departing planes and the bustle of fellow travellers jockeying for food and drink.

> *At times I think I cannot wait to see you then I realise I would wait forever if I had to.*

I wish we were together right now.

I am thinking of you always.

It's my job to worry about you so limit the Vespers... please?

I was sitting by the fire tonight and feeling rather down. I know we will be fine but we had such a good time in Seattle together it seems so unfair for us to be apart. Then I thought, just get on with it, Hawes.

Been watching Brideshead. The boys are in Venice. Very good but very sad.

This is when I miss you most, not in the bad times but in the happy times that we cannot share.

I feel like the cat that got the cream with my American.

I really hope you are having a good day in Fiskardo. I am missing you more and more and cannot imagine what I will feel like after you visit.

I've been messing about with the photos from my Seattle visit. We were truly happy then but I feel we are even better now.

I'm content that you make me happy. I have no worries on that front. I would like to think that I can make you happy and that you will tell me if there is anything I do which upsets you.

I'm going in the tub now to have a glass of wine and listen to Chet Baker.

I feel fine with everything. It is always a drag to arrive home and adjust to having no one to talk to. Kisses from Plough Cottage.

Just had a great five-mile run with hills and no stopping. The mist is on the water and I loved it. How nerdy is that?

I'm missing our long chats but at least we'll have lots to discuss after you arrive in 'Blighty'.

I did a long run in the gym, lifted weights. How good am I?

I am home and about to watch a 'movie' – to be American about it.

I assumed Sara remained waist-deep in the double murder investigation that had preoccupied her before I left so I sent only a text: *Waiting for departure. All is well. Hair long. Got three weeks' beard growth. Am brown as Italian shoe leather. Cannot wait to wrap my arms around you!* After buckling in and before take-off I checked one final time before turning off the phone. No reply. *Good*, I thought, *I played it correctly.* I knew Sara well enough to know she drew an almost impenetrable line between work and pleasure. The two should never mix. And that… suited me perfectly.

A long immigration line ensured a lengthy delay but I was cleared eventually, making my way through a set of double doors where an additional barrier corralled passengers into a narrower passageway before being set free. I spotted Sara immediately. There was no hiding behind columns this time.

She looked fantastic – bright smile, expressive eyes and an air of confidence knowing her foreigner stood on British soil. We hugged and kissed as if it were the first time.

"Darling, oh my, you are so brown and feel wonderful… and hot… and scratchy with that beard but rugged! You're looking like that movie hero of yours. What's his name?"

"You mean Jerimiah Johnson, the 1840s mountain man who shunned society to hunt 'grizz'? I'll take it."

"Oh, of course, Jerimiah 'Liver Eatin'' Johnson. How *could* I forget?"

"I'm only hunting lanky, ginger-haired Brits, long in the body, and by the looks of it, I set my traps correctly."

"Edward, honestly. I thought the Greek sun would have baked some of that rudeness out of you."

"Too early in the season. From what locals told me, only August's heat bakes out rudeness, crudeness, orneriness and complacency."

"Any idea if it works on sarcasm?"

Ahhhh, I had missed her wisecracking. An entire week of repartee was in the offing. Once in the car, Sara handed me a snack: a homemade scone warm from the oven, a banana, an apple and a flask of water. I devoured all three and sipped the water while enjoying the view as she drove the scenic back roads to Eynsford. The Kent countryside was pretty. Red-brick homes with red-tiled roofs, Tudor cottages, some with thatched roofs, and the cone-shaped Oast houses reflecting the county's hop-growing heritage, commingled nicely under thick foliage from ancient English oak trees. After an hour we reached the narrow brick and stone arched bridge crossing the River Darent that figured so prominently in pictures Sara had sent earlier. Directly ahead was Plough Cottage – the classic waddle and daub-constructed home from 1490 that I first saw in a real estate brochure seven months earlier.

"Gosh, it resembles a Hollywood set, Sara. It really does."

"This isn't Hollywood. It's the real thing actually. You're in England."

"I'll be damned."

The door entry was low, forcing me to bend down twelve inches to walk in unscathed. Once inside, however, the cottage exposed its historical charms. The oak wall and ceiling beams separated by ancient plaster painted off-white caught my immediate attention, followed by an Inglenook fireplace that occupied three-quarters of the supporting, right-side wall. Carved deep within its firewalls were three non-functional bread ovens that had been sealed a hundred years ago. The fireplace mantel oozed antiquity. The beam was twelve inches thick and eight feet long. The growth circles indicated the tree had been at least three hundred years old when felled so, taking into account the cottage was five hundred years old, I was touching an over eight hundred-year-old piece of English oak – that had continued serving its secondary purpose exceedingly well.

Sara had planned a full first day. Arriving at Victoria Station we set off immediately to tour museums and view historical sites. Fortunately from Sara's days of 'walking the beat', she knew every crevasse, alley and shortcut throughout Soho, Mayfair, Chelsea, Westminster and the City of London. Her sense of direction was so exact, I thought the Met Police had imbedded a sat nav chip into her upper right arm. We remained far removed from the crowded main streets. I would have failed and failed miserably if Sara forced me to replicate the walks by myself.

At St Paul's Cathedral we huffed and puffed our way up 528 steps to the outer dome to view the London panorama. The time clock indeed was turned back in Whitehall at the Cabinet War Rooms. The originality of the entire bunker – from the sugar cubes sitting aside a teacup and Churchill's bedroom to the Remington Noiseless typewriters used by secretaries and stenographers and the Trans-Atlantic Telephone Room where Churchill spoke in secret to FDR were truly impressive. The Map Room, in fact, remained exactly as it had been in 1945 when the clerk turned off the lights and left the building. This was one occasion, I thought, where the overused cliché 'time stood still' seemed appropriate. It had in this instance. Sara understood my interest in the Great War so after leaving the Cabinet War Rooms we walked around the corner to the Cenotaph. Its visual and emotional austerity didn't celebrate victory but a questioning inarticulateness. Its solemnity was impressive.

Ever attentive to my historical interests, Sara force marched me along the banks of the Thames until we stood outside the Tate Britain. She pointed out that, although destroyed in the film *Spectre*, MI-6's headquarters remained solidly intact on the south side of the river, still opened for clandestine operations.

"A new exhibit showcasing your famed 'Bloomsbury Lot' opened recently to fab reviews. Thought you'd want to have a nose."

"Am I going in alone?"

"Oh, no, don't worry. I'll do my best to endure the insufferable."

"Demonstrating the proverbial 'stiff upper lip', I suppose."

"That's all tosh, you know. We don't like to complain. And we don't like hearing others complain either. That's all."

It was thrilling to view paintings I only had read descriptions of or seen in art books. The genuine article remained preferable despite the availability of online images. The overt simplicity of Vanessa Bell's *Studland Beach* (1912) transcended the generations. I found the works of the elusive

Dora Carrington expressive. *The Mill at Tidmarsh, Berkshire* (1918), the *Portrait of Annie Stiles* (1921) and the famous portrait of *Lytton Strachey Reading* (1916) didn't disappoint. All seemed a bit melancholy, but on reflection I realised I had interposed her tragic death on her early work. There was no disputing the relevance of Mark Gertler's famous anti-war work, *The Merry-Go-Round* (1916). His controversial *Creation of Eve* (1914) caught the reflective eyes of two well-dressed and poised octogenarians. Sara and I remained in place hoping to overhear their reaction.

"Oh, my, Beatrice, poor Eve looks as she'd been shot from a cannon."

"Yes, I see what you mean. A co-worker from the agency with whom I shared a flat after the war looked strikingly similar. Used to prance around the place like a wildcat – arms outstretched and without a stitch on… obviously proud of her figure *a la* Eartha Kitt. Something I never quite understood."

"Was that Caroline?"

"No, no, it was Mavis. You never knew her – physically confident and uproariously funny. Went off to Monaco and the south of France with a Frenchman who owned a yacht and never was heard from again."

"Well, at least it's warm there."

Sara and I could hardly contain ourselves. These ladies reflected a vanishing breed of Brit. Decorous with a bit of 'soft voice' condescension thrown in for spiciness. Glad I experienced them.

Completing an exciting day touring London necessitated finding a bar. I attempted to impress Sara with a list comprised months earlier – the Connaught, the Savoy – both the American Bar and the Beaufort Bar, Brown's Hotel Bar, Claridge's Bar as well as The Fumoir. She nixed them all: the Connaught was filled with loud, overly impressed-with-themselves nobs; the American Bar at the Savoy capitalised too heavily on its Jazz Age history in a Disney-like kind of way; the Beaufort was over-subscribed by 'ladies who luncheon'; Brown's had been remodelled so it resembled a business-class airport lounge; and Claridge's, well, Sara had arrested a guy in the bar years earlier for dodgy behaviour. She thought his actions so unhygienic it put her off returning socially.

"Don't be discouraged, MDA. I know an intimate place that tourists, proper wrongins and Americans couldn't possibly be familiar. It's in Mayfair but tucked in a close behind the Ritz, if you believe it!"

"You've walked me through London's tapered back streets in a manner only a detective would know. I'm confident whatever watering hole you've chosen will border on the secretive. The more unknown it is by the masses the better I'll like it."

"Don't be rude, Edward... 'the masses'. Honestly."

"I was going to say 'the unwashed' but thought you'd take offence."

Emerging from the tube at Piccadilly we hurried through Jermyn Street, passing the eponymous stores of Fortnum & Mason, Floris, Dunhill, Turnbull & Asser and Crockett & Jones. Eventually we crossed St James's Street onto Park Place. A short distance on the left was Sara's chosen venue: St James's Hotel and Club, specifically William's Bar. Housed in an old Victorian building constructed in 1857, it had opened initially as a club appealing to foreign diplomats. Only recently did its clientele include travellers capable of covering the tab.

The bar exuded class. An eclectic array of wood framed oil paintings from the 1920s – 1960s garnished the walls. Tufted gold sofas with cylinder-shaped cushions aligned the perimeter, melding perfectly with the single-seat club chairs fashioned in black and tan velvet. The bar accentuated by yellow-gold back-lighting worked well with six black glass tables adorned with stoneware bud vases. Classic jazz mixed occasionally with the melodious crooner played overhead. I soon discovered, however, that William's Bar served a purpose beyond booze and jazz. The environment is best summarised by what it is and what it is not. It was quiet and intimate. It was not a venue favoured by the Instagram or Facebook set. It was a place to hide if necessary, to be alone if desired. It was not a location for attention-seekers. It was a sanctuary for contemplation. It was not a venue for viewing the ridiculousness of humanity. It was an establishment whose clientele valued anonymity. Sara had chosen wisely. We settled in nicely after ordering our customary drinks: gin and tonic with lemon and Vesper martini. The barman excused himself after he confirmed we didn't desire anything else. He needed to prepare drinks for a private function on the first floor. We were alone. Hearing Dean Martin's 'Memories Are Made of This' prompted a conversation I didn't think possible at age fifty-two.

"Have you thought about the potential? Could be exciting. We'd have so much to offer a child… and the freedom to do, what I imagine, would be a fabulous job."

"Sometimes, before dozing off to sleep the last few months, I thought about the possibilities. But because age, condition and quality probably would limit success I've put it out of my mind. Kinda wasteful to pine for or to lament something that can't happen. Sounds cliché, but I've learned life offers one guarantee: there is no guarantee. Others have suffered far worse. That's why I've never brought it up. Thought the topic might surface someday if we continued seeing each other. I mean, you're young, fit… why wouldn't it? It's natural. It's important."

"Yes, but not having a child doesn't diminish the potential for a brilliant life."

"Oh, of course. Totally agree. Seems odd but couples I've known who appear the happiest, the most connected and the most fulfilled don't have children – whether by nature or personal decision. The important thing is they didn't squander time because of what they couldn't have. They focused their energy developing themselves as individuals and as a couple and became closer for it."

"So you're against trying?"

"No, no, not at all, but disappointment could be damaging. At least that's what doctors have told me. IMF is available nowadays so that's an option, I suppose."

"You mean IVF not IMF."

"Yeah, sorry. Don't think the International Monetary Fund would be concerned if we pursued In Vitro Fertilisation. What was I thinking?"

"I'm probably in the minority but I'm a bit uncomfortable with IVF."

"I'm ignorant of the whole process to be honest. What concerns you?"

"Two things. One – it's expensive and success isn't guaranteed so our bank account and emotions would sit beside the other on a rollercoaster. And second – and I only know this from a colleague who experienced IVF – two eggs are fertilised. The doctor choses the one most sustainable – for the lack of a better word – and discards the other."

"I see. So—"

"It's the unnaturalness of the whole thing. I'm giving permission for someone to choose, replacing natural probability."

"Isn't that the purpose?"

"Yes, but… then there's the moral issue, not to mention the angst created if the process failed. A bit too Orwellian."

"I understand. Don't like tampering with nature personally. From what you described it fits nicely with the greediness of our times. *I want it so I will do anything to have it.* Sometimes it's best to embrace what we have and accept what we don't. Makes for a less anxious life. And who knows, perhaps nature will take pity if we choose that path."

"Maybe so, but it's a troubling issue."

"There is something else, Sara. While we'd both experience emotional turbulence only you would endure the physical. Failure could wreak havoc. I wouldn't want you to experience such a life-changing event. It's too unfair, too selfish if I pressed the issue."

"Not even to secure a 'Lee' lineage?"

"Absolutely not. Not concerned in the least. Our enjoyment with each other is paramount. Little else matters."

"Edward, Edward… we have so much in common. It's… it's, well, if it wasn't believable it would be disconcerting. We don't give importance to unimportant things yet tackle important issues with fervid earnestness. And do so together."

"Well, you're easy to talk to, Sara – frank, honest with the requisite amount of sarcasm thrown in so I don't develop a 'big head'. Who wouldn't enjoy it?"

"I could think of many. And don't ask names because I won't divulge a vowel or a consonant regardless of many gin and tonics find their way to our table."

Finishing one last drink, Sara recommended Andrew Edmunds for dinner, an out-of-the-way bistro in Soho. I enjoyed listening and watching people as we made our way to the restaurant. Soho displayed a bit of everything – tragedy, comedy, drama and, depending on one's point of view, a pinch of eroticism. The atmosphere and food at Andrew Edmunds couldn't have been nicer. Nine tables competed for space in a narrow room. The only lights were single candles atop a wine bottle placed in the middle of each table. The woodland smells of wild garlic, truffles and grilled fish competed nicely with the distinctiveness of rosemary, wild mushrooms and baked chicken. The thought of dessert became an obligation when the aroma of apple-cinnamon crumble and mint chocolate soufflé made their way to an adjacent table. After a coffee and Vin Santo to settle the meal we began walking to Victoria Station via the back streets Sara knew so well. Along the way in the distance we kept hearing songs from the movie *Grease*. The clarity and volume increased as we navigated the crooked streets. Once we emerged from a darkened alley into an open area directly ahead was a blinking neon sign for The Stag, a well-known gay nightclub. The door opened as we walked by, necessitating me to have a nose. On stage were several revellers dressed as the 'Pink Ladies' singing 'Beauty School Drop-Out'. Thinking I was speaking to Sara, I wondered who would wear the skin-tight leather pants and perform 'You're the One That I Want'.

"Why don't you come in and find out?"

It was one of the 'Pink Ladies' standing far from the entrance smoking a cigarette. I became a bit nervous for the first time in a long while. What do I say?

"No… but thanks very much. We're in, ah… a bit of a rush to catch the last train from Victoria sadly. You sound wonderful, though."

"Well, Edward, that should teach you not to stick a nose so far in the door, won't it?"

The incident spurred us on. Five minutes remained before the train departed. Once relaxed in an empty train coach and with Sara asleep against my shoulder, all I thought about was our developing closeness. The memory of this day, of all days, was worth preserving.

Sara concocted a surprise for my last day. All she divulged the night before was we'd have to leave early in the morning.

To be in compliance I found myself with Sara at 8-am driving on a narrow country road. Horse riders and tall hedgerows prevented speeds exceeding 30-mph. After an hour I viewed the destination from a distant hill: Chartwell, Winston Churchill's country home near the village of Westerham in Kent.

"This is wonderful. Thank you. My parents admired and respected him a lot. Mom used to regal me with stories of ol'Winston's pugnacity before America entered the war. His warnings of Hitler's rise in the '30s. His speeches during the Battle of Britain. And, of course, the famed Iron Curtain speech in Fulton, Missouri – of all places – at the beginning of the Cold War."

"I'm sorry we couldn't enjoy our usual slow rise to greet morning but I wanted to arrive before tour coaches offloaded bushels of Americans, otherwise it becomes too overpowering, too overpopulated. And not nearly as enjoyable."

"No worries. Older Americans in particular can be exhausting. They relish bringing attention to themselves. I'm sure we'll see women displaying tacky symbols of Americana and men unabashedly wearing the 'Full Cleveland.'"

"What do you mean, 'Full Cleveland'?"

"Well... let's see, how to describe... It's a unique fashion style made popular by the World War II generation. It will disappear when they're through with life. At its purest, the 'Full Cleveland' consists of white, patent-leather shoes, knee-length black or white socks, double-knit short trousers and a solid colour polyester shirt. An absolute fashion disaster. Recent modifications permit plain street shoes and regular-length socks. A loosening of the rules unfortunately doesn't conceal its hideousness. That remains at full throttle."

"Lorrrrrd. I'll have to call the fashion police if we see anyone dressed like that."

"To be honest, I'd be disappointed if, on a hot day such as today, a coach full of Americans didn't yield at least one 'Full Cleveland'. In a surreal kind of way you've got to admire it: the ultimate fashion *faux pas* with a faithful, albeit diminished following."

While Sara presented her National Trust membership card, I picked up a travel brochure. Titled 'AMERICAN VISITORS', it highlighted specific items in the house – objects, letters and photographs – that chronicled the growing closeness throughout the war between Britain and America. I took my pen and blotted out the 'S', leaving only 'AMERICAN VISITOR', and placed it inside the breast pocket of my blazer so only it remained visible. Our early arrival enabled us to see most rooms alone. Churchill's study was particularly interesting. It was here in the 1930s that he wrote *The World Crisis*, a slightly biased history of the Great War. As we continued touring several room guides welcomed me, asked where I lived in the States and hoped I'd enjoy England. Although privy to the conversation, Sara never asked how they identified me as American. After two hours we left the house to view the surrounding gardens. One particular vantage point offered a panoramic view of the gardens and the house so I asked Sara to include me in the picture. As Sara took the shot the prominence of 'AMERICAN VISITOR' caught her eye.

"Oh, Edward, honestly. Now I understand why everyone knew you were an American. I had no idea. Lorrrrd. What are you like? You resemble a young, public school boy wearing a name badge in case you become lost."

"I like self-deprecating humour. If you can't laugh at yourself you probably shouldn't be around others, don't you think?"

"Perhaps, but right now you should turn around and look to the front... at the coach that's off-loading passengers."

"A potential target rich environment of 'Full Clevelands'. Be on the lookout, Sara, be on the lookout, for that rare breed, that genuine specimen of Americana."

As if on cue, an American couple walked by. The lady wore a bejewelled American flag broach and a 'Sarah Palin for President – 2012' baseball cap. Her husband didn't disappoint. He sported a 'Full Cleveland' including a patent-leather white belt that matched his shoes. His not-so-subtle adherence to a political philosophy was a pin badge of crossed flintlock rifles crowned with the letters 'NRA'. That told much of what I needed to know. We overheard them talking as we made our way to the car.

"Churchill and Roosevelt got along great. And Reagan and Thatcher… close friends. They singlehandedly brought our nations together. Can't imagine Obama getting along with any English leader."

"Of course he won't. How could he? He wasn't even born in America."

"Now you've heard it, Sara. The genuine ignorance of Yanks abroad is not remarkably different from Yanks at home. Difficult to digest, but I'm guessing it's only going to get worse."

"Well, then, take that AMERICAN VISITOR advertisement out of your pocket!"

I placed it neatly inside the car's glove box. Thought I'd keep it as a unique 'cross-cultural' memento.

The last evening at Plough Cottage Sara and I discussed the future – our future – something we hadn't done since our intimately personal conversation at William's Bar. An east wind had brought its distinctive brand of summer coolness so we started a fire in the Inglenook, opened a bottle of Vacqueyras and enjoyed the light dinner Sara had prepared.

"I've been thinking about our relationship, Sara. It's genuine. It's unique. It's intense. And for all the provocativeness inherent in a trans-Atlantic romance, it's also unsettling. I'm too young to retire and so are you. Who between us is bold enough to pull chocks, leave their job, sell their home for a life destination unknown – and it is unknown despite naive cries that 'love conquers all' – we both know it doesn't. The answer: neither one."

"Don't you think your presentation a bit harsh?"

"I'm sorry. I don't mean it to be. Too brutally honest, I guess. It's just… well, you know how I like to plan. To see the future. To know where I'm headed. I see us together… but I have difficulty uncovering the path that will get me there. To make 'us' a reality."

"I understand but relationships revolve around spontaneity more than precise planning. I'm not worried. I know my life destination – at least I think I do. Prickly issues resolve themselves over time. And if yours doesn't, well, then, it probably wasn't meant to happen. Please don't be impatient."

"I thought that would be your response so hear me out on what might be a workable albeit temporary solution. What if I worked part-time? I'm certain my boss would agree, especially since it involves a cut in pay and benefits. I'd work two and a half weeks in Seattle and spend the remaining time at Plough. Who knows, maybe I'd find new clients in the UK. Your career isn't impacted. Your healthcare remains intact. In fact, with me on the scene handling house chores, gardening, food shopping and whatnot, your life will be less stressful and more fulfilling. I know mine would be."

The heat of the fire coupled with the red wine had made Sara's freckled cheeks turn rosy. After a reflective stare into the flames, she gathered her thoughts.

"The idea of living together half the time, I think, would be too disruptive. We would be constantly unsettled – at least I'd be. If together all the time then the time spent away would be fine – give us space – but not if you're coming and going. I'm open to ideas but afraid I'd no more than get used to us and you'd be back on a plane. And I'm not greedy about money but... the cost alone doesn't make it worthwhile. A significant portion of whatever you earned would be spent on air travel."

"I'm not prepared to leave America totally – not yet anyway. Obama has given serious-thinking Americans genuine hope. The nation seems to be making positive and corrective changes. The country is regaining its élan. This scenario has me earning money, sharing the financial burden, and... our self-contained safety nets remain intact. No one is displaced. No one sacrifices too much."

"I know. I appreciate that, but it's important for you to feel comfortable with me in England. Your suitcase needs to be empty of worries. The same would be true if I moved to Seattle – too much disruption, me flying back and forth to England twice a month. Relationships require stability, especially new ones. Whether we admit it or not, both of us crave assurance from the other that there never will be and never could be anyone else. No person, no event, no condition could come between us. A seemingly impossible guarantee few obtain so they stop looking, but it's something uncompromisingly essential for me."

"I realise that, believe me, I understand. That's only one of many reasons I cherish you. Remember... Fritzy refers to it as an emotional structure – incorporating the obvious architectural metaphor."

"Yes, I remember. And it makes perfect sense. But I've become so used to being alone it would be fabulous to have you full time. I'd love you on site. I'm never bored with my own company but miss having someone to discuss everything with at times. You may not be aware, but it's pretty challenging debating with yourself."

"Oh, I don't know, I enjoy debating myself. I always win."
"You are funny."
"But seriously... I guess we'll continue dividing our time between two continents until one of us has an epiphany, until one of us – me, in particular – stops planning, stops anticipating and finds contentedness."
"I'm hoping that discovery comes soon. I can't help thinking after a period of time, certainly after we've made the decision, spending years apart is simply wasting precious time. We'd lose more than we'd gain."

Sara's kernels of wisdom never disappointed. It also reflected the distinctive British propensity to discipline someone verbally without them taking immediate offence; an attribute worth learning. She had administered a soft blow to the head without even clinching a fist. There was no denying Sara felt confident in her life destination. The next decision was mine to make. The relationship was mine to win. It also was mine to lose.

I had an early-morning departure the next day so Sara and I climbed into bed earlier than normal. She fell asleep immediately. I remained coiled, tight as a banjo string, as my mind busily processed the last month. My four-week holiday had been a cultural awakening. Greece, to me, was inherently unique. Comparisons couldn't be made. Attempts would prove inadequate. And England, well, it illustrated better than anywhere I had visited the broad differences between the Old World and the New World. I tallied the dissimilarities while trying to doze off: make do and mend vs. disposability; Church of England ecumenism vs. American evangelical intolerance; retrofit and refurbish vs. tear down and build new; quiet conversation vs. boisterous bloviating; 'interesting perspective' vs. 'this is how it's done'; walking and using public transport vs. incessant vehicle use; limited retail hours vs. open fourteen-hours a day; tradition vs. no tradition; respecting the past vs. ignoring the past; anti-social behaviour vs. anything goes; and finally, beneficial for the community vs. beneficial for the individual.

A more important experience than both Greece and England, of course, was Sara. Our growing closeness had strengthened the possibility of achieving what we both desired. Although comparing our relationship to a two-for-one commodity deal was inappropriate, I accepted that's how it could appear to friends. More challenging than how they perceived events, however, was determining whether I had conflated affection with the desire to escape America. Was my departure inevitable or was I using Sara merely as a pathway towards a yet unrealised new life? I didn't find the answer that night nor the nights that followed. The dilemma became the cussedness of my life.

NINE

THE COOP AT NETHERBY HALL, CUMBRIA

Throughout summer and early autumn, Sara and I kept to the schedule first outlined in New York. She spent a week in August while I reciprocated with a visit in September. These meetings corroborated that something unique was developing. A relative ease and comfort existed between us. Trust became implicit. Humour omnipresent. And an air of unpretentious simplicity shrouded any need to be around others. The desire for one to visit the other in October or November had weighed heavily, but we were too overburdened by work. The ensuing ten weeks became the longest time since New York that we hadn't seen one another. We tootled along the best we could, never complaining or lamenting our positions. One certainty remained, however: the prolonged absence would ensure a splendid Christmas.

Two weeks before I left to celebrate what Sara labelled

as a 'Dickensian Christmas', the natural-born citizen issue of President Obama unfortunately gained prominence among Republicans. Soon it blossomed into a rallying cry for far-right political fundraising and the upcoming midterm elections. Sarah Palin, in particular, openly questioned Obama's birth records. She thought Republicans had addressed the issue too timidly during the '08 campaign when she was Senator John McCain's running mate. Others jumped in eventually – including the insufferable Donald Trump, who, a few years later, would parlay the racist lie into a presidential campaign. I took little note of these events initially, only laughing in abhorrent disgust. The seriousness of this quirk that metastasised into a political and social malignancy lay in the future. I remained focused on Sara.

The night before departing the weather proved warm for Seattle. The dense fog belied the normal feeling of coolness. I prepared my signature Vesper martini, keyed up Wynton Marsalis's *Standard Time, Intimacy Calling* and sat outside on the deck. As usual for a late night, a brawl had commenced outside the infamous whisky bar across from my building on Second Avenue. Being nine floors up didn't obscure my line of sight. Not only could I see as events unfolded, I heard with crystal clarity the raucous voices screaming profanities and threats intermixed with Christmas carols. It seemed a man and a woman dressed as Mr and Mrs Claus had taken offence to being thrown out of the illustrious establishment and proceeded to pound on the large, plate-glass windows. It wasn't their boisterousness that caught mine or passers-by's attention. It was their clothes – well, actually, their lack of clothes. 'Mr Claus' had on his signature Santa hat, white whiskers and gold spectacles but nothing else. Poor 'Mrs Claus' wore only her signature hat. Despite the warmness of the night their bodies displayed all the physical signs of being cold. Two police cruisers with four personnel soon arrived. They took hold of the 'Clauses'. Told them to spread their legs and place hands over their head and against the windows they had been beating earlier. Realising they were only drunk and posed little threat, an officer went to his car and returned with two grey blankets of which the fish-belly white Clauses graciously accepted. As an officer loaded 'Mrs Claus' into the backseat, she stopped momentarily and shouted, "God bless us, everyone!" As if on cue, 'Mr Claus' joined in: "Merry Christmas to all and to all a good night."

With so many trips under our belts, the flights, the immigration cues and questioning, and luggage nut-roll had become rote. Only the embrace and welcoming kiss continued to excite. We had agreed earlier that to save time and avoid heavy traffic we wouldn't return to Plough Cottage. We began the trek northward directly from Heathrow. Of course, in Sara's inimitable way, she didn't divulge where we were spending the holiday. I squeezed out only the slightest hint of a confession.

"It will be full of history, a shared personal literary and cultural landmark, and a cosy accommodation that will create lasting memories."

As she opened the boot to store my suitcase I saw a hefty-sized box.

"I decided to acknowledge the ninetieth anniversary of the American Congress passing the Volstead Act. Putting it on its head. In other words, we won't suffer the indignity of a dry household this Christmas."

She lifted the box lids to reveal several narrow-necked bottles of fine wines and champagnes, single-malt Scotches, English gins and an exquisite bottle of rare, French Normandy calvados bottled *before* the war.

"Obviously impressed with your knowledge of early twentieth-century American history, but I'm really taken by the booze you've purchased. The quality is difficult if not impossible to find in the States... and frightfully expensive, if even available."

"Since you understand British history, I thought the least I could do was develop a broad-brush appreciation for our 'former' colonies. And the wines and all, well... just say I have a friend with connections."

"I won't ask anything more."

"Oh, it's nothing untoward or clandestine. Don't be too impressed. A little is okay, though."

"I look forward to uncorking a bottle while quizzing you on the causes of the American Revolution, specifically your analysis of what historians often refer to as Britain's 'benign neglect.'"

"Oh, Edward, honestly. Don't be rude!"

"I thought I was being pedantic rather than rude."

"I think I'm detecting a heightened level of incorrigibleness that must be drummed out of you – somehow, anyhow. You've been away from me too long."

"You've got a week to recast me. Better start cracking."

Although experiencing the British countryside from inside a car driving along the motorway has limitations, it nonetheless oozed a certain rustic peacefulness. Crass billboards and fast food eateries did not clog the roadsides or compete with the scenery. And, for the most part, fellow drivers seemed well-mannered, lacking any sense of aggressiveness. We didn't experience speeding, tailgating, horn blowing or road rage, making me believe such behaviour may belong exclusively to Americans. Four hours into the journey Sara announced we had arrived at our first destination: Castle Howard, near the hamlet of Ganthorpe in North Yorkshire.

"Here we are, Edward – how did I describe it – 'our shared personal literary and cultural landmark'. How's that for exciting?"

"I'm truly dumbfounded... pinch me hard so I know

I'm actually here! Unbelievable... and that's not American hyperbole. Thank you."

"Ouch!"

"I do what I'm told."

"That is what Americans refer to as a 'figure of speech', Sara. Guess I'll be more careful in the future."

"There's wisdom in that statement."

"Your sarcasm is totally out of hand. We both have been separated from the other for too long."

The estate appeared exactly as it had almost thirty years earlier when the television series of Evelyn Waugh's classic *Brideshead Revisited* premiered. We walked the grounds. Milled around the site of the temporary army encampment. Sauntered up the single-tracked lane on the castle's south front where Captain Charles Ryder viewed 'Brideshead' for the first time since his agonising break from Julia years earlier. Sat by the imposing Atlas Fountain, remembering it as essential backdrop to the intense discussions between Charles and Julia as well as the frivolous, light-hearted banter of Charles and Sebastian during their languorous days at Oxford. Relaxed on the steps of the Temple of the Four Winds to take in the sprawling landscape and watch the swans swim uncaringly in the nearby lake. Castle Howard's interior, of course, evoked a cavalcade of memorable scenes from the television production. The Great Hall, in particular, brought back wonderful memories. Much to Sara's embarrassment, I jokingly asked a room steward the location of Nanny Hawkins's room.

"I probably shouldn't do this but since we have few visitors today, please come with me."

We followed him along a corridor aligned with marble busts of historic Greek and Roman philosophers, poets and emperors, finally making our way through a ceiling height door that entered into a small room.

"Recognise the hearth? Can't you imagine Nanny sitting near on her cushioned chair knitting while remonstrating Sebastian for his undignified behaviour in London?"

"Interesting. In the series her room is perceived to be quite small. And this, well, is incredibly spacious."

"The director paired it down deliberately with decorated panels and other bits of furniture to make it homely. He loved the mantel, feeling it integral to Nanny's character and a place of refuge and comfort for Sebastian. Unsurprisingly, I suppose, the chair remains in use, residing in one of our back offices. A bit worn and tattered but ever so comfortable."

After thanking the man for bending the rules for our benefit, Sara and I went outside, walked slowly down the elongated steps towards the boxwood gardens surrounding the Atlas Fountain.

"Amazing what happens when you ask."

"American confidence plays havoc with my English sensibilities."

"Please continue to be yourself. I have no need or little desire for you to change."

"Thank you. But I will admit… it was exciting and a bit naughty to go behind the scenes."

In an odd but significant way Castle Howard made me reflect on plans I had made as a young man serving in the army. I recalled a few lines from *Brideshead Revisited* that had been committed to memory years earlier: *The languor of youth – how unique and quintessential it is! How quickly, how irrecoverably, lost!*[1] Procrastination and the passage of time, it seemed, might have scuttled my more ambitious intentions.

---

1   Evelyn Waugh, *Brideshead Revisited, The Sacred and Profane Memories of Captain Charles Ryder* (Boston: Little, Brown and Company, 1945), p. 79.

Ever the stern taskmaster, Sara encouraged us onward before the late December sky descended into darkness. An hour later, as the remaining bits of sun disappeared to the west, the moon appeared on the horizon, casting a florescent beam of light over the countryside. Minutes later I saw mileage signs for Hadrian's Wall and Housesteads Roman Fortress.

"We're almost at our destination, Edward."

"I don't believe it... Hadrian's Wall. You are absolutely *full* of surprises, Sara. I'm so, so... impressed. It's something every American school kid learns about by at least age ten."

I leaned to my right and kissed her cheek.

"Don't interfere with the driver. You'll cause an accident. Honestly."

Suddenly on my left, I saw a lone tree standing between a natural break in the hills. The moon had cast enough light so I could actually see parts of Hadrian's Wall descending down one hill and up the other.

"That's Sycamore Gap, darling. Won't be long now. The little pub we're staying at, Twice Brewed, is further along the Military Road. It's plain and rustic but a colleague said the food and ale are wonderful. After a good night's sleep we'll walk alongside the wall to the fortress and have a nose. Up for it?"

"I'm up for everything... hot food, fine ale, a soft bed, a ginger woman long in the body lying next to me and a leg-extending hike in the morning. To paraphrase George Gershwin – *who could ask for anything more?*"

"Don't be rude."

After a much-anticipated sleep and a hearty breakfast we began the three-mile hike to Housesteads, one of the most northern frontier posts of the Roman Empire, ca. AD 122. The well-worn trail hugged the undulating Hadrian's Wall, making the walk feel twice as long and three times as challenging. What normally would have taken less than an hour morphed into ninety minutes. A horizontal rain, courtesy of a biting east wind from Norway, pelted us soon after arriving. Touted to be the most complete example of a Roman fort in Britain, it didn't disappoint. More than simply moss-covered rocks on the ground. Using imagination and a bit of interpolation we could visualise how the designs of the barracks, granaries, bakery, baths, hospital, the commanding officer's house and the interval towers were reflected in what remained. The remote location and barren landscape made me pity the eight hundred Roman soldiers stationed here centuries earlier – far removed from their native blue skies, soothing sun, and plentiful fruits and nourishing vegetables. They must have missed home. As we made our way on the now slippery and sloppy trail along the wall, a low-lying fog moved in from Scotland. Cold and wet and barely able to see more than fifteen paces to the front, we made it safely to the car eventually.

I began to appreciate that like ales, cheeses, puddings and accents, the weather in Britain quickly changes within a sixty- or seventy-mile radius. We encountered blue skies, bright sun and a mild breeze after travelling west for about an hour, a complete reversal of what we'd experienced earlier. Soon we arrived at a down-healed village in Cumbria close to the Scottish border. Sara obviously saw my look of disappointment but assured me that I should relax; the village didn't mirror the location nor the quality of our accommodation. I started to doubt her reassuring words, however, after she turned onto a single-tracked farm road riddled with potholes. For two miles we drove at a maximum speed of five miles per hour. Gradually a luxurious Georgian estate appeared far on the horizon.

"That's Netherby Hall, Edward… but we're not staying there. Disappointed?"

"Ahhh, no, not exactly. Bit sprawling for two, don't you think?"

As Sara manoeuvred the car onto another tracked road, our lodgings finally came into view: a reddish, two-storey stone structure conjoined by two Gothic towers sitting next to the fast-flowing River Esk. Known as Coop House, it was built in 1750 by the owner of nearby Netherby Hall. He intended it as a place for his family and future generations to enjoy the river and to catch salmon and sea trout aided by the nearby weir. A bevy of swans and a gaggle of geese soon joined hundreds of grazing sheep enjoying themselves in the nearby fields.

A cosy interior increased our hopes for a relaxed Christmas. A small but efficient coal and wood-burning fireplace, a spacious living room with a comfortable sofa and overstuffed chair, a fully equipped galley-like kitchen, and a large bathtub outfitted with a waterfall shower head offered all the comforts necessary for a week-long visit. The bedroom, which overlooked both the river and the grazing field, supported a bed and a night table with little space or need for anything else. The building's most welcoming asset: no television, no access to the internet or to email. We could ignore the outside world and blame our selfishness on the house. We were blissfully alone.

Curious about our immediate surroundings, we walked about a mile along the river's edge, experiencing cranes, kingfishers and the occasional leaping salmon. Soon we came upon a narrow suspension bridge designed exclusively for foot traffic. We crossed, walked through a cluster of trees to find a quaint, stand-alone church. Still operational, Kirkandrews-Upon-Esk had been rebuilt in 1775 on the foundations of the original twelfth-century structure. Designed by a student of the eponymous architect Sir Giles Gilbert Scott, the simple

Georgian exterior complemented the lavish Baroque interior perfectly. Located in an area regarded for centuries as debatable land, questions of ownership persisted until 1603, when the unification of England and Scotland settled the matter.

We repeated this walk often throughout our stay, sometimes venturing in the opposite direction along the river through scrub brush intermixed with beautiful birch trees. One sunny afternoon we ventured north-east along the river, following its twists and turns and curves until we reached the border. The site obviously was well known because there was a small foot bridge with a sign indicating where to place your feet to experience divided loyalty – the left foot in England while the right foot remained in Scotland.

We returned regularly to the Coop before dark, conscience of the winter sun's early disappearance. A warm fire, a good book, and a couple glasses of the fine wines and Calvados Sara brought made for comfortable afternoons and relaxing evenings. All this, of course, was aided and abetted since the first night by the lights and a few choice ornaments Sara placed on a gnarly, moss-covered branch found on the ground outside.

"You said we'd have a Dickensian Christmas, Sara, and that 'Bob Cratchit' tree certainly enhances the ambiance. Only thing missing, I'm afraid, is a small wooden crutch leaning in the far corner."

"Honestly. Mocking the Cratchits and poor Tiny Tim."

"Not at all. Not at all. After *Tale of Two Cities*, it's my favourite work of Dickens. The reader develops a tremendous empathy for the Cratchit family. A rare book that's always worth another read… especially this time of year."

"Oh, I agree. Marvellous story…"

Sara got up and added another log to the fire, refilled her wine glass and reclaimed her seat on the sofa. As she glanced at the Gothic-framed picture window facing the river, she gently touched her upper lip with an index finger. I had seen this often. She was thinking.

"I'm happy and content here, Edward. And I hope you are, too."

"Very much so. You've chosen a wonderfully isolated and romantic spot."

"You've always taking the lead asking deep questions so this time... well, thought I'd have a go. Mind awfully?"

"Fire away, Sara, fire away."

"Now you may not be able to answer quickly... could require some thought but that's okay. What is or has been the happiest time of your life?"

"I've got that one covered surprisingly."

"Of course. Answers at the ready, in the breach, just waiting to be... sorry, that's not kind."

"That's fine, don't worry. Humour and sarcasm are sport. And you, my dear, excel at both."

"Don't know if that's a compliment but I'll take it. Thanks."

"You see, the reason I don't have to struggle with a response is I return to that time often – for grounding, for inspiration, for understanding. And the life philosophy – for the lack of a better word – I developed in this period has come into its own recently. So the immediate answer: My four years as a university undergraduate."

"I thought it would be connected somehow with history or education."

"They were wonderful years. I was alone. Only me. No one held expectations for me except myself. I didn't have to impress or be responsible to others the way I had been when younger. And by others I mean parents, the community, the Boy Scout Troop, the church, even my saxophone teacher. I concentrated solely on academics. University professors didn't mollycoddle. They assisted in every way possible but only if you demonstrated interest and took the initiative. I embraced their approach. The pureness of that ethic appealed to me. But in a refreshing way, I also understood society had no interest in what I did, how I did it or whether I accomplished anything – except, of course, if I broke the law or morphed into a public nuisance. I began to appreciate that not being accountable to or dependent on others defined individual freedom. All responsibility for success or failure belonged to me, no one else. Despite constant pleas from friends who encouraged me to, *enhance the campus experience*, I refused to pledge a fraternity, believing it too superficial, too temporal, too adolescent. It would interfere with achieving academic excellence."

"Ever consider you may be looking through sepia-coloured glasses?"

"I did initially. Yes. A year after graduating and while travelling to my first army posting after earning my aviator wings, I thought about why I so enjoyed university life. Somewhere while driving through the Bitterroot Mountains in Montana – probably near Lolo Pass – I developed the concept of simple contentedness. Then the larger world intervened and pushed the idea aside so I stored it in some atavistic cranny of my brain, hoping it would remerge someday. Since the only thing we own is our past I've tried recently to resurrect it, to eke out some deeper meaning from life experiences. Remember when we stayed at Fritzy's place on San Juan Island and how I lamented not being able to act, to follow through? So, you see, it can't be labelled nostalgic."

"Oh, dear, you *have* thought long and hard on this. And, yes, I remember discussing isolation and solitude – physical and emotional… and your frustration. Didn't realise though the idea first percolated in your head so long ago."

"Of course, that freedom, that independence I experienced as an undergrad never recurred. Work created responsibilities. It demanded working with and for others. Self was subordinated to the organisation where egos, backstabbing, intrigue, competition, boredom, aggression and laziness abounded. I'm not whining but that's reality. Can't be avoided. Christ, even Michelangelo had to please the Pope! But after thirty-plus years, I've reached a position in life where I could experience absolute freedom… and simple contentedness for the *second* time. I'm hopeful this time that thinking and talking won't run too far ahead of doing."

"The similarities between us don't seem to end, Edward. Two experiences stand out most in my life. Camping in the Yorkshire Dales National Park as a young girl during family holidays had a huge impact. It wasn't the family component necessarily, but the freedom to walk and to roam on my own and be surrounded by nature. I loved the rugged openness of the countryside. The endless lines of dry-stone walls cascading up and down hills cleverly delineating boundaries. The tea-coloured streams and rivers cutting their way through hillsides and onward to the valleys below. Although the wildlife in the Dales was not as dramatic as in other parts of the world to me it was perfect. Birds of prey such as falcons and hawks, barn and tawny owls, pheasants, grouse and wide varieties of migratory birds. During the early summer months several kinds of bats appeared. I often stayed up late to watch their nightly routine. And as peculiar as it sounds, I even was drawn in by the intense smell of the muck. There's no denying… it's unique."

"Do you visit every summer?"

"Pretty much… maybe ten, twelve times."

"Now I appreciate why you plan to retire there. Seems breaming with everything you value and enjoy."

"The second time period occurred during my first two years with the police. I walked the beat alone, kitted out in a dark blue skirt and tunic, a leather shoulder handbag and Dr Martens shoes. Armed with a 'woman-sized' truncheon, I resembled Olive Oyl of Popeye fame. I was stationed at Bow Street Station in Covent Garden. Sounds odd, I suppose, but it was there where I experienced absolute independence for the first time. I followed procedures obviously, but anything that occurred on the street – robbery, burglary, murder, prostitution, disorderly conduct, anti-social behaviour – was my responsibility. You didn't patrol with a partner so if things become dangerously sticky, I called for support, otherwise I handled everything myself. Similar to your experience, it was up to me – on my own to make of it what I wished. That kind of freedom was so heady. I don't believe twenty-year-olds experience this today. Parents and mobile phones won't allow it."

"Don't remember where I read this but it seems fairly accurate, in view of our recent reveals: *You learn everything important in life by age twenty-five.*"

"I guess we were fortunate realising the value of contentedness within ourselves so young."

"For many being alone means abject loneliness."

"I can't accept that. Not an option really. Couldn't possibly be bored with myself."

"People will get bored of me long before I become bored with myself."

"Oh, Edward, honestly."

We organised our calendars for the coming year soon after returning to Plough Cottage, deciding to share the burden equally – four visits each for a joint total of eight. We agreed also that the host could continue working during the other's visit. Sara's holiday allotment far exceeded mine, but even she couldn't take off eight weeks. And besides, we thought the visitor could explore on their own, become disoriented and subsequently lost in their adopted city.

"I'll be curious how you feel about Seattle in February, Sara. It's shrouded in grey – concrete buildings, low ceilings, fog and clouds overflowing with miserable rain. Sometimes there won't be sun for weeks. Dense fog weaves its way through every urban crevice, often remaining days if not weeks. When I first reported for duty in the army, I didn't see Mt Rainier for six weeks. The ironic thing: Gray Army Airfield – and no, I'm not making-up the name – is positioned at the base of the Cascade Mountains. I had to ask my platoon sergeant where the volcano was exactly."

"I'm flexible. I can cope for a week. And who knows, maybe the greyness will inch me ever closer towards drinking Scotch."

"Well then, from a selfish point of view, it'll be worth it."

"Shame you couldn't stay for New Year's Eve."

"I know, but the special priced fare was too good not to act. To stay another day would have added another $600. Airline companies do it deliberately, you know."

"To be honest, Edward, I couldn't give a monkey's about New Year's. Never appealed to me actually. Another manufactured holiday where everyone is supposed to act passionately. Similar to Valentine's Day."

"Funny we never talked about it before I made the reservation… but I agree. Great potential for a wasted evening."

"Guess my so-called regretting sounds rather fraudulent now."

"No, not at all. Don't worry. We've only known each other one year – so we can't be expected to have covered every topic… despite our perverse fondness for talk."

She sat on the edge of the bed while I packed the few items returning with me to Seattle. The majority of clothes, boots, shoes and books I brought remained behind. A near-empty suitcase allowed me to pack what I considered so far to be the best of England: Dorset Simply Nutty Muesli, Hop Shop Lavender Farm Honey and Rococo Truffles from London.

"We can't be too glum, Edward. I'll see you in seven weeks."

"And to quote a beautiful British friend of mine, 'That's nothing!'"

Sara had volunteered to work New Year's Eve. She felt it the least she could do in fairness to her colleagues who covered Christmas Eve, Christmas Day and Boxing Day. It made even greater sense with me leaving in the early evening. She dropped me off outside Victoria Station. Because we had shared our farewells prior to leaving Plough Cottage, we suspended with any last-minute public demonstration. A grab of the suitcase, a meaningful kiss and then goodbye. Once comfortably settled on the Heathrow Express, I reflected on our relationship. I didn't know what Sara derived or hoped to achieve with me but her presence in my life provided a beautiful way to cope with an increasingly absurd world.

TEN

LONDON

I RETURNED BOYISHLY HAPPY from this trip and the many others that followed. Sara also had sacrificed in the intervening years, frequently making five-day turnaround flights to Seattle. The tally between us: thirty-two flights in four years. Despite the obvious logistical and financial commitment, I found difficulty solidifying what must assuredly had been expected by Sara, her friends, even Fritzy. I couldn't shake my much-maligned proclivity towards predetermining outcomes. Couldn't crack the mould to which I had been cast so long ago.

By late autumn 2012, America had replaced with reasoned intellect the most egregious bravados of George W. Bush. The nation, it seemed, had regained a modicum of respect on the world stage. Significant portions of the horrors of the early twentieth-first-century had been corrected. Barrack Obama seemed positioned for certain re-election. An indescribable calm had fallen over the land... well, at least in Seattle, requiring me to make a decision.

Some things, I decided, must be done in person despite their awkwardness. I couldn't end our relationship with a lengthy phone conversation – too inconsiderate. An explanatory letter would be inappropriate – too unfeeling regardless of the words chosen. So I visited London to tell Sara goodbye. I thought it best if we met someplace neither had been, not wanting to spoil memories from some of London's finest hotel bars, low-end and high-end restaurants or our favourite bench in a remote spot in Regent's Park. Perhaps I presumed too much. Maybe she'd want to forget. But selfishly I didn't want my memories soiled. I hoped mine could be cocooned in my reverie, untrammelled by sorrow.

After lengthy research I decided on Knight's Bar, directly above Simpson's on the Strand close to the eponymous Savoy Hotel. As a hardened vegetarian I doubted Sara had visited simply because it has remained the quintessential restaurant for classic British meat dishes since 1828. The bar was intimate, isolated and far removed from the smells and toil of the restaurant. I thought it perfect.

Thinking we'd be alone and unlikely to be disturbed by others desirous of a good time, I decided half two would be a quiet time to rendezvous. I arrived thirty minutes early. Sure enough it was empty. The place seemed cosier than portrayed on the website. The wrap-around bar had a black and gold chessboard motif, reflecting Simpson's heritage as the epicentre of nineteenth-century chess-playing. The design of two-seat sofas and oversized armchairs evoked the Jazz Age as did the trad jazz recordings playing overhead. The green and gold furnishings meshed perfectly with the black glass and bronze circular tables. Full-length curtains muffled outside noises. The discrete ambiance of the room and soft lighting didn't demand attention. Sara should find it comfortable. And as pathetic as it sounds, the environment wouldn't flippantly dismiss what we had shared. I chose a remote table in the far-left corner. I summoned the waiter and ordered the usual Vesper. Fifteen minutes later I ordered another, sat back and waited. Undergoing two root canal surgeries simultaneously would be preferable to what I had to do.

Sara arrived at exactly half two and, seeing me in the far corner, half-smiled and sauntered over. She waved off the solicitous bartender. Perhaps it was my nerves, but her radiance brightened the room. There was no denying she looked fabulous. Sara never lacked confidence but this afternoon she evoked a feeling as if no task was too difficult. She'd survive regardless of the outcome. But I understood her better than anyone. I knew Sara's other side. She had a sensitive soul. Underneath the tungsten armour was a heart filled with emotion and hope and love. And I was about to puncture it. Me, the ultimate deterministic man, inflicting pain on the woman I love... not loved... but still love today, in this London bar on the Strand.

Since we were alone I needed an embrace but I could tell immediately from Sara's expression she'd resent any display of affection. She sat next to me on the sofa instead of in the facing chair. I understood why, of course: Sara anticipated an emotionally tense and possibly contentious conversation and, respectful of privacy, didn't want anyone overhearing. Like most things she did for or to me, I appreciated it. Down deep, however, I knew she had engineered this manoeuvre for self-protection.

"I probably have read the ending already, Edward, but I'm curious as to why. When you cancelled Christmas in Cornwall two weeks ago I knew something was up... and it wasn't going to end nicely, especially for me. Using work as an excuse seemed too transparent and fake."

"We both lose, Sara. So much promise, so much hope and we couldn't put it together. I hope you understand it's not your fault. You cannot be blamed."

"I know where to place the blame. What you haven't answered is why. Why now?"

"Well, three reasons, I think."

"Lorrrrrrrd. I'll need a drink if this morphs into one of your trademarked narratives."

I went up to the bar and ordered Sara a double gin and tonic with lime and another Vesper. Not wanting to be in the midst of discussion when the barman came, we waited quietly. No words were spoken. We simply stared at one another. I continued once drinks were served.

"You're probably unaware, Sara, but years ago, prior to our New York meeting, ol' Fritzy didn't think the relationship would amount to much. He dismissed it frankly. We'd simply use each another to solve unresolved personal issues and move on. He changed his mind, however, after hearing about our New York experience. He began thinking instead that we'd move towards a symbiotic relationship where both would derive some meaningfulness. He remained convinced it wouldn't last but all was not lost. After running its course we would have achieved something – you know, his 'heightened level of emotional intelligence' in which he continues to believe. A state of mind that could benefit us in the future with someone new, someone different. And because we had achieved it together we'd separate without rancour or malice. Sadness, naturally, but neither of us will have suffered the bitterness of ingratitude. How did he phrase it… *you will have absorbed her message and she yours.* I guess we'll never know if and when the other reaches that lauded level of contentedness."

"A four-year relationship is a long time. If you didn't think we were a viable combination why couldn't you have the courtesy – the decency – to call it quits much earlier? You were in your early fifties when we met. I was thirty-nine. Look what's been wasted. You're fifty-six. I'm in my early-forties. How many trans-Atlantic flights were there? What about all the plans we made? Remember the holidays we spent together – Lisbon, Oxford, Cambridge, Paris, Rome, south of France, Lake Garda? And what about..."

"Don't neglect the US trips – being chased by grizzly bears in the Grand Tetons, driving through Wind River Canyon into Thermopolis, Wyoming, hiking in Mt Rainier National Park, attending the Pendleton Round-Up, talking with Nez Perce Indians, following the Natchez Trace to hear live jazz in New Orleans and..."

"Yes, but now looking back, and I hate saying it... how much money did we waste on those trips? And what about the emotional tally? It may not affect you but for me it will be..."

"Haven't thought that far ahead but the aftershock will last years. I'm certain of that. I'll probably never heal."

"So what are you saying, shared misery will provide comfort?"

"No, misery offers nothing but reflective remorse... It is so necessary for me to explain myself, Sara. It's important for you, too. May I continue?"

"Fine. I'll try not to interject."

"Interrupt at any time. The second reason was the state of America. I remember telling you in Chicago that after 'W' was re-elected in '04 I came mighty close to pulling chocks and fleeing to Canada. Really damn near. But I couldn't act unilaterally. When we met in December Obama had been elected a month earlier so optimism flourished. No pressing need to leave. The great ship of state, so to speak, had righted itself. I would have left had he lost. And since he was re-elected a few weeks ago I feel more confident about the country than I have in years. The stench of Bush, Cheney and company remains but it's not as pungent. Their reign may only have been aberrant behaviour. So, really, I couldn't leave America now, Sara. The nation is no longer dominated by the incompetence of 'W' and his neo-con henchmen."

"How can you conflate the two? Isn't our relationship more important than how good or how shitty the state of American politics?"

"Of course it is. Infinitely more important, but if the country had continued being as fucked-up and lost as it was under 'W', it would have been a cinch to ditch everything – the job, the career, the condo, health insurance, and retirement savings and investments – and move to England. The state of America would have fuelled the move."

"A significant part of finding inner contentedness and simplicity is lightening the load, living with less and experiencing what's pure, what's real. You've sought that kind of life for donkey's years and we came damn close to achieving it, but you couldn't commit. How disappointing."

"Perhaps I'm a fraud deep down, Sara, too concerned about the necessities of modern life: a job, healthcare and financial security. That's the way America moulds its citizens unfortunately. I'm one of its finished products. The system doesn't permit deviation."

"Isn't it high time you accept you've never fit nicely into that mould? It's anathema to you and you know it. It can't be that difficult. That lot of bohemians from history you so admire found little trouble dumping America during prosperous times and moving abroad."

"Well, I'll give you that. Makes me respect them more actually. Unlike me, they had the courage of their convictions. But none left America to get married. They married Brits after living in England several years. Not to be pedantic, and it's frightfully irrelevant in view of our shared angst, but it isn't possible nowadays for an American to just arrive in Britain and start a new life. If we had met while I was working in England or France or even Greece it wouldn't have been such an all-consuming issue."

"I like your pedantic edge sometimes. It always made me laugh because I knew you only were conveying facts and not trying to impress. I'll miss that... I think."

"Thanks for toning down the intensity, Sara. Dark humour works during troubled times. But seriously, if after arriving in England and something happened between us in two or three years, how would I recover? Could I recover? I would have resigned from my job years earlier, transferred my entire financial wealth to England and had no health insurance. On top of that, having sold my condo unit, I'd have nowhere to live. I can't imagine returning to the States at age fifty-eight or so. Impossible. Wouldn't happen."

"You could have remained in England. The government wouldn't break down the door and force you to leave. I love you from my nose to my toes and I think we would have been happy... but if the worst happened, you wouldn't be abandoned. You know me well enough to appreciate my inner core."

"Yes, and you know mine, but human wants and desires change. I need total assurance."

"I'm sure you were acutely aware that most days I never spoke to anyone outside of work or business interactions. A strange way to live, of course, but I looked forward to the possibility of us. Appears you doubt yourself more than the remote possibility of me having doubts about you at a later date. What you've forgot through all your anguished ramblings is that living with little and wanting less increases dependency on each other. And I'm betting an entirely new form of devotion, respect and love becomes ascendant. That's what I was hoping. That's what I was anticipating."

"I was too, Sara, I thought my impatience with conventions would push me through to the other side. I've wanted to desperately... for decades, but I can't break this self-imposed, determinism of mine... planning, knowing what's ahead, anticipating failure and how to recover – predicting outcomes before events happen. Surprises don't amuse me. I've thirsted for the simple life you described. And I wanted to share it with you, only you... but when pushed... I'm a coward, I suppose. I could ruin your life reconstituting mine. I've been unable to toss aside everything, drop out and live contentedly. The increased uncertainty brought by leaving the States and marrying was too great. Nothing was guaranteed. I lacked control."

"I understood your concerns and appreciated your issues. You were carrying some heavy burdens, but as I constantly reminded you – on pain of death, I would never be unfaithful. Never. I could not seek comfort in others by way of infidelity. I would never be with another man. I was yours alone. I longed for you to be as secure, as confident and as happy with me as I was with you. It's obvious now you never reached that level of assuredness. After everything we had talked about in these intervening years I thought I was important to you. But I was wrong. If the fear of marrying is too great, too uncertain, then you aren't ready for me."

"I love you. You're incredibly important to me, but if something happened, if you left... I couldn't withstand the physical repercussions that surely would follow. Simply too great. Perhaps the residue from a trust broken long ago disintegrates into bits too small to rebuild with someone new. I don't know. I honestly don't know. There was an acronym used in the army when a piece of equipment, an operation or a procedure wouldn't function properly – it was FUBAR: Fucked-Up Beyond All Recognition. Maybe I'm just FUBAR'd."

"Are you going to allow one event from the past to control your entire future? Don't answer. I'll answer it for you: ridiculous."

"But as I've explained, this is one of three issues I'm grappling with."

"I agreed to meet because I wanted to hear your reasons – three of them it turns out – and try to understand. I wanted to explain my views as well, not to convince you otherwise, but why we would have been successful. I'm afraid you'll realise I was correct years from now, Edward, when… you're surrounded by books, swilling booze all day, living in a damp apartment, alone. But to *appear* optimistic, let's hope we'll benefit from Fritzy's 'heightened level of emotional intelligence' and find that special person and settle in that special place. But appearances are deceiving. And since you aren't an optimist I'm guessing our separate but equal prognosis probably won't have legs… Well, I must get a wiggle on so I'll say, *Goodbye*. I abhor the ending but I respect your courage to talk face to face. When are you returning? Spending a few days in London?"

"No, actually I leave tonight on the redeye. I came over only for the day to say, *Goodbye* and *Thank you*. You are a remarkable and lovely woman. I'd write a book about you, Sara, if I were a novelist and not an historian. And honestly, if only one finds contentedness I hope it's you. I sincerely hope it's you. You so deserve it."

I reached to shake her hand but she pushed it aside. She pulled herself close and kissed me. She stood up, wiped her eyes, gathered her belongings and turned towards me.

"I won't forget the times we had. We were two one-offs that had become whole."

I stood and watched as she walked the length of the room. She looked towards me one last time before turning left to exit. I offered a reflective wave, sat down and thought: *What a contemptible ass. I've ceremoniously thrown away and destroyed any semblance of a contented life and, what's worse, I've destabilised Sara's something awful. I'll pay for this. My God, I shall pay for this.* If on cue, the original 1939 version of 'Don't Worry 'Bout Me' performed by Hal Kemp's orchestra started in the background. The irony wasn't lost. It was Sinatra's version of the same song that was playing when Sara tapped me on the shoulder at Jilly's four years earlier. The inevitability of a solitary winter was upon me.

ELEVEN

SEATTLE

"Table eleven is set for tonight. We'll meet at half seven."

"RESPECT. Looking forward to it… sadly."

Despite the indecisiveness of Trump's election, his 2016 Electoral College victory made my long-held desire to leave America a reality. The amorality of his entire being guaranteed the administration would be tethered to fiendish corruption, bountiful lies, conflict-of-interest malfeasances and outward betrayals. The two-bit grifter had been elevated to primetime. The country would descend rapidly into the moral dead zone.

After selling most of my possessions, I hired a professional moving company to manage the remnants. Two days before leaving I scheduled a seminar – a kind of final exam – at Fontana and the eponymous table eleven. I thought initially the evening might be tinged by melancholy but remained optimistic that after a few glasses of house wine we'd seize upon the significance of the moment. Our repartee would regain momentum. I shouldn't have worried. The singularity of our relationship couldn't be ignored.

I walked down Second Avenue to Blanchard as I had done for ten years of meetings with Fritzy. True to form, he had arrived early. His signature bike, now host to an all-conquering rust, leaned against the iron fence. Gian Carlo offered a hug as I walked in.

"Chris told me a few weeks ago you were leaving. Moving to a Greek island. I am sad. All here are sad. No more monthly seminars."

And with that he led me, as usual, to table eleven; however, this time it was different. A white shroud covered the table. Fritzy was standing to the left smiling. Gian Carlo pranced ahead, grabbing the forward most corner of the shroud with two fingers.

"I no good at speeches. The plaque says all… forever."

Whereupon he flung off the cloth to reveal an engraved copper plaque secured at the head of the antique table:

Table 11
Host to Monthly Esoteric 'Seminars' between Edward Lee and Chris Sunderland 2007 – 2017

I was taken aback and slightly embarrassed.

"You realise, don't you, Gian Carlo, I'm not going. I've decided to remain in Seattle…"

"No, you don't. I know that smile too well. You are, what do I say, 'pulling my legs.'"

"Ahhhh, you're correct. You do know me. Thanks so very much. I'm humbled by your generosity, not only for the plaque but more importantly for your kindness, for your humour and for your love of making every guest feel important. I shall never forget Fontana or you, Gian Carlo."

"*E allora.*"

Chris and I sat in our respective chairs. I poured each a tall glass of house red.

"I'm as surprised as you, Buttons. Gian Carlo did this all on his own. When I confirmed the reservation he asked me to arrive ten minutes early. He wanted to show me something. I thought it would be a vintage bottle of special wine he planned to open."

"Touching, isn't it? Keeps the memory long after we are dead and gone."

"Certainly will. Each time I dine at this table I'll reflect on our discussions, our laughs, our craziness. And as my body deteriorates and my mind fades and I grow forgetful of what happened here, Gian Carlo can point to the plaque. What a gift. What a gift... What... a... gift."

"Can you imagine what people will conjure in their minds decades from now when Fontana is no longer and the furnishings are for sale in an antique store? *Who were those guys? What comprised an esoteric seminar?* The sheen of the copper will have been covered by a green patina. And whomever purchases it... wonder if they'll keep the plaque attached?"

"The answers are not for us to know, Buttons. *That* is what makes the gift unique."

"You're spot on, Fritzy, spot on. Now, I think we've bloviated enough about immortality... however fleeting... so, let's move, ever so cautiously yet expeditiously, to ordering our splendid meal."

"I'm all in, Buttons. All in."

We both selected the romaine lettuce with homemade dressing and croutons with a generous sprinkling of parmesan cheese. I opted for homemade ravioli filled with veal and special spices. Fritzy sunk his teeth into a lamb tenderloin with figs in a marsala wine sauce, topped with Italian goat's cheese... from Gian Carlo's family estate in Umbria. We chose a double affogato each for dessert. Fontana added crumbled biscotti to the top, making this exquisite dessert more special.

"Damn, Buttons, if I weren't ill I'd leave, too. Trump's entire being doesn't bode well for the Republic. I'm concerned. He's dangerous. Trump's ignorance is exceeded only by the ignorance of his supporters. You were around in the '60s but... much too young to be a nuisance. My classmates and I were old enough. We hit the streets. We demonstrated. We had sit-ins. Railed against the Vietnam War. Fought for civil rights and against racial discrimination. Promoted the Equal Rights Amendment. I think history does or will consider them admirable positions. While we may have failed achieving all our objectives, our voices became so loud and our causes judged so right, that eventually society changed. Not everything, but one hell of a lot. I fear with Trump the country will regress... and quickly. Will his version of white nationalism gain ground? That, of course, raises the questions: will intelligent, tolerant Americans – which I hope remain in the majority – take to the streets? Will we practise civil disobedience? Will we boycott? And, if need be, will we riot?"

"I agree with your perspective on the '60s, Fritzy. I'm pessimistic unfortunately about the future. There won't be meaningful demonstrations against Trump and the GOP. Not going to occur. Americans are literally fat and figuratively happy. They're not moved by righteous causes anymore. As long as the economy moves forward, the stock market climbs and individual 401K plans increase in value, the average American will have difficulty attributing or linking his antics to any constitutional crisis. Keeping in mind, of course, civics, American history – or any history for that matter – are no longer required courses at university. The educated today wouldn't know enough to realise if and when their government was teetering on the abyss."

"If your prediction comes to pass... America would no longer be the juggernaut for positiveness. Probably make me reconsider cancer a gift instead of a curse, as selfish and perverse as that sounds."

"Hell, Fritzy, moving to Greece is based on selfishness."

"Permit me to paraphrase a beautiful French girlfriend of mine from university: 'Explain me, Buttons.'"

"America is tired. The country couldn't elect someone as daft as Trump unless it were bored with itself, tired of stretching, tired of learning and tired of growing. I no longer belong. I find the incessant emphasis on appearance stifling – basically everything about you *but* physical appearance ironically. You know, all of those ideas we've shared, debated about and talked over for a decade. And because I'm not responsible to anyone or to anything – company, institution or individual – I'm free to leave. Having lived frugally and invested well the past thirty-seven years, I'm rich with what actor Humphrey Bogart referred to as 'fuck you money' – the financial independence to make unfettered choices. There is more to life than remaining in America. I've served my country. Survived helicopter engine failures. Battled testicular cancer. Rebooted an out-of-control heart. Events won't control me any longer. I would become preoccupied living in Trump's America. Guarantee he won't be a 'No Drama Obama'. I'm afraid there will be incessant drama all the time with this shameless self-promoter. He'd consume my every day. Christ, just re-read his inaugural address – full of hate and vitriol. No more, Fritzy. Is it un-American to cross over? Leave before the flood? Probably. Do I give a damn what others think? Yeah, probably – at a level somewhere between a grain and a pinch. And besides, I've always thought patriotism wins first prize as the most overrated virtue. It's the epitome of provincialism. I'll be simultaneously saddened but contented to swim in the sea, lie on the rocks and watch America go to hell."

"Terse and pithy, Buttons. You've obviously have battled this out in your head long ago. Well done. I remember we both were disillusioned with Bush, Cheney, Rumsfeld and company, and how you thought seriously of moving to Canada. Going so far as visiting the consulate and completing the paperwork, if I recall. You just didn't follow through."

"That's right. Lacked the courage; however, now for some reason, I detect a genuine sense of urgency. Don't know why. I just do. To paraphrase what you advised years ago, Fritzy: *The world has ended and it's up to me to make my life anew.* And I'm doing so. I'm confident life in the Greek fishing village will be so fulfilling that when it's time to die, I die clean. No strings. No regrets. No pining. And most importantly, not laying in sawdust unaware of my surroundings."

"The winding down of life is often not cheerful, Buttons. It's damn difficult usually. If we could drop off quietly like autumn leaves that would be pleasant – for me, you and everyone else. I'm not a betting man but I'd wager our lives probably won't end neat and orderly. We won't detach gently from the branch of life and float softy to the ground onto a bed of luscious moss. But I agree with you, more importantly than how we died is how we lived. That is something only we can answer honestly by ourselves, alone in the privacy of our own room. It's what we did with the years given us that's important, not how many years we stood erect."

"Seems you have been ruminating a lot, too, Fritzy."

"Terminal illnesses bring requirements. I thought if I buckled-down and reflected, I'd garner a few extra credit points, you know, an extended reprieve from sitting across from the black cat too soon."

"As usual, Fritzy, you're leading the vanguard, isolating the insolent noise of life and replacing it with the disembodied voice of reason. Remarkable."

"Well, Buttons…"

Before he finished, Gian Carlo approached with an unopened, limited edition bottle of Metaxa Angels' Treasure.

"In celebration of Greece I present bottle to you, Edward. Not good obviously as Vecchia Romagna Riserva, but I don't want to dampen your love of Greek. For you and Chris to drink. Now. What is left, you keep. You take away."

Whereupon he turned and returned rapidly to the kitchen.

"He may be a bit upset, Buttons. The whole staff enjoyed our loyalty the past ten years. And my imminent departure compounds the distress. Italians love tradition and dislike change, you know. We've become disrupters, I'm afraid."

"Oh, my. Then it's incumbent on you to come for the occasional dinner for as long as possible. And something else, there is no way we can finish this bottle tonight. You take home whatever is left, Fritzy. Once I'm comfortable in Fiskardo we'll synchronise a time – via text – to toast each other with a glass of Metaxa. It's *the* after-dinner brandy in the village so I won't have difficulty acquiring a bottle."

"Buttons… your proclivity toward romantic classicism is surpassed only by your dogmatic determinism. Splendid idea. Simply splendid."

"Ahhh, determinism no longer defines me. Belongs to the ash heap of my personal history. How else could I be moving to a Greek fishing village? And don't worry about the ten-hour time difference, Fritzy. For you, I'd drink anytime, anywhere, anyplace… bar none. I'll bring a flask to 'the rocks' if necessary."

"Just increasing the heat in the room. Judging whether you still were paying attention. Proud of the adjustments you've made, Buttons. Execution proved uncomfortable but you persevered. You've earned my admiration yet again."

"Thank you. And Fritzy... I shall miss you in Fiskardo. Please understand my melancholy will endure indefinitely after your last word. You shall remain a void, housed permanently in my pantheon of fabulous friends."

After refilling our brandy glasses we agreed to lighten the conversation.

"So what's the low-down on logistics? Your determinism may be a memory but your analness for planning and detail remains intact."

"Quite right. Quite right. My route of flight isn't too awful. Direct to London and then three hours to Argostoli. A voluntary lay-over in London makes it civil."

"Think you might contact Sara? You know, find out what she's been up to."

"Interesting you remember her."

"Couldn't possibly forget. How could I? She was memorable. Possessed an ignitable spark unlike few women I've encountered."

"To answer your question, I'd love to, Fritzy, but Sara – to use the film or literary metaphor – doesn't 'do' sequels. She always found them shoddy and repetitive. Wouldn't have any intention to relive what we shared five years ago. Not in her make-up. Sara's lost to the ages, I'm afraid. Besides, and as you so aptly described, a woman of her calibre probably is married and living in a forlorn area of Yorkshire or Northumberland. Contact would be considered an unwelcomed intrusion."

"A shame you didn't put it together. If you remember correctly, I didn't think it could be sustained. But you'd both achieve a higher level of emotional intelligence which could be used at another time with another person. Perhaps you'll meet someone in Greece."

"I don't know if I'm capable of..."

"How do you plan to spend the day in that isolated fishing village of yours?"

"Not worried in the least. Bit different, I guess, from Seattle... read, run, swim naked, soak up the sun, write, enjoy classic jazz, hone martini-making, play my saxophone with reckless esprit and... reminiscence about life. Sounds odd, but I find that cathartic. Memories sustain life, you know."

"That's splendid, but what about women? Put my theory into practice. Greek women can be... well, rather exotic, if I recall. Limited inhibitions. Alluring eyes. Thick hair. Olive hues. Intense, physical passion with minimal need for breaks. All shrouded, of course, in the seductive scents and musical sounds of the ancient world. Simply wonderful."

"What *have* you been reading? Bet the Metaxa has mixed with your cocktail for merriment."

"Buttons, please, what did you utter moments ago... *memories sustain life?* Well, then, my friend, I speak with authority and... shall rest my case."

"Perhaps a dalliance then – if conducting a cross-cultural study – otherwise no relationships. I want to live alone, unaffected by others."

"Buttons, Buttons, Buttons, you're not Francis of Assisi."

"Agreed. Just want to live in the world but not of it – that indescribable state of being, somewhere between dropping out and checking out."

"Ahhhhhhh, I'd envy that lifestyle. Certainly the food, the heat and the sea draw me, but that philosophy is... well, something from a bygone era. Perhaps you'll accomplish what previous aspirants have tried but failed to do. You'll have ample opportunities and varied choices. Sink your teeth deep into the bone of life, Buttons. Splendid."

"I'll agree about ample opportunities but as far as variety

– you may think I have numerous choices, but only one of them will be right. The challenge is finding it and once I do, hold on and don't let go."

"Keep me informed on your 'natural selection' process. I'll be curious about the results."

"I will but it may never materialise. And I'm totally prepared for that."

I poured us each another glass of Metaxa. There were no other customers. Respecting it was the last time we'd see each other, Gian Carlo didn't hint or indicate we needed to leave. Even the cooking staff adjourned to a distant room.

"I'm amazed, Fritzy, at how well the 'cocktail for merriment' has worked. You would have exited long ago without it."

"Well, we certainly wouldn't have shared this celebratory dinner together. Only a cornucopia of medicines made that possible. The concoction plays hell with my energy level but I'm here, critiquing the farce that has become America and… seeing you off to ancient lands."

"Well, Fritzy, your situation reminds me of a favourite song by Dianne Reeve called 'Into Each Life Some Rain Must Fall.'"

Whereupon I reached into my leather backpack and brought out a package wrapped in a most undiscernible manner. I placed it besides his brandy glass.

"I have found these works of literature invaluable in deciphering life. Perhaps they will offer some sustenance, helping to strengthen your fragile hold. And, ah… just so you know… all are first editions."

He unwrapped the package carefully, placing each book alongside the other on the table: Richard Aldington's *Life for Life's Sake*; W. Somerset Maughm's *The Razor's Edge*; and Ernest Hemingway's *Across the River and Into the Trees*.

"Thank you. I'm honoured. I remember you considered these, what was the term, 'consequential literary works' that you've read often."

"I did and I still do. But that's my opinion. Contemporary critics didn't think much of them. Many judged *Across the River* as Papa's second worst book. For me, however, they ask the questions necessary to evaluate your own life. They mix well with Metaxa, by the way."

"And with a jigger of the dulcet sounds of Paul Desmond's sax and a hefty slice of 'The Bird's' bebop thrown in, I'll have some stellar reads. Thank you."

"Now that's what I'm talking about, Fritzy. Good man."

We talked a while longer. Repeated stories from our youth that we had shared probably countless times before. He added heat and spice by reciting his numerous university liaisons, including one with an English literature graduate teaching assistant from England that I never had heard before. It seemed particularly saucy and the ending, well, it had Fritzy stamped all over it. I, on the other hand, could regale him only with army stories – from the ass-tightening excitement of flying 120 knots, fifty feet above the ground, to the debasement of monitoring 293 men urinating in a bottle to be in accordance with drug and alcohol standards. We called it a night at half past midnight. I thanked Gian Carlo for everything. Told him to continue serving only his best food and finest wines to Chris. He promised he would. Once outside, I stood by, holding the books and Metaxa, while Fritzy unlocked his bike.

"This is it my friend. Writing will continue in earnest but we won't see each other ever again."

"Thank you for your genuineness, bon ami camaraderie and wise counsel. Never to be forgotten."

We only exchanged firm hand-shakes. Fritzy did not offer his trademarked hug this time. I watched as he coasted downhill to First Avenue. In the past he'd turn right without looking back. It was different this time. I watched as he dismounted, turned towards me and offered a military salute. After I returned the gesture he peddled away. The irony, of course, was I never thought Chris knew that since his diagnosis I always had watched as he descended towards First Avenue. What was never mentioned for years was finally revealed… but only at the end. Even then no words were spoken.

I walked slowly up Second Avenue, storing the sights, sounds and smells of Seattle so as to recall them in the future, if desired. The allure of the dark blue sky and early-morning sea air encroaching across Elliott Bay was marred by the loud ranting of several drunk, overweight men sitting outside a dive bar wearing red, 'Make America Great Again' baseball caps. I was in no condition to confront them nor pass by, knowing they'd relish confrontation. So I crossed the street. Minutes later, while sitting on the deck outside my unit, I put on my iPod, opened a bottle of sparking water and keyed up Ben Webster's 1967 recording of Ellington's 'Solitude'. A defining era of my life had ended. I'd never be the same again. Ever.

TWELVE

FISKARDO

I woke early that August day. The weather seemed uncharacteristically cool so I went for a longer than normal run, finishing at 'the rocks' and completing what had become my daily regimen since April. Not a sound was heard. The four fishing boats servicing Fiskardo had returned long before sunrise. It seemed too early for recreational boaters to launch, especially after a night of heavy partying. I was alone. I was satisfied. This craggy bit merging into the Ionian belonged to me. The water revived me immediately upon entering, gently messaging the deteriorating disc in my lower back. After swimming for twenty minutes I navigated out of the water. As I stretched out to absorb the morning sun waiting for my running kit to dry, I remember thinking: *If this morning is a harbinger... it will be a fabulous day.*

I walked along the harbour towards my flat being greeted by the various vendors with whom I had become acquainted. They were busily setting tables, sweeping the pavement outside their shops or relaxing with a cup of coffee before the rush of tourists disturbed the solitude. The preferred greeting amongst my Greek friends, it seemed, was, "Fresh from your 'rocks', Edouardos?" I don't know if they had got together and agreed to ask me that instead of, "How are you today, Edouardos?" Even if they hadn't, I found the similarity amusing. Most were privy to my preferences and habits: Vespers, Mythos, 'the rocks', reading, writing and – in complete agreement with Sartre, *Hell is other people* – a solitary table or chair removed from others.

I spent what remained of the morning and early afternoon writing a manuscript that probably would never reach an editor's desk. I lacked the abilities of a novelist but possessed the desire so I continued churning out eight hundred to one thousand words a day. I tried my best to avoid that ubiquitous nut-roll of incoherence posing as art. So each Sunday I edited the prior week's efforts which usually meant halving the word count. I kept this lame attempt to myself for two reasons. I was slightly embarrassed to admit working on a manuscript, confident most people – including Fritzy – wouldn't understand. I often imagined him remonstrating me: *Buttons, you're an historian and a damn good one. Non-fiction is your expertise, not novels. Christ.* The more serious reason was it weighed heavily towards the personal. I didn't want to feel obliged to divulge content when people asked the proverbial question: *What's it about?* So I never mentioned it… to friend and foe alike.

Sometime around one o'clock I hit my stride. The ideas, the words and the memories came easily. I continued until almost five, when I realised if I didn't hurry I'd have to compete with others vying for a table at Tselenti's. Being a regular had its privileges. I knew my table wouldn't be taken this early… but only if I stopped writing, showered, changed into some decent clothes – basically, got my ass into fifth gear. Ten minutes later I grabbed my book, checked myself in a forgiving mirror and locked the door.

Having not eaten since early morning I was anxiously looking forward to a fabulous meal. The staff had placed a reserved sign on my table positioned against the front of the building on the far-right side. The same table I'd occupied regularly since first visiting in 2009. I asked Mr Tselenti if he'd play a personal favourite, Erik Satie's *Gnossienne No. 1* – a word invented by the composer and associated with the myth of Theseus, Ariadne and the Minotaur at Knossos, the Neolithic ruin in Crete. It never failed to set the mood, always sending me adrift. The music commenced. I opened my book and sipped the white Robola wine recommended earlier by Mrs Tselenti. After finishing half a glass someone questioningly called my name. As I raised my head the most comforting sensation came over me. I'd recognise that one-of-a-kind accent anywhere. Eighteen years of the north of England mixed with thirty-plus years of London produced a hybrid elixir unlike any other.

"Sara? Oh, my God!"

I stood up and, without seeking permission, gave her a bear-like hug and kissed both cheeks. She didn't recoil but she didn't reciprocate. Why should she? She looked utterly fantastic. Her sun-kissed skin made for a rich amber tone melding perfectly with her auburn hair. The darker colour amplified her eyes. What years ago held a glint of lapis now appeared alluringly like amethyst. Truly captivating. Her height obviously had not changed. Legs began at the shoulders enabling her, as she professed so often, 'to be long in the body'.

"Oh, my... I can't believe it. I'm... I'm, well, hell. I'm dumbfounded. God, you look absolutely wonderful... beautiful actually. Are you on holiday?"

"Oh, don't be ridiculous. I'm falling apart. Everything's dropping. I even have to colour my hair now and then. I'm a bit lumpy, not nearly as limber as I used to be. Kind of convinced myself I'm wild… but manicured. Anyway, I remember you trumpeting Fiskardo so often to all who would listen, that after you gave me the 'heave-ho' and we ceased 'being an item of discussion', I thought I'd investigate. Visited in early May about four years ago, not long after we said our goodbyes actually. Had a wonderful time. Was looking for rustic solitude and natural simplicity and found it. Kept returning, eventually deciding I'd relocate here when retired and be grandfathered in before Britain left the EU. And that was about three years ago."

"Well, whatta ya know, Sara Hawes formerly of England, now living in Fiskardo! I'm impressed to say the least. The wild but manicured mindset appears to be working."

"Don't be daft. So how long are you visiting, Edward?"

"I live here too – or getting ready to – believe it or not. Been here almost five months."

"Well, to paraphrase you, *Whatta ya know*, Edward Lee formerly of America, now living in Fiskardo. I'm *more* than impressed. You wear it well, a bit thicker but you still have your hair. Not bad, not bad at all for what, about sixty?"

"Yeah, thanks. Almost sixty. I try to keep the fat at bay, sometimes I win but usually lose. I'm hoping to become more fit and healthy now that I'm in Greece. The heat, the sea and the local Robola should reap great dividends."

"Ahhh, Robola… couldn't find anything healthier."

I didn't pursue it but got the feeling she hadn't lost her penchant for sarcasm. It remained intact.

"So, tell me, if I couldn't influence the decision to disown your country, who or what did?"

"Well… it was American politics – specifically Trump

and his ignorant supporters that propelled me towards expatriatism."

"Oh, my, so Obama winning a second term kept you in America and us apart, and Trump winning got you to leave and... live in Greece. It must be truly awful for someone like yourself becoming an expat."

"Actually, it isn't awful at all. Been festering deep within, I guess, for years if not decades. But don't get me started. You don't want to hear all that."

"Trump acts like an absolute bully and buffoon on the world stage."

"What a minute. I think I'm experiencing a flashback to December 2008 at... The Original Pancake House."

"Whatever are you talking about, Edward?"

"Don't you remember? You failed to show up as promised so I had to ring and roust you out of bed."

"Oh, that's right. And I had forgotten my spectacles and had to ask the waitress where you were sitting. Lorrrrrd."

"Exactly. And after apologising profusely you pointedly asked, *So what was it about Bush unilaterally invading another country?* Took me aback initially, but soon realised you were testing me, gauging my knowledge, my level of interest and political persuasion. Canny, to say the least."

"So, for both continuity's and old time's sake then, don't you think Trump acts like an absolute bully and buffoon on the world stage?"

"Still the same old determined Sara, aren't you? Well, yes, he does... unabashedly but my concerns go deeper, much deeper. As you're aware, Greece has elements of ineptness like America, there's just far less bullshit – no fake patriotism, no religious zealotry and no sanctimonious moralism. I began planning my departure two days after the election. And the rationale to leave the States permanently became incredibly easy after Charlottesville. His racial animus praises inequality while elevating hatred. I'm beginning to think he embodies the decades-long accumulation of white grievance and anger. Trump threatens the liberal order. He criminalises his opponents, labels them evil, un-American and, in some instances, treasonous. He chastises the news media, calls it the 'enemy of the people' and mocks the First Amendment. And finally, his brand of crony capitalism benefits him and his family first and foremost. He leaves morsels for the nation to peck at and squabble over. And we are supposed to be grateful? Sounds odd, but with Trump you're not off base to think the darkest motivations and most heinous explanations for his behaviour. I had enough. The nation no longer behaves like the progressive nation I had known. I'd become a stranger in a strange land. Idealism is dead. Tolerance left long ago. Respect is ignored. Intellect is ridiculed. And because the politics of hate triumphed in '16, democracy has entered a harsh winter where spring may never emerge. He wasn't elected to govern and elevate. He was chosen to grieve and destroy and, by the looks of it, he'll succeed. No matter how or when his presidency ends, the spectre of illiberalism will haunt America and its politics for generations. The box of horrors has been opened and it'll be difficult, if not impossible, to seal."

"Any chance people will recognise their mistake?"

"It doesn't look promising. Much of the country suffers from cultural dementia. Most lack the moral courage to regain what they frittered away. Millions don't understand basic civics nor appreciate how Trump's destroying the system's foundations by belittling and disrespecting everything and everybody that came before. I lack the patience to wait and the will to fight, especially with the Republican Party's complicity. I think, in hindsight, 'W' and Trump are bookends – where the real America resides. In between sat Obama the aberration, the American aspiration. Depressingly sad. It's funny, pathetic actually, but when I see an American flag a surge of patriotism rises deep within, but… well, that feeling is for what the country was, not for what it is today. I behaved too cautiously – terribly indecisively – with you five years ago. I learned something by that action. Living in the past had become my future. I vowed not to disappoint myself a second time so I left. The easiest decision I have ever made. Sorry, a bit long-winded but once you add olive oil to a hot pan it splatters."

"Oh, don't apologise. Who knows, perhaps you're a visionary. Maybe others will leave as well."

"Kinda doubt I'm a visionary. I'm more like the man of 'day before yesterday' than the man of 'day after tomorrow'. And besides, if it's true that everyone is as clever as they are, minus how clever they think they are, then I've probably got a negative score."

"You are funny, Edward. But who knows, your predictions were spot on years ago. It is terrible what's going on in the States. Fond memories for how it used to be. I remember our shared interest in politics and current affairs. I liked that about us. I must admit, however, since living here I pay scant attention. It's absent from any concerns of mine. The pace and quality of life doesn't open itself to current events. Both nations are in a right mess. Britain's suffering from atrophy while America's plagued by incontinence. I couldn't be bothered."

"That's the reason I moved here, the quest for that peaceful and balanced life we had talked about so often. Current events won't consume me anymore. I've had enough. And please understand, Sara, as I said at Knight's Bar if you remember, you cannot be blamed in any way for my indecisiveness. If we share time together I'll explain more fully. I regret what I did.

Damn stupid. Disgusting really. We were excellent together. Almost perfect. I have thought about you so often, so very, very often; wondering what you were up to. Anytime I heard 'Scotland Yard' mentioned in the news, I'd reminisce about our years together. The passage of time certainly determines which memories are kept. And with you, I've probably kept them all. Crowded memories."

"Well, if I didn't want to see you I wouldn't have approached you, would I? That's the second time I've interrupted your drinking."

"And *long may it continue*, to quote a close friend from long ago. Was it another flip-of-the-coin moment?"

"No, I felt fairly confident it was you, ironically by the way you sit when reading: deeply immersed, pencil in hand making notes. Who else could possibly do that? Would have been damn embarrassing if it hadn't been, though."

"Ahhh, if it hadn't, I'm sure the guy would have been flattered. So, are you by yourself?"

"Is that a tactful way of asking if I'm married or living with someone?"

"Don't know how tactful it was – you know I never mastered English subtlety; it wasn't my specialty – but… yes."

"No, I'm alone. Had a brief romp in London. A temporary explosion of insanity, predictably fizzling out as soon as it began. Then I moved here. Well, actually I live in the 'ghost town' in the hills overlooking Fiskardo."

"Oh, my God, not Psilithrias, down the hill from Antipata?"

"Yes, exactly. You're familiar with it?"

"Of course I am. Hike by each time I visit Antipata for lunch and an ultra-frosty Mythos. But there's nothing there – at least there wasn't."

"So you visit The Old Stone House Taverna? It's a cute place. I like it. There is a wonderfully friendly tabby cat who hangs about. She always grabs the empty chair next to me. Not quite as friendly as ol' Bix at the Algonquin – remember him – but fairly close."

"Of course, I remember Bix Beiderbecke. A class act. The original Jazz Cat. About Psilithrias—"

"Oh, yes. I got a brilliant deal on, well – as you know – an abandoned property. Two walls remained but everything else was built from scratch – including rebuilding the two walls! It's an entirely new place essentially. But the best thing is I've got a detached building, almost as big as the living quarters, which serves as my studio!"

"That's wonderful, Sara. You've got a pottery. Truly fantastic. I remember you mentioned living in the Yorkshire Dales and doing hand-building, throwing or whatever. I suppose the only thing that's different is you're on a Greek island in the Ionian."

"There is a bit more… Remember how I desired a certain 'oneness with nature'? Well, although the house is new, I've opted for a pseudo-primitive existence, meaning no electricity. Water comes from an ancient well on the property. The main source of heat comes from the huge fireplace on one side of the ground floor. When it is cold – only about two months a year – I heat my bath-water in a huge caldron by the fire otherwise I bathe in the Ionian. But I do have an outside shower head attached to the house that comes in handy on extremely hot days or when I'm layered in clay. I did sell out and purchase a gas burner for cooking, but overall it's rough and wild. In fact, my pottery wheel is a mid-nineteenth-century kick wheel. My foot provides the synergy that propels the rotation. Archaic, yes, but wonderful to work with. Fab results. I travel to Maganos and use a friend's kiln for firing and to Sami to fire larger items. It's worked better than I ever thought. I'm currently constructing an outside wood-burning kiln for salt-glazing but, because it's an open fire and extremely hot, I'll use it only in the wetter months."

Suddenly Mrs Tselenti approached. After hugging Sara she turned to me.

"Edouardos, you know the gorgeous Miss Sara, the 'Potter in the Hills'?"

"Well, yes, Mrs Tselenti, Sara and I have known one other about nine years but haven't been in contact for some time. I believe we're having a small reunion."

"I bring another bottle of Robola. No charge."

"So she knows you, Edward?"

"Oh, God, yes. I ate at Tselenti's every time I visited. For me there wasn't anywhere else. I adore the atmosphere, the food and the music. I relish the time and the space but only get charged for the food. Wonderful."

"Funny, I feel similarly. I don't dine out much but when I do I always visit Tselenti's. Sometimes if the weather's bad and you stay late enough Tselenti's host one raucous party inside. Sometimes the police come and shut it down. Sad, really."

"Yeah, I know. Experienced a few of them. It depends on the make-up of the crowd. The boaters that show up are wealthy, burned-red Brits who have been at sea too long. And they like their music loud. Good fun, though. I remember my last evening four years ago Mr Tselenti indulged in a homage to the American West. He did it purposely for me. I couldn't believe the variety. He played everything: *How the West Was Won*, *The Alamo*, *The Way West*, *The Big Country*, *Once Upon a Time in the West*, *Dances with Wolves*, *Legends of the Fall*, *Fistful of Dollars*, *Hang 'Em High* and *Unforgiven*. Believe it or not, he played the theme song from *The Man Who Shot Liberty Valance* sung by Gene Pitney. I hadn't heard that song in probably fifty years. Truly impressive.

"Another evening Mr Tselenti came over and told me: *Tonight I play only American music*. He disappeared behind his massive audio control station in the back of the restaurant and plated-up two hours of American memories from the 1950s – 1980s. Some I hadn't heard for decades. But the naughtiest thing Tselenti's encourage, Sara, is serving a free dessert every evening, regardless of what or how much I spent for dinner: lemon-lime tart, Ekmek Kataifi, crepe suzette, chocolate crepe with caramelised hazelnuts or pistachio ice cream. I've learned it's not the place to dine if you want to drop a stone or two. They will desist only if I insist – and I mean insist – I'm too full. Of course, five minutes pass and a waiter drops off another glass of Robola… no charge. What lovely people."

"No doubt Kastas understands his loyal, American customer fairly well. I've discovered once Greeks befriend you, there's no end to the generosities they'll bestow. Well done. You've made an excellent impression."

"They think I'm a bit odd, a character, so to speak, because I still maintain a routine begun years earlier. And the staff seemed to have committed it to memory. After being seated they deliver a large bottle of San Pellegrino and a glass of white Robola. Finishing dinner I go inside, sit at an isolated table for two on the far right-hand side and read until around eleven. The staff laugh, telling each other, *Edouardos is in the library*. The head waiter, Lara, ensures my glass of white Robola is never empty. I feel special indeed."

"What are you like, Edward? Honestly."

"One evening a few weeks ago I had finished eating and was preparing to enter the library when Lara approached looking a bit panicky. It seemed a writer from New Zealand had taken my spot to work on a magazine article. She apologised, chastising herself for not paying closer attention. She looked shocked when I asked if she would ask him to move. She stared at me, trying her best to come up with a polite response. Told her I only was kidding and not to worry. I took the other single table at the far end of the restaurant. She felt relieved."

"Lorrrrd, wonder how they'll react if we ever dine together? Your routine will be broken."

"Now *that's* something I'd look forward to."

"So you've been here for about five months. Are you renting or thinking seriously about buying a home, a flat or what?"

"I'm still an American citizen unfortunately, so I remain in Greece for three months, leave for a month and return for another three months. So nine months of the year I'll be in Fiskardo. The other three will be spent slumming in the States. Haven't figured out the state side of things exactly. I'm renting a flat not far from the bakery called Nitsa's Place. It's surrounded by a varying array of climbing vines, Mediterranean fauna including apricot, orange and lemon trees. My first-floor flat is hidden, tucked in the rear. Has French doors and a small deck overlooking the lush gardens of the tall Venetian building. I find the ethereal atmosphere nourishing. The rent's affordable and the smell of freshly baked bread each morning is a pleasant alternative to an alarm clock. I'm signing a three-year lease in a couple days when the owner returns from Athens."

Feeling comfortable and content with our situation, I asked Sara if she could join me for dinner at half seven. Thought we could test the reaction of Tselenti's staff.

"Edward, thank you, and you are kind, but I have an appointment with a customer in Asos that has brilliant potential. They've even invited me to dinner. But, yes, let's catch up. I'd be disappointed if we didn't. We've got so much to talk about. But that is for another time with a larger bottle of wine, maybe a magnum. How about the day after tomorrow? If free, why not make your way to Psilithrias for lunch? It will be light but I promise it will be fresh and nutritious. Plenty of fine Greek wine and succulent olives will be on hand."

"That, sounds, well, perfect in every way, Sara. How do I find your humble but primitive abode?"

"Don't be rude, Edward… or should I call you, Edouardos?"

"You can call me *aaanything* you want."

"There's that rudeness again. Hold all comments until you've seen it. Honestly. You obviously know to walk up the steep hill until you see the village sign along the road. Take it and follow the footpath to the left. At the 'Y' take the path on the right. Follow about five hundred yards and you'll see the house. It sits alone, nothing on either side or in front, only the studio located in the rear garden. An intricately carved, sun-bleached stone sign with the name of the house sits atop a rock wall on the footpath. It's filled with bits of amethyst spelling out *Keramoskepi*, which roughly – and very crudely – translates to 'Stoneware Cottage.'"

"That sounds easy enough. I can almost picture it in my mind, except for the house, of course. I'll look forward to it, Sara. Thanks for inviting me."

"Listen, I've got to get a wiggle on."

As she gathered her belongings I stood, feeling as I had years earlier beside the elevator of her Chicago hotel. I wondered how she felt. To make us both comfortable we shook hands, but before we let go, I pulled her close towards me and kissed her forehead. Nothing had changed… it all came back to me.

"Naughty boy. See you day after tomorrow."

And with that she turned and walked hurriedly towards the car park. I watched until she was out of sight. What presence. What confidence.

I sat down in my chair and poured another glass of wine. Mrs Tselenti came over, hovering bedside the table, desperately wanting to talk.

"Miss Sara a wonderful woman, Edouardos. Her pottery is beautiful. But she stays by herself in pretty house. No male friends, I think. I don't ask but difficult to understand."

"Sometimes people are happy and secure within themselves, Mrs Tselenti. They may 'like' to have someone in their lives but they don't 'need' them. Contentedness can be found by other means."

"I guess, yes. Still difficult to understand. She such a pleasant woman… enjoy dinner, Edouardos."

Just then the waiter brought dinner – tzatziki, courgette croquettes, and a walnut, pear and blue cheese salad, the perfect trifecta of Greek food. The place was brimming as I completed my meal. I thought of leaving, feeling it disrespectful to occupy a table of four, but decided against it. I ordered a small carafe of white Robola instead. Fate, it seemed, had muddied well-conceived plans and created a scenario I never had considered. I could only wonder if it possible for us to care for one another a second time. Much had changed: we were older, we were poorer, we were settled, but our bohemian-like lifestyles and life philosophies, as usual, appeared in sync. About half a carafe into what was becoming a late evening I realised that whatever I said to her, I needed to taste my words before I spit them out. I wasn't going to return to America nor she to Britain. We had found each other only accidentally on a small Ionian island and, regardless of what may or may not transpire, we needed to be cautious. We had individual lives to live. I likened it to walking barefoot on the jagged rocks hugging the Cephalonia shoreline, a mixture of pain and beauty. The bill paid, I meandered back to the flat thinking: *Here I am, a month away from turning sixty to find myself again standing on the precipice* with Sara Hawes, a woman I never should have shown my back to five years earlier. *An unforgettable woman.*

After entering the flat I opened the French doors to let in the sea breeze. The crowds had trickled down to almost nothing, only the muffled noise of boaters drinking and reflecting on their latest sea adventures. I keyed up Duke Ellington's *Unknown Session*, mixed a Vesper and reflected on the evening's events, attempting desperately to place in context, hoping to extract small kernels of understanding.

About halfway through the second martini I realised I had repeated exactly what my father had done almost thirty years earlier: procrastinated. Neglect killed him. After suffering debilitating pains in his hips and ischium bones, finding it difficult to sit, to lay down or to walk at his preferred double-time pace, he visited the doctor after two years of consistent pain. He was too late. Terminal prostate cancer had metastasised to the bone. He died twenty-seven months later on my thirty-second birthday. Throughout life I had tried to garner nuggets of wisdom from my experiences and those of others. At age thirty-two my father gifted me an unintended life lesson: at its worst procrastination will kill you and, if it doesn't kill you, it will lessen your enjoyment of life. Whatever you want to do, whatever you're going to do, do it. Sounds simple. It isn't. I certainly didn't follow through with Sara. And for that, I am solely to blame. If offered a second go, I won't screw it up. I can't.

I only realised it was morning when the smell of freshly baked bread wafted into the flat. Although exhausted I seemed close to grasping what may lay ahead for Sara and me. Perhaps Fritzy was right years earlier when he predicted that while the relationship would fail, we'd develop a heightened level of emotional intelligence that could be used in the future. He obviously thought I'd find someone new – it wouldn't be

Sara – but it may be only years later. We had come through it, but had we come through it the same? Would earlier emotions resurface?

Remembering Sara was a stickler for promptness I set off early. I figured she'd be well stocked with fine Greek wines so I brought two bottles of champagne knowing they'd go down smoothly. I had little difficulty finding *Keramoskepi*. Her skill explaining directions remained intact. The steep climb coupled with August's extreme heat made me appear as if I had been rode hard and put away wet. The exterior of the house with its terracotta roof tiles and natural reddish-white rock recognised island and Greek culture without appearing kitsch-like. The front entrance was located in the middle while on the right-hand side were twelve steps that appeared to lead to an uncovered sundeck or patio. Where considerable scrub brush and debris concealed other ruins, Sara had cleared and planted olive trees, jasmine, lavender and an English-Greek herb garden complete with oregano, dill, fennel and basil. A stone path on the left-hand side led around to what I assumed was the pottery studio. Excited, but full of trepidation about what the day could bring, I used the door knocker Sara obviously had designed – a large, unpolished piece of amethyst secured in a bronze casing mounted on a massive, roughhewn olive wood door. She answered immediately.

"Were you checking me out like in New York? Seeing if I'd skulk about and have a nose?"

"No, actually I was going on the footpath to see if you were about. And here you are, on time."

"And here I am on time but wet and smelly. Sounds crass and I don't mean to appear presumptuous, but could I use your outside shower? I think we'd enjoy the day more if I were clean and dry and wearing fresh clothes."

"Not a problem, Edward. Had an acquaintance decades ago in London who after arriving always – and I mean always – needed the toilet. Never knew if it was nerves or dodgy digestion. Must say, it kinda dampened the mood… Anyway, everything you need is on the shower shelf. Follow the path on your left. Help yourself. Everything is natural and made locally. But… well, I don't have any men's clothes and mine won't fit obviously."

"Don't worry. You know I anticipate. Never a step forward without knowing what's ahead. I bought a change of clothes."

"Of course, I forgot, 'anal retentive' Edward. No forward movement without prior planning. Now that wasn't exactly fair, was it?"

"No offence taken. It's worked to my advantage a few times… like now. But honestly, on important life issues I've altered all previous predilections. Hell, that's why I'm in Fiskardo."

"Brilliant. Enjoy. I want to hear about this epiphany."

As forewarned, the shower was cold, frigidly so, but its position amongst olive trees and the smell of jasmine enticed me to stay, not to leave. I dried off, put on clean clothes, and walked to the front and entered the house. I was transfixed by the design. Sara was sitting comfortably in an oversized leather chair by an unlit fire. Behind her was an olive wood mantel as long as the width of the house. The mosaic floor offered no comparisons. Tiny one-inch stoneware tiles covered the area. In the centre and in all four corners were additional mosaics using a glaze, I learned later, that Sara had developed – the Ionian, reflecting the ginger soil and the lapis sea. Each design replicated vessels she had crafted. Three different-sized pots dominated the middle of the floor while in the corners four Greek-inspired vases pitched at a forty-five-degree angled towards the centre. Three walls had recessed niches displaying what I presumed to be Sara's favourite or most recent creative efforts. Backlighting from small candles placed behind each piece created a shadowy backdrop. I recovered my visual balance and walked over and kissed her gently on the head.

"This is stunning. And that isn't American hyperbole. Incredibly impressed at your artistic élan. And this mantel… where or how did it get here?"

"Well, thank you. Glad you like it. I enjoyed watching your facial expressions as you walked about. Made me giggle. It's truly home to me. The mantel… well, workmen uncovered it when levelling the ground prior to pouring cement. It's original to the house believe it or not. Through the years as the house crumbled, the mantel collapsed, covering over with debris, soil and undergrowth. We reclaimed it and, except for a small deformity needing filling, it was turned, sanded and French polished. When the fire is going, the flickering effect on the wood is hypnotic. I guess I like large mantels. This one is about six hundred years old, two hundred years younger than the one at Plough Cottage."

She gave a complete tour of the house. A functional kitchen was in the rear overlooking the studio. The cabinet doors consisted of customised, reclaimed front doors from abandoned homes. A narrow stone staircase led to the first floor, consisting solely of one bedroom and a large bathroom equipped with toilet and oversized sink.

"But the bathroom lacks the coveted 'Sara Hawes' tub."

"I've got one downstairs. You saw the two wooden doors on either side of the fireplace? The left-hand side stores wood and the right-hand side is where the copper Bateau bath is stored. I place it near the fireplace in winter and fill it with heated water from a cauldron suspended over the flames. The bath remains warm being so close to the flames, so I can enjoy a toasty-hot bath in a romantic setting while enjoying a glass of red Robola. I insert a long tube at the base after finishing and run it through the wall to outside. The water collects in a stone-like sump where it eventually evaporates. On a day like today, it would be gone in under two days. Takes a bit longer in winter."

"Is this something the architect recommended?"

"No, I invented this piece of kit actually. The architect was impressed. But to be honest, Edward, I've become so used to the outside shower I only use the bath between December and early February. Otherwise it's a cold shower or the Ionian."

Inlaid bookcases formed two of four walls in her bedroom. They were stuffed with books and art pottery. French doors led outside to the open-air patio. A wicker sofa and two chairs with thick cushions and an in-ground fire pit hinted this was a place to enjoy cool evenings or damp mornings. On the right were the stone steps I saw when arriving that lead to the front of the house. The elevated position of the patio permitted a clear view to the east towards the mountains of Ithaca. Returning to the bedroom I was struck by the half-read book on the nightstand beside her bed. Its distinctive blue cover was familiar – my own book on Britain's difficulty accepting architectural modernisms published three years earlier. She noticed my interest.

"I love the way you write. Reflects a hell of a lot of work. Congratulations."

"You're probably the fourth person I know who's read it. I'm glad it's out there... if only for posterity and as a benefit to future historians. I accomplished my goal. Now I realise, Sara, that artists consider their studio a sanctuary but would you feel comfortable giving a tour?"

"Only if you promise not to touch anything."

"I *do* believe my mother taught me well."

I thought the studio would be of wood construction but it wasn't. Similar to the house it was built of natural reddish-white stone with terracotta roof tiles. This was a considered studio, not a fey or amateurish attempt. To compensate for no electricity three of the walls were glass. The longest glass window was a sliding door that opened to half its full length. I thought immediately Sara had borrowed the idea from when we stayed at Fritzy's house on San Juan Island eight years earlier. Except for the pitched roof, it looked stunningly similar to Philip Johnson's Glass House. She said at certain times of the day the light becomes so intense she had to install blinds. Inside were all the trappings of a potter – wrapped bundles of clay stacked neatly in the overhead loft; plenty of wood shelving containing pottery at different levels of completion; and, of course, the manual kick wheel Sara had talked so excitingly about two days earlier. Its crude simplicity belied what it produced. Upon reflection I realised it owed far more to the talent of the potter who threw and turned the clay than the machine. A pegboard above the workbench contained a varying array of wood, metal tools and brushes used for relief design, glazing and finishing. The only non-pottery item was a battery-powered satellite radio. Sara didn't use it to keep abreast of world events as she had done so religiously years earlier. Now she tuned it to only one station: Swiss Jazz – one of the world's finest jazz stations. It added a unique artistic rhythm to her work. About one hundred feet away was the initial layout of the wood-burning kiln she planned to use for salt-glazing. As she locked the door I noticed a black slate sign suspended from the door knob that I hadn't spotted earlier. It stated simply: 'POTTER AT WORK'.

Sara asked if I wanted to eat inside or outside on the patio. I felt foolish to prefer inside, but the Hellenic beauty of the ground floor required it be used today of all days – reacquaintance day. Then I remembered the ground floor lacked a table.

"If it's too troubling, Sara, we can dine outside. No use rearranging furniture."

"Oh, don't be silly. There's a table on the ground floor. You think I roll out a Persian rug, cross my legs and eat food with my fingers from a ceramic bowl?"

"I suppose my visual perception was overloaded. I never saw a table."

"Well, it's inside the wall. Called a pocket table and includes two benches on either side. The walls are so thick the architect recommended it. And to prevent the wood from being damaged the interior of the wall is lined with thick wool. Ingenious, I thought."

Sara lifted a recessed brass handle on the side of the table, extended it five feet, unlatched two legs secured underneath the table-top and placed them firmly on the mosaic floor. The support for the opposite end was within the wall itself. She accessed two benches on either side of the table in a similar fashion and retrieved two bespoke cushions that fit atop each bench.

"What a fascinating piece of furniture. Absolutely remarkable. Creates a minimalist space resembling an Adolf Loos design."

After setting the table using her hand thrown plates and beakers, Sara served the food – a variety of Greek cheeses, a selection of olives, red tomatoes and fresh sea bass garnished with pomegranate sauce. To my utter surprise she also had made courgette croquettes.

"I adore courgette croquettes, my favourite item on Tselenti's menu except, of course, for the whole red snapper or sea bass."

"I like them, too. Vasilia gave me the recipe under a shroud of secrecy. Told me to never speak of it, as it had been passed down by four generations of Kastas's family."

"Now *that's* something. You've definitely made a friend."

"They've purchased several pots for their private quarters upstairs above the restaurant. Vasilia loves the Ionian style, believes it artistically reflects the island. So I feel well complimented."

"I agree with her. Completely evokes the aura of Cephalonia."

While nimbly uncorking an extra special bottle of white Robola, Sara said something that preoccupied me long afterward.

"You know, Edward, somewhat consequentially I have you to thank for my life here. Had we not met, had you not visited Fiskardo and had you not turned away from the idea of us, I'd be hunkered down somewhere in the Yorkshire Dales. I have all this because of you. So, a belated thank you."

I didn't know exactly how to respond so I offered a toast.

"To the rose-lipped maiden of Fiskardo. May she always be contented, unaffected by whatever disruptions life presents."

We clinked our stoneware beakers together – well, the clink sounded more like two rocks clashing but a festive sound nonetheless.

"Where did 'rose-lipped maiden' come from?"

"Remember on San Juan Island… you used it to toast our last evening as we stood by the fire drinking champagne."

"Lorrrrrd. Your memory astounds me. All those details catalogued and so readily accessible. Fab."

"Shame on me, Sara, for not taking the initiative as you've done. I should have acted differently. So much wasted time. So much lost opportunity. I've learned if procrastination doesn't kill you, it will lessen your enjoyment of life."

"That's rather prophetic. Now where did *that* come from?"

"I didn't read or find it anywhere. Sadly it's something I discerned as my father lay dying. Wisdom garnered from anguish and personal pain. I haven't followed it as dutifully as I should sadly."

"You're here, Edward. That's important. It's a long way round the corner sometimes, isn't it?"

"Indecisiveness prolonged my path. Ironically it took America choosing a first-class loser with a fourth-rate intellect – a bottom feeder – and the complicity of the Republican Party before I realised my America had been co-opted. Trump and his sycophantic staff continued assaulting what little bit of decency and dignity remained of the presidency. He and his cronies are slipperier than a bunch of eels in a bucket of Vaseline. They annihilated shame. Disgustingly sad. And the American people either willingly or unknowingly chose this course. If willingly then I had no choice but leave. If unknowingly then the stupidity of the electorate comprised largely of half-educated mouth-breathers, should never be underestimated again, easily justifying a departure. Either way the only solution was to low crawl through an opening, scale the wall and emerge on the other side as an expat. The desire to live simply is a philosophy lost on most Americans. The country has all the comforts but little of what is essential. I accept Greece has issues but it is wonderful, a far sight better than America with its penchant for money and morality that caters to morons."

"How about you, Sara, when or how did you lose your attachment to the 'old lion and unicorn'?"

"As you know, the austerity measures inflicted on the police and the social welfare programmes by the Conservatives that started during the financial crisis only worsened over time. Resources at the Met were stretched so thin, if a piece of silk cloth, you could have seen through it. I became really furious at Cameron's government, in particular the Home Secretary and the Police Commissioner. The Home Secretary served as Cameron's lap-dog and was complicit in destroying the organisational structure of the police – sold police properties and stations throughout London; dismantled the training school at Hendon; forced the Commissioner to report to the London mayor instead of directly to the Home Secretary; making the force vulnerable to the whims of elected politicians. That's the last thing we need. Of course, the worst was that the Commissioner followed Cameron's directives unflinchingly because he coveted an appointment to the House of Lords. It was horrible, truly pathetic. And I haven't touched on the individual issues: benefit cuts as well as increasing the service requirement to forty years. I was grandfathered into the last scheme fortunately, so I left a few years short of thirty. Thank God. How could I have done my job at sixty years old? Honestly."

"Sounds awful. Luckily you squeaked through on the old benefits scheme."

"I feel fortunate. Of course, Cameron's Big Society programme was laughable at best. He closed the libraries. Attempted to privatise the forests. Sold the country's financial interest in Eurostar. Privatised Royal Mail. Diminished public transport in rural areas. Permitted fracking and on, and on, and on. My concerns increased dramatically with the EU referendum, especially the way both sides campaigned using uninformative and adolescent tactics. The public received no knowledgeable benefits. Even worse – the issue was determined by simple majority. How can the government think an issue of such importance that will impact generations of Brits, be decided so flippantly, so simply? Refreshing that seventy-two per cent of eligible voters participated, but regardless of which side won, a seventy per cent plurality should have been required. If that wasn't achieved then the vote should have been declared null and void. And look what's happened – paralysis.

The *coup-de-grace* occurred the day after the referendum. Big Dave walked out of No 10, announced his resignation, turned around and whistled a little ditty sauntering back into No 10. Can you imagine after the fall of France in June 1940, Churchill telling Parliament that Germany obviously would achieve victory so there's no need to resist or to fight and then resigning? Cameron, Osborne… they're Eton's and Oxford's finest? Think the nation deserves a refund. Now the country's saddled with May as Prime Minister – the lap-dog. Glad to be totally out of it. No doubts. No regrets. No second thoughts. I made the correct and, for me personally, the sane decision."

"Ironic, isn't it, two nations so sullied, their governments propelled us to flee. Citizens have an obligation towards their government, but government also has a covenant, a duty to its citizens. I kept the faith. It was the American government that didn't. I also believe something else. You know there is that all-too-human tendency as time passes to look wistfully at the past. But I can tell you one thing: I won't ever yearn for or be romantic or even nostalgic about America. I've severed that relationship. In all fairness, though, the country disowned me long before I reciprocated. It had become a foreign country but yet again, I acted too slowly."

"Well, unlike you, I've never been idealistic about anything, certainly not my country. I haven't discussed politics with anyone in a long while, Edward. And as much as I enjoy it… can we transition to more pleasant topics. Is that possible?"

"Of course, certainly. I, too, haven't talked politics with anyone since I left. Kinda good though to articulate it out loud. Reinforces my decisions. But, yes, how about something beautifully unique… like your pottery and your life in Greece?"

"Being alone, feeling content and living naturally are essential to my creative process. I believe, at least I hope, the work reflects tenderness and passion. It's not contrived. It's genuine and considered. I throw, turn, glaze and fire what inspires me, not what sells. As I said long ago, I'm not fussed about being a struggling potter. The struggle begets beauty and simplicity."

"It's certainly unique. I like it. A homage to the ancient Greeks with requisite amounts of modern design. No Spartan warriors, no naked nymphs or leapfrogging men but subtle glazes reflecting the area's rustic landscape. Any gallery showings, yet?"

"I've got my first showing in autumn at a gallery near the Castle of Saint George in the hills overlooking Argostoli. The organisation found me surprisingly. I didn't know anything about it. I have asked, but certainly Vasilia was involved somehow. The Tselentis know everybody and everything that occurs on the island. So what about you, how do you occupy time?"

"Well, I'm not mouldering. Run a lot more and swim. Collect the sun at 'the rocks' and work on a manuscript."

"What's it about?"

"Knocking around some ideas; the proverbial 'work in progress'. Borrowing a bit from Hemingway... *I hope to live it up to write it down.* Probably won't happen, though."

"And what and where are 'the rocks'?"

I explained discovering it years earlier and why I felt drawn to them – their isolation and ruggedness force an undisciplined entry into the sea. The beautiful location set against a mountainous backdrop invited contemplation. A spot that softened problems and smoothed emotions. Fearing I had exaggerated their importance, I stopped.

"Promise to take me sometime? Seems wonderful. I'm intimidated by waves but I might give it a try as long as you're about."

"It's a date then."

I soaked up the environment, taking it all in while Sara retrieved another bottle of Robola. My ginger friend – my British confidant – had been churned through the grist mill and emerged contented with life. Good for her. She had blown through my selfish indecisiveness, deservedly so, I reflected.

Sara refilled our glasses and sat down. She seemed preoccupied by something or somebody. She had something to say.

"Once settled, Edward, I reflected on the difficulty of retiring early, selling Plough Cottage and most possessions, departing England, leaving friends, abandoning family. Fraught by myriad concerns which couldn't be addressed easily or quickly. So, what I'm offering, I guess, is an empirical understanding for the challenges you faced five years ago about leaving America – the turmoil, the angst and the inherent precariousness of it all. I don't think I grasped the totality until I did it myself."

"Thanks, appreciate that but deep down – and only after two years of serious reflection – I learned my priorities were back-ass backwards. I had lacked the courage of conviction for our wants, for our desires. I put me ahead of us. You stated it perfectly at Knight's Bar: *Isn't our relationship more important than how good or how shitty the state of American politics?* Above anything or everything else, that statement alone should have convinced me I was on a one-way path to a dead end. I've had to live with that poor decision. You expected more but I didn't deliver. For that, I'm unabashedly ashamed."

"That's all in the past. You're here now. That's what's important."

"Here's a story you may enjoy. When Trump was elected in '16 I made immediate plans to leave. He offered no assurances his presidency would be any different from his campaign or the way he had managed his business. I couldn't conceive of living near or working with people who put such slime in office. I responded to an editorial in the New York Times a month after the inauguration. It was titled 'I Have Performed a Selfish Act'. I recounted how I had wanted to leave the country since '04 after 'W' was re-elected but demurred. The desire festered quietly but deep within until Trump's victory and subsequent absurd behaviour forced my hand. My parting comment to readers: *I have assumed the coveted title of expat, never to return... ever.* And guess what? It received 460 recommends. Better yet, it was chosen as one of the editor's top picks. Showed there were a hell of a lot of Americans who weren't relishing what the 'Orange Man' would bringeth. Positioned thousands upon thousands of miles away, I'm not one of them fortunately. I no longer give a damn."

"We've voluntarily removed ourselves from our countries to experience contented simplicity. My elusive dream fortunately came true: a holistic naturalism void of complex choices."

"That brings me to an important point, Sara. It's something I've thought about long into the night after our meeting at Tselenti's. We've relocated and, it seems, neither one has the faintest desire to return or move elsewhere. We should proceed cautiously if we continue to visit each other. To act rashly would spoil what took so long to achieve. We must lead individual lives which may or may not involve the other in the future. Needlessly applying pressure to recreate the past will undo the good surrounding our reacquaintance. Does this make any sense at all?"

"You do, yes. It's pragmatic. We're experienced at life. At our respective ages we should approach our association by relishing the sheer madness we find ourselves, not dwelling on rejection from years earlier. Cherish it actually. I remember my advice from the first visit to Seattle. It's as apropos today as then: *Let's just do whatever feels right.*"

"I remember that toast. By adhering to it our relationship achieved a spontaneous fluidity and an equity of purpose, a shared desire. It enabled something natural and truer to our instincts. A special time."

"We're in a spartan environment with a renewed spirit for life. As the Brits say, let's see what the 'warm south' has in store."

And with that Sara retrieved another bottle of Robola. I felt neither awkward nor anxious. As naively wishful as it appeared we had picked up where we left it… *before* Knight's Bar. Our fondness for talking and listening remained intact, vitally important if the relationship developed legs.

After pouring a glass and getting resettled, I asked Sara something intrusive but it was another issue that had preoccupied me since Tselenti's.

"How do you handle the lack of emotional physicality?"

"That's rather personal, isn't it?… I've blanked it out at my age. Compartmentalised it. Put it to bed, so to speak… no pun intended. What do you have to say for yourself?"

"I certainly haven't kept up with the PMCS since Knight's Bar. The only thing I've brought to bed is a good book. Bordering on monkishness at this stage, I suppose – transcribing texts, pressing grapes, distilling brandy."

"PMCS – what the hell is that?"

"Preventive Maintenance Checks and Services."

"Lorrrrrd, Edward. Honestly."

"Seriously… I've learned one only can find genuine intimacy with someone they love. If love isn't present, it's best either to abstain or remain alone. A man can rationalise any physical relationship as intimate but only he knows whether his actions are honest and true or the selfish manoeuvrings of an opportunistic cad. I'd argue that a man who's had numerous dalliances will be incapable of developing a loyal and fulfilling relationship with one woman. It's simply impossible."

"Well, you remain a 'one-off' – charmingly out of sync with your generation and several others, I think."

"For a brief, shining moment I thought you'd lost your sarcasm."

"I can't lose it. It's innate."

"I'm so excited to write Fritzy about us. He'll be astounded, rushing to proffer brotherly advice."

"Oh, my, I never asked. Just assumed he had died years ago. Wasn't his cancer terminal?"

"It was, it was. He volunteered to take some experimental drugs – a potent cocktail of several cutting edge but unapproved substances. Surprisingly the cancer ceased spreading so it's only a task of managing what remains. The cocktail drains him physically but, in true Fritzy style, he argues: *By all indications and evidence presented, I prefer walking around tired than lying down... dead.*"

"Hasn't lost his humour. What a character. Glad for him and for you. Your excellent friend remains amongst the living."

"Exactly. Difficult to say goodbye, though. But we did have one hell of a final seminar at table eleven – similar to taking a midterm, a final and an oral exam all on the same day. Lasted into the wee small hours. He joyously accepts responsibility for pointing me towards the road less travelled."

"Where there is need, there is desire. That's what got you to the rugged peacefulness of Fiskardo, Edward."

"I wanted... well, we both needed to refocus our lives and reached out to a small Ionian island for assistance... and was accepted."

Despite our history I didn't want to outstay the welcome. We had achieved a lot by digging deep below the surface. Surely there will be other days, I thought. Sara's perceptiveness picked up on my uneasy readiness to leave.

"It's been fab getting reacquainted. Might still have it. Thank you."

"Incredibly enjoyable day. Here it is half eight and I feel as if I've only arrived. If that's not a testament to friendship than I don't know what is."

As I rose from my chair Sara came over and hugged me warmly.

"Not to be presumptuous but... may I kiss you?"

The lightness and tenderness of her kiss made me want to freeze it forever so I could reimagine it at another time and another place as utter and unrepeatable contentment.

"I must confess something before you leave. I wasn't on my way to the footpath looking for you. I was lighting the candles, setting the mood, preparing for your arrival and standing next to the door appraising the ambiance when you knocked. I wanted it perfect. Didn't want to faff about after you'd arrived. Sorry to say, I may even have been trying to impress you."

"Don't apologise. You did impress me. You've always impressed me... never one to sing the same song twice."

A fresh breeze coming off the water and travelling up the hill towards Psilithrias made for a pleasant return to Fiskardo. My head was so cramped with thoughts and ideas about Sara that a short journey seemed even shorter. Once home I put on Stan Getz's *Café Montmartre*, made a Vesper, sat on the deck and pondered the day. It seemed we had emerged from the relationship tsunami unscathed. Scars that remained weren't outwardly visible, although she did possess an heir of confident independence and self-containment. But overall, no residue of rancour or malice or ingratitude – as Fritzy had predicted years earlier. I think it showed not only how close we had been but how good we had been together. I felt also exceedingly positive about myself. My obsession had vanished for needing predetermined confirmation that beginning afresh with Sara would be worth the effort. This may have been because we lived close and couldn't help seeing one another occasionally – ignoring the fact, of course, it took five months for the first accidental encounter. I also thought – and sincerely hoped – a by-product of leaving America was that I had broken the impenetrable mould that had stifled freedom and unconventionality throughout life. Its dominance belonged to the ash heap of personal history.

Sara contacted me a week later. She had reached a point where several pots needed firing and, because her contact in Maganos was on holiday for another week, she thought a swim off 'the rocks' was in order. We met at Tselenti's for a Mythos prior to sweating it out while walking to 'the rocks'. More than any other day, on hot days a frosty-cold Mythos was essential. It never disappointed. Upon meeting, I noticed Sara strangely wasn't flushed or even mildly overheated.

"I know you're not one to sweat, Sara, but the walk from Psilithrias would have taken a bit of a toll, surely."

"I didn't walk. I drove."

"Didn't know you had a car."

"Not a car, a gold Vespa. It's fab."

"Where's your helmet?"

"Don't use one. Only goggles to keep bugs from my eyes. Nobody wears helmets here. Too hot and too uncomfortable."

"I can't wait to see my ginger friend at the controls of a Vespa complete with goggles tooling around the countryside. Would never see that in the UK or the US, for that matter."

"Isn't that part of the reason we're here – freedom mixed with personal responsibility with minimal intrusion from others?"

"It is. It is. I try and wipe off as much of America from my tongue as I can but some still clings. Another one of the constrictive aspects of US society. I'll get there eventually. Don't worry."

Sara surprisingly had never visited 'the rocks'. She knew the approximate location but never ventured towards the rugged shoreline. She had no difficulty navigating the steep descent. After taking off our backpacks, hiking boots and sweaty socks we sat down with the sun directly overhead gazing at the horizon towards Ithaca. The sea looked calm and welcoming.

"Look at that scene. Has remained unchanged for millennium. We're only a drop in the bluest sea, Sara. Nothing more, nothing less."

"I never held illusions of anything different."

"It's taken me a lifetime to appreciate that, to feel content with the transitory and temporal nature of life. When we're young we think opportunities abound – they're nothing if not plentiful – naively believing promise and potential are endless. *If I don't try this activity or accept this appointment or attend this school another opportunity, perhaps a better one, will materialise.* In reality most opportunities, particularly the best opportunity, come once. If you don't embrace it… it'll disappear and won't return. Promise and potential are fickle and won't be there when you need or want them. We don't learn this, if we learn it at all, until middle-aged. And, of course, by then it's too late: suddenly the realisation of what could have been becomes what will never be. Now… perhaps I better dive in before I become too philosophical and sound like a complete nabob."

"You lack the pedigree for a nattering nabob."

"Perhaps, then, I'm only a natter."

I removed my sweaty clothes and walked towards the 'bread loaf pan' entry point.

"Edward, Lorrrrrrd, put on some pants. People could see you."

"I'm careful. My wares aren't exposed to passing boats. It's so freeing, so natural. You should try it."

"Swim naked? Not my cup of tea. Did it once in a pool. Wasn't impressed. May have been the chlorine."

"I thought you were bohemian?"

"Swimming naked in the sea makes one bohemian?"

"No, but it's an insouciant state of mind with a genuine connection to nature. Now if you don't stop talking someone will sail by. Seeing me standing buck naked surely will cause distress – for them and me! They may run aground."

Upon surfacing and turning towards the rocky shore I saw Sara cautiously walking towards 'bread loaf pan' without a stitch on.

"Edward, please look away. I suffer a bit of the *National Geographic* these days. That's what age does for you."

I laughed out loud, repeating to myself, *National Geographic*. Her lament had no effect on me. She looked stunning. Except for one minor slip her water entry was flawless. After swimming the two hundred yards towards me she treaded water.

"Goodness, I'm so buoyant. Everything floats! I'll have to say… it *is* nice. Feels different. I'm so, so… unencumbered. Bloody marvellous."

After fifteen minutes of swimming, floating and treading water we decided to return to shore.

"I'm sure you have a plan that prevents anyone seeing us?"

"Nope, I swim over and get out. It's their problem if they enjoy gawking at a middle-aged man."

"Honestly, maybe you can do that but a woman…well, everyone records everything nowadays. I could end up on YouTube as 'Droopy Ginger Woman Emerges from Sea.'"

"Only kidding, Sara. I look around and gauge the proximity of boats or ferries on the horizon. I listen for the sounds of motorboats or ferry boarding announcements from Fiskardo. Because sound bounces off water so clearly you can hear the boats long before you see them. If it looks and sounds clear I swim over to the jagged rock that juts into the water, approximate when the incoming waves will hit the shore and slowly get out of the water and onto the large white rock directly in front of us. Watch. It's simple. Honestly."

I exited and turned to watch and to encourage Sara. I reconfirmed there were no boats close by. Except for some difficulty grabbing hold of the protruding, jagged rock she made a smooth exit. Once on shore she ran to our clothes pile, wrapped my shirt around her, sat down and began giggling.

"That was fab, Edward. Wonderful."

"It's primitively refreshing."

"I'll agree with you on that. Thank you."

I stretched out on a flat, low rock that shielded us from being seen from the sea. Sara nestled nearby so we could feel the cool breeze and absorb the hot sun. She became too hot and removed her shirt. Before nodding off to sleep I lifted her left hand and kissed it.

After eating a light dinner at Tselenti's, including drinking requisite amounts of white Robola, Sara asked to see the flat. Fortunately I had cleaned and straightened it earlier. Embarrassment wouldn't be mine. Seemed strange having Sara in my living space again. Her detective eye wasted little time identifying items brought from Seattle. The artwork, the filled bookcases and the desk had made the transition. She picked up also on two new items that hadn't come from America: cat water and food bowls.

"You never said you had a cat. Fab."

"I don't actually. 'Chet' – as in Baker – is a non-paying, occasional border. I befriended this ginger tom kitten a few months ago at Tselenti's. He almost nicked an entire lamb shank off the plate of an unsuspecting customer. Chet was airborne, neck extended, paws spread, close to achieving success before the gentleman realised the ol' boy's intentions. I took an instant liking and unbeknownst to me he followed me home one evening. I let him in, well, he entered confidentially on his own. Offered him water, a few leftover bits and that was it. Chet avails himself of my hospitality about four days a week. The other three days he must spend with a lady because when he first arrives Chet smells heavily of perfume. He loves the lushness of the deck. It's high and surround by fruit trees so he's probably harkening back to his ancestors' languid days on the savannah. He's a wonderful critter to have about. A bit arrogant but I respect that. Using habit as a guide, he'll make the scene sometime after half ten."

"I think I'll love, Chet. Great name. And I like the flat. Smaller than Seattle but quainter. The wall colours reflect a cool Mediterraneanism. You'll appreciate it when winter rains arrive, wondering if the summer sun was an alcohol-induced mirage."

While preparing drinks I put on the classic *John Coltrane and Johnny Hartman* to set the mood – perfection for a late summer evening. Having re-read *The Great Gatsby* for the first time in forty-five years, I decided on a drink reminiscent of the era: a gin rickey. The cocktail of choice amongst Gatsby's friendly neighbour, disloyal friends and ne'er-do-well opportunists. Surprisingly a gin rickey highball was the only drink my racetrack-loving grandmother enlivened. She lived in clover in the early '20s, so there was a bit of family lore connected to the drink.

"So, whatta ya think?"

"Refreshing. After finishing a few they'll re-enter from the back door, I imagine, knocking me on my bum. Stealthily, of course."

"Tolerance shouldn't be an issue."

"There's that naughtiness again… I'll have another, please."

I gently kissed her lips as she took the drink.

"Thanks for coming today. I realise 'the rocks' isn't a beach full of lush sand or soft shingles, but it also lacks the bothersome and the attention-seeking. It's peaceful, quiet, almost abandoned – only me, unforgiving rocks and the cool sea. Your presence added a femininity reflected in Pre-Raphaelite paintings. Simply exquisite. Thank you."

"You do speak tosh sometimes, Edward, but thanks. I thoroughly enjoyed it. Wouldn't go it alone, though. Too dangerous. You should be ever so careful."

Habitually on time, Chet made his presence known by pawing at the bottom of the front door. In he came, meowing loudly as if chastising me for taking too long to open the door. He spotted Sara immediately, stopped, looked her over, meowed and hopped on her lap, head-butting her left hand.

"Chet knows class when he smells it."

"Honestly, this is one confident boy. Can see how he almost nicked that man's lamb dish."

"If you don't mind, I've learned Chet is partial, not to his namesake sadly, but to Stan Kenton, specifically 'Tampico' and 'The Peanut Vendor' from 1945 and 1947 respectively. Mind if I play them? He adores June Christy's voice and the crescendo in 'The Peanut Vendor' relaxes him surprisingly. They both share a 'south of the border' kind of vibe."

"Couldn't disappoint, Chet."

Time passed quickly. It was soon past midnight. I didn't know how or if I should ask Sara her plans for returning home. Too dark to walk. Too much alcohol for the Vespa.

"Do you feel comfortable staying over?"

"I think it would be a shame not to, don't you?"

Answering a question with a question. Another one of Sara's innumerable talents.

I woke late the next morning. Chet had exited earlier from the deck via the lemon tree. And since Sara didn't budge, I walked to the bakery and bought fresh bread and a large tin of Cephalonian honey. No movement or sound was heard from the bedroom while I prepared coffee, but as I poured the dark brew into my cup I heard a winsome voice in the background.

"I can smell the coffee but I can't taste it."

"Oh, I see. Guests are supposed to be served in bed."

"That would be ever so nice. You certainly haven't lost your intuitiveness."

"That request didn't require intuition. Angling more towards British subtlety, I believe."

As Sara pulled herself together I accessed email and printed the lone message. It was from Fritzy. I read it first in the unlikely event he had written something untoward about Sara. He hadn't. As she returned to bed, I presented her with a fresh coffee and Fritzy's latest epistle:

Dear Buttons—

My first thought reading your letter was my 'cocktail for merriment' had affected comprehension. Rereading I learned the mind wasn't deceitful. You and lovely Sara Hawes are reunited, have rediscovered one another on the road less travelled! My sincere and heartfelt congratulations, Buttons. Any pearls of wisdom I could offer at this juncture probably would be rendered useless within a month. The emotional intelligence you achieved with Sara was earmarked towards someone new. Relocating to Greece I imagined in my non-drugged state you'd befriend a lovely exotic Greek woman who dressed traditionally and played the bouzouki. (I guess it's the romantic in me, Buttons.) But I'm out of my ken now. It's possible, I suppose, what you and Sara found years ago will rise from the depths of dormancy and shower you with all good things. I needn't remind you to tread lightly, my dear boy, but I shall… tread lightly. I'm sure you've both changed in the intervening years. But I am impressed by the free swimming at what you refer to as 'the rocks'. I have found being naked in nature and isolated from humanity the closest we moderns can get to being feral – except, of course, eating raw meat of a deer or caribou we brought down ourselves.

Live large, live free and don't hold back, Buttons. Experience everything Greece and Sara can offer. Despite full larders, stuffed wardrobes and boundless possessions, the intellectual emptiness of America increases exponentially each passing day. There is nothing for you here. A wasteland of what could have been.

After rereading the above paragraph, I think I should conclude on a more positive note. Therefore, when faced with a decision, unsure what to do, just ask yourself the rudimentary question: 'What would ol' Fritzy do?' If answered honestly, you'll soon find yourself waist-deep in something or somebody new and exciting. Love to you both.

I remain, as always,
Fritzy

"The 'cocktail for merriment' hasn't affected his humour, Edward. May even have increased it. What a character. Honestly."

"It's extended his life so I'm sure any activity he pursues is raised to the tenth power. Hope he's writing down his thoughts. Could be enlightening."

"Since you mentioned writing, I've noticed a five-inch-high stack of typed papers on the corner of the desk, weighted down with what appears to be a sun-bleached stone from 'the rocks'. Sure you don't want to divulge its content?"

"No, not yet. All in good time, Sara, all in good time. Writers don't let others read their work until it's completed. Only when they feel confident in the quality will writers permit a chosen few to review a manuscript. Of course, there is an important caveat with this statement: it presupposes I'm a writer."

"It's similar to pottery, I guess. I don't like others reviewing or commenting on work until it's finished and then only if I'm pleased with the results. I get it. I was a bit too inquisitive. Sorry."

"Don't worry. Deep down I'm just trying to get some fun out of life. I've pretty much reconciled I won't receive any reward for my toil. But I'm fine with that. Sometimes it may be more important to write it down than get it published. Somebody will read it someday. After all, a lot of people run five, six or more miles a day. I did in my younger years. Doesn't mean I was bound for the Olympics or itching to compete. I ran because it was cathartic. It exercised my brain. Made me feel whole. I feel similarly about writing."

"Won't you be discouraged if you can't find a publisher?"

"Initially, yes, but rejection won't fester. I can't and won't let it."

"Doesn't sound like the Edward I remember."

"I can only say this perhaps because I'm not working and living on savings, but that's why I'm here – life for life's sake. It's wonderful not pursuing something – a better job, a fancier house or membership in an exclusive club where no one knows your name. Doing something for self-fulfilment and personal enrichment is the ultimate luxury. And the best thing about it, Sara… doesn't bring attention to myself. In this self-absorbed era, the significance of being insignificant is unappreciated and undervalued. I live in the world but not of it… and I'm thriving."

"And doing it alone only increases the intensity."

"Oh, I don't know, experiencing it with someone who feels similarly would be wonderful."

"Yes... perhaps. Being alone, I think, has made me a better person. In fact, I know it has."

I was taken back a bit by her nonchalance but didn't ask for an explanation. After finishing another coffee, I asked Sara if she'd mind if I went for a short run before the afternoon heat arrived.

"That would be fine, Edward. Would give me time to shower, enjoy another coffee and have a nose. See if I can find anything interesting."

"You'll be disappointed. Won't find anything incriminating. All that made its way to the bin before leaving Seattle, but you might enjoy the small photo album on the bottom shelf of the art deco bookcase."

And with that I was gone. My route took me south through Fiskardo and along the coast road to Foki Beach and Taverna. I continued up a steep hill for about fifteen minutes before I became too winded and couldn't take anymore. Regaining my breath, I reversed course for a leisurely return to the flat. I was gone for forty-five minutes. I entered my flat after cooling down a bit outside the building. The place was quiet. Sara was gone but had left a note on the table: *Sorry to leave without saying goodbye but totally forgot I'm supposed to meet the gallery owner regarding the autumn showing. I'll be late unless I get a wiggle on. She's buying me lunch at the Myrtos Beach Taverna. What am I like? Don't have time to even change clothes! And, Edward, what are you like? The photo album of our time together – all labelled with dates and locations. Made me happy and sad simultaneously. Let's dine together some evening soon at Tselenti's...* 'The Potter in the Hills'

I devoted entire days to writing in the weeks that followed. I ventured out only for the occasional dinner with Sara at

Tselenti's. We shared stories from the past and updated the other on our hoped-for successes. The shared enjoyment of Fiskardo dominated most evenings. These discussions, of course, were made more enjoyable by consuming copious amounts of Robola complemented by Mr Tselenti's jazz playlist – the most eclectic selection east of the Adriatic. One evening I admitted to Sara that the manuscript, although still a work in progress, had advanced to a semi-satisfied level. Careful not to divulge too much, I confessed somewhat sheepishly that the final chapter was the only remaining hiccup.

Days later, while listening to Johnny Hodges's *Used to Be Duke* and Louis Armstrong's *The Best of the Hot Five and Hot Seven*, I decided the quickest way to complete the manuscript was to spend more time with Sara. The experience would crystallise my thoughts, bring everything together. And besides, Sara's excitement about her approaching gallery show had become contagious. I thought she might enlist me with a basic or menial task – anything so she could focus solely on her pots. Knowing her penchant for organisation and planning, everything probably would be completed weeks in advance but I thought I'd ask, if for no other reason than politeness.

"That's kind, Edward, but everything's handled. You know me… leave nothing to chance or to others. But if you still want to help, and if not too much to ask, mind working on the wood-burning kiln? I've only staked out the perimeter. All the materials are there – cement, fire brick, rebar, ceramic fibre tiles. The angle iron and connecting rods that keep the kiln stationary have been pre-cut to exact measurements. All that remains is the assembly. I'd like it completed before Christmas, if possible, so it can be used this winter."

"Certainly, but remember what you said years ago?"

"No, but I'm guessing that grizzly bear trap memory of yours will remind me."

"*You're not practical, Edward.*"

"Ahhh, yes, true, but I have a book with instructions and drawings so you won't be too far removed from your comfort zone. You like books."

"Your sarcasm hasn't diminished in the intervening years. It's even more biting than before. Well done."

"You've also made great strides. Congratulations."

I walked behind the pottery and removed the tarp covering the materials.

"Gosh, Sara, how did you get these fire bricks here? How many are there… 150? Certainly you didn't carry them individually from the access road? That would have taken days."

"A lot of questions in rapid succession. Let's see, close on the number… there are exactly 175. And, don't be silly, of course I didn't carry them individually. I hired the two young children of the couple who own The Old Stone House Taverna."

"You what?"

"Oh, Edward, you are gullible. Of course I didn't. The husband of my friend in Maganos has a small vehicle – similar to a golf cart. They're used on the island at isolated construction sites. It took about four trips. Four hours later everything had been offloaded and neatly stacked."

"Well then, I'd better get cracking. Wouldn't want my pay docked."

Two or three hours passed before Sara inspected my work. She seemed impressed by my ability to read, to follow instructions and to remain flexible.

"Fab progress but if the foundation is here, why have you constructed the kiln using *all* the fire bricks over there?"

"Made a 'dry run' on the design, Sara. Wanted to ensure I laid the bricks correctly and everything fit snugly before becoming permanent. I'll relocate the bricks in the same order after the foundation dries in a few days. The roof will be done *in situ* obviously, but shouldn't be too much of a problem. Fingers crossed, of course."

"That explains why you're sweating like a farm animal. Lorrrrrd. Want to clean up using the outside shower? If not, then beat feet to Fiskardo, otherwise I've prepared an early dinner for us... but only if you're presentable."

"I'll be damned, easiest offer I've had in days. Why do you think I brought a change of clothes?"

"Go get washed-up then. All this wittering. Honestly."

"Is the water, soap and shampoo deducted from my wage?"

"If you don't get a wiggle on it most certainly will."

After the late afternoon lunch I told Sara I'd return in two days to complete the job. While she didn't seem disappointed I was leaving, she did encourage me to bring a couple changes of clothes and necessary toiletries when I returned. She thought I could spend a few days at *Keramoskepi* instead of traipsing back-and-forth. Lacking all pretence of inventing any kind of excuse, I accepted immediately – as if Sara had doubts. Thought it could be a wonderfully creative and relaxing time for us both.

It was an unseasonably hot October day when I returned. I used the warmth to my advantage when repositioning and aligning the fire bricks into position, viewing the autumnal heat as a gift, a chance to lose weight before the inevitable gain complicit with winter.

I longed for the shower after a full day's work. Sara remained hunkered next to her wheel, throwing and turning clay into objects of desire. And with the 'POTTER AT WORK' sign dangling from the door handle, I knew not to disturb her. The cascading cold water felt clean and refreshing. And the tea-mint shampoo invigorated me. Having showered so often at *Keramoskepi* the coldness of the water no longer bothered me.

"Room for a small one?"

"I don't have on my glasses but I'll certainly make room if you're a naked, ginger woman long in the body. But you can't touch. I'm clean and you're… well, covered in muck."

"You're not going to let a bit of potter's clay come between us, are you? Of course not."

Later that evening we enjoyed a fire on the patio outside the bedroom. The scent of pine lingered in the air; a bonus brought by warm afternoons. The brightness of a full moon and the orange flames cancelled any need for candles. Except for the distant call of a scops owl, the only sound was the flickering of the fire and the occasional popping of wood.

"While gathering firewood and waiting for the preverbal cement to dry, I reflected a bit on past relationships – or influences – that moved me towards the uncommonness of this life. As we've discussed already, the state of America was the immediate cause but I went back further, to certain persons, to events in some cases, which instilled the desire for difference. For the first time I realised there were a lot of similarities. They made me question. They offered alternatives. It was kind of enlightening. Enjoyed it. How about with you; has anyone or anything, in particular, influenced your decision for this discretionary life at Psilithrias?"

"Oh dear, you still excel at asking the easy questions, don't you? Many relationships were temporary but the influences of some became permanent, even life-altering. Mind awfully sharing your influences first?"

"No, that's fine, I understand. Thoughts and ideas like that aren't exactly perched on the edge of your lips waiting to be set free. You may laugh at my first influences but unsurprisingly they're from history."

"I'd be disappointed if they weren't, to be honest. You'd never abandon Clio."

"Well... the first group are the American and Edwardian Bohemians who gained notoriety – most of it negative – prior to and immediately after World War I. The other are the American expats of the '20s and '30s. That much-clichéd menagerie of artists, writers, musicians and wanderers whom university students even today try to emulate during sojourns abroad. I've studied these characters for years, since high school actually. Read their books, viewed their paintings and visited the places where they thrived. All seemed attuned to life's effervescence. They rejected what was expected, exchanging it for the improbable. And by detaching themselves from the hum-drum conformity of the times, they found contentment in aloneness or in a select coterie of believers. I think members of both groups led a kind of soft-rebellion for decades – not against specific individuals – but the inadequate and boring ethos of the larger society."

"Did they succeed? Find contentedness? Experience happiness?"

"Yeah, some became noteworthy, even notorious. Some were driven to drink or early death; others committed suicide. But I don't dwell on how they finished life, I concentrate on how they lived it. They didn't spend their final years in a care home not knowing who they were and being force-fed through a tube. They put meat on the bone when they were young. Longevity didn't concern them in the least. So they didn't, to use the modern vernacular, sell out. They possessed the courage of conviction regardless of the questionable places that courage took them. There is something genuine in that. Something worth considering. Pure. It's almost noble."

"Interesting. And please don't take this the wrong way, but for the first time I'm seeing bits of them in you. How strange... all those years I spent mocking 'your lot.'"

"That's okay. Don't worry. I always thought your reaction rather amusing. Other influences included three university history professors from undergraduate and graduate school. They nourished my intellectual curiosity during the day but also provided something they probably weren't even aware of at other times. Needless to say, I never told them because it didn't concern history. It concerned lifestyle choices. Not shattering choices, but unpretentious ones that over time have made a difference. Their singular attention to their particular era of historical interest made me understand the necessity of expertise. They frowned on dilettantism. And because scholarship required lifelong devotion, the quest for understanding could never cease. Their impact affected me in other ways, too – namely, embracing genuineness and simplicity. Possessions reflecting status held minimal value. They chucked aside most symbols of material success. One professor emphasised the luxury of freshly baked bread and homemade preserves. He took immense pride in the heirloom antiquity of his mahogany bookcases. From another I learned to mix a gin and tonic properly as well as always choosing cloth-bound books over soft covers, the latter being wasted money. Most importantly, he emphasised the necessity of personal integrity and the uncompromising acceptance of civil rights. The third professor thought serious conversation imperative at cocktail receptions and dinner parties. Listening to claptrap and drinking Scotch younger than twelve-years shouldn't be tolerated. And most importantly, jazz music – as the only original American art form – needed to be studied and appreciated. Failing that, it should serve, as *de rigueur* for background music during 'intelligent' conversations lasting into the wee small hours."

"Did you ever tell them of their impact?"

"No, never did. Two have died and the last one is quite

elderly. I thanked them in the acknowledgements section of my book. So… gone but certainly not forgotten."

"In many ways you probably didn't take a full accounting until years later, after the sand dial had shifted."

"Probably right. My influences – the Bohemians, the expats, the professors – had been percolating for some time and only came together after befriending Fritzy. He understood my interests, my desires… as well as my much-maligned determinism. The vigour of his personality and life experiences became the catalyst propelling me forward onto the road less travelled."

"It's wonderful all these people got you to Fiskardo, but they let us down five years ago, didn't they?"

"Well, I—"

"Sorry, I'm not being fair."

"Nope, the blame's entirely on me. *I* let us down. If we were ever to have tomorrow…"

I stopped. It wasn't the time or the place to discuss my or, hopefully, our plans. Sara deserved better. I'd been holding my affections for some time. It would have to wait a bit longer. So I placed three logs on a mellowing fire and redirected the conversation.

"You're up, Sara. What influences have affected your life?"

"Unlike you, Edward, I don't admire personalities necessarily from the past. When I look at historical figures, I wonder more about what they were really like. Numerous people have changed the world, but their accomplishments didn't occur in a vacuum. I'm far more curious to understand what experiences and who else influenced them and why. On a personal level and somewhat amusingly – at least I hope so – if I like someone for their work – an artist, a performer, a singer or even an author – I'll try my best not to learn anything about their personality. Fearful I won't like them if they divulge too much. I stood in line once to get an autographed CD of Suzanne Vega. She's a wonderful American folk singer, about your age. Seemed pleasant on stage and all, but I made a huge effort to limit conversation. I feared she'd say or do something that would lessen my love for her music. I expect everyone to have huge flaws. So the less I know about them, the more content and happier I'll be. In that way the illusion is complete, so to speak."

"Okay, understand your reluctance to embrace historical and contemporary figures. But for someone who's achieved your level of success... well, that had to have germinated by someone or some event."

"Always interrupting. Honestly. I haven't finished. Yes, I have been influenced by living people."

"Sorry, typical impatience, I guess."

"My grandmother, Sara – known to all as Sadie – was smart and proud and possessed a wonderful wit. I was named after her. She was a small girl when her mother died in the 1918 flu epidemic. By the early 1920s, Northern Ireland had reached such a boiling point that her father left with Sadie and her siblings for the north of England. May sound cliché, but she made fun out of the littlest things. She always found time to take me out. To do things together – just she and I. And what memorable times we had. We'd first hop on a bus into Sunderland and then catch the train to Newcastle – every year a few days before Christmas. Ate lunch in her favourite old-fashioned tea-room. And we always shopped at Fenwick's but never bought anything. She simply didn't have the money. The store was large and had numerous exits so, if you weren't attentive and took the wrong exit, you'd end up in a different part of the city. We always got disoriented, never remembering exactly which entrance we had used. She never became frazzled. We thought it so funny all we could do was laugh. To this day I feel grateful for her special attention. She made me feel happy and wonderfully content. Unfortunately she died when I was only fourteen. I think of her often, still recalling with genuine fondness the special times we shared.

"As you know already, I travelled to America at aged eighteen to teach pottery in a Vermont summer camp. The experience changed my life. I saw how big, interesting and grand the world is. Many of the people I met instilled me with such a sense of confidence, I started believing I could to do whatever I wanted in life – which was something. One friend in particular, Peter, was a student at Yale University. Even though he and his friends were intelligent and privileged in life opportunities, deep down they were exactly like me. They loved art. They played music. They enjoyed books. And they were interested in hearing my opinions. It felt good. I felt valued. It made me appreciate that although opportunity and the luck of birth offered huge advantages out of the 'starting gate', with hard work, focus and determination I could be successful, too. That's when I decided to go out and make my own luck. I've never looked back or been intimidated by anyone with more intelligence or greater wealth. And besides, as I learned long ago, money will buy almost anything… but truth. So there you have it, Edward, the people and events that unknowingly led me towards this fabulous discretionary life in Psilithrias."

"History, life… are full of complex ironies, aren't they? If I hadn't unilaterally destroyed what we had five years ago, we'd be living in Yorkshire or somewhere in the Pacific Northwest, certainly not in Greece. A shared, unrealised destiny from the past seems to have brought us to Fiskardo."

"The maligned riddle of life."

"If read in a book I'd have to say it was a contrived narrative for the self-absorbed literati to enjoy."

"This time I'll have to with agree with your cynicism, Edward."

We slept late the next morning. A gradual start to the day suited us. After a dose of Greek yogurt and fresh peaches with honey we went to work: Sara to the pottery and I to the kiln. By day's end the roof was completed. I also had gathered what I presumed to be enough dried wood cut to the exact dimensions so Sara could give the kiln a go in about a week's time. She was impressed with the speed and quality of the work.

"You certainly excel at following directions. Thank you so much. Looks fab. Can't wait to test it. I've got some pots that are in the drying stage, so perfect timing."

"I even dated the cornerstone, so to speak... in Greek: 'TO ETOS 2017', meaning 'the year'."

"How clever. You're full of surprises, aren't you? Thank you."

While Sara probably wouldn't have minded if I stayed another day, I decided three nights and four days was enough. And besides, too many questions were ricocheting in my head. I wanted to be alone. I needed to think. Returning to the flat I prepared a much-desired Vesper, keyed up Nancy Wilson's emotional rendition of 'The Folks Who Live on the Hill' followed by Philip Glass's minimalist album *Glassworks* and relaxed on the deck. As the October sun slowly concealed itself behind Fiskardo's rooftops, I reflected on events from the last few days.

I felt invigorated. Reconnecting with Sara certainly had amplified the goodness and excitement of living in Cephalonia. The four days spent with her solidified my feelings. Her signature *joie de vie* had intensified now that she had retired and was throwing pots. And her humour and puckish behaviour had achieved an enviable level of spontaneity. Attributes I knew I'd never possess. In the past she spoke with abandon on important and frivolous issues. Her responses now, however, seemed cautious and measured. It certainly didn't bother me. I accepted it as part of her growing maturity. I had experienced something similar ten years earlier. But I also detected a heightened level of disquietude. It seemed obvious that, while many comfortable aspects of our prior relationship had survived, other elements either had disappeared or seemed irrelevant. At fleeting moments I thought Sara felt a bit uneasy around me, unsure of her emotional and physical feelings. The sense of oneness in which we had taken such pride and cherished years earlier, had been replaced by a calculated and fervid individualism. The five-year separation had made us rely on no one but ourselves. And, of course, life events only had hardened this dependency. But at its core, I believed our sense of oneness probably could rise to the top. It would be different, though, more pragmatic and less musing than before.

Four days before Sara's gallery showing I accepted her invitation to go on what she described as a small trip close to home. Sara's friend loaned us a dinghy for a late afternoon excursion to a postage stamp-sized island called Daskalio located between Cephalonia and Ithaca. Locals referred to it by its ancient name, Asteris. The ancient chapel of St Nicholas occupied most of the island's limited space. We packed the necessary essentials – food, water, wine, blankets, candles and sleeping bags. As dusk transitioned to evening the sky illuminated with a boundless array of stars. No wonder the ancient Greeks were drawn to astronomy, I thought. They could experience a reality-based planetarium every evening. When we decided the day had come to a close we snuggled beside one another and fell quickly to sleep. It had been a good day.

We woke early. The wind had changed direction, enabling us to hear goat collar bells from along the nearby shore. Sara arose from underneath the blanket and walked towards the pebble beach. She removed her shirt and entered the still water. Rays from the morning sun cast a saffron-coloured glow on her feminine figure. After swimming a few yards, she turned towards shore and encouraged me to join her.

"It's lovely. So refreshing and cool. Come join me."

Needing little prodding, I entered the water and swam towards her. She placed her arms around my shoulders and started giggling.

"Edward, not too perceptive, are you? Why *are* you wearing shorts?"

I fumbled around, treading water while simultaneously discarding the shorts. Sara laughed throughout my aquatic ballet. The performance completed, she swam over and wrapped her legs around my waist. We swam back towards land after a while and sat on the shore gazing at the blue sea and salmon-coloured mountains of Ithaca dominating the eastern horizon. The shared silence allowed me to organise my thoughts.

"To describe my previous action as foolish, Sara, is insufficient. I have debated with myself and have argued with myself constantly, sometimes aloud, sometimes in silence. We had few arguments, no trust issues and no disagreements about life's fundamentals. Love, respect and admiration flourished. Selfish indecisiveness was the culprit. Lacking faith to step out without seeing what's ahead. Fritzy was right; my life had become too predetermined, too predictable. And while I tried desperately to change, I failed. I failed miserably. But our separation must cease. Today. On this island in the Ionian. I've procrastinated too long. I'm no longer distracted by America. What is going on in that society is going on in that society. It never will have anything to do with me. You are my country now, Sara. It is time to take leave of my homeland.

To make an exit. To make it wide. To make it clean. And... to make it permanent."

I paused, wondering what she was thinking.

She looked at me encouragingly as her red hair dried in the early morning Greek sun.

"Go on then."

"As you know, prior to leaving for Fiskardo months ago, I sold the condo unit and most possessions, keeping only sentimental items and family heirlooms. Although logistically difficult, I also opened an account with an international bank to handle retirement and investment funds and social security deposits. You weren't aware but weeks ago I began the consequential process of ceasing to be an American: I've returned my US passport to the consulate in Athens and in the final stages of becoming a citizen of Greece. So, you see, I've handled two of three reasons why I broke it off five years ago."

"And these actions mean, what, exactly?"

I couldn't tell whether she was irritated or leading me on, knowing exactly where I was headed despite the long-winded narrative to which she had become accustomed. So I hesitated a bit.

"I could only do this... because I had no responsibilities to anyone or to anything. By luck and the forgiving kindness of your angels who looked after us in the past, we found each other... for the *second* time. All my prior failings brought me to you again, Sara. A beautifully wrapped package I never fully opened. Well, I've unwrapped it and want to grab hold and cherish the only thing good about life... I promise a union founded on love and the essentials for a simple life. Contentment in a discontented world. Will you marry me?"

Only the water lapping against the rocks intermixed with the occasional squawk of a gliding seagull disturbed the quiet.

Sara remained still, staring at Ithaca and pondering. After a lengthy pause she turned towards me with a straight face that lacked her characteristic smile.

"No, Edward, I simply can't. I've refocused my life since retiring and leaving England. I'm free. I'm content and want to remain so. Having you about all the time would be a disruption, upsetting the balance I've created. You'd swallow and devour my freedom, my contentedness – not maliciously, of course, but simply by being you."

A paralysing numbness consumed me.

"Remember what you said when you first took me to 'the rocks'? *The best opportunity comes once. If you don't embrace it, it will disappear and won't be there when you need or want it.* At the risk of appearing arrogant, that was me, Edward, five years ago at Knight's Bar. I *was* the opportunity you didn't take. So, yes, what could have been, sadly will never be. Although we've rediscovered each other, we can't recreate what existed prior to Knight's Bar. That belongs to the history – yours and mine. And this is one time that history's relevance would prevent me from moving forward. I'm a different person now. I must be alone to succeed. I've set a course and am moving in a direction that's fulfilling. I've found my decade-long search for contentedness, for solitude. If happiness is the gauge for success then I'm well underway to achieving my goal. But I must do it alone... so let's keep things as they are. I'd like to think we'd remain good friends – more than friends actually – prioritising time for cocktails, dinners, trips, the occasional romp. Please try to understand... I need you to understand... Say something, please? Anything. Oh, Edward... don't shut down... I can't listen to your silence."

Prostrate with shock, I couldn't speak. Too early to process Sara's comments. I only understood that by turning away from the first chance to be with her had determined she could walk away from the second. We packed the dinghy and pushed off. Silence preoccupied me as we headed around 'the rocks' towards the harbour. What I had imagined as an exhilarating life with Sara had disintegrated. The oneness created by the union of two had become impossible.

AFTERWORD

8 December 2017

Dear Chris – or should I address you as – Fritzy,
 I have sad news concerning our dear friend, Edward. He passed away nine days ago while swimming at what he called 'the rocks' – his favourite spot in Fiskardo. A place he visited regularly to swim or simply to collect the sun and enjoy the isolation. I'm sure he's told you about his numerous adventures at the site. We visited a few times together and while I enjoyed it, the place was certainly more meaningful to him than to me.
 I delayed notifying you immediately after it happened because, based on the location and no obvious signs of foul play, questions remained as to how he died. Was it an accident or suicide? Having not heard from him for weeks I asked the restaurant workers along the pier if they had seen him returning from his morning run. They hadn't seen him

for at least two days so I became concerned and hurried to 'the rocks'. I found his body suspended from the tall, jagged rock that abuts the sea. His medical alert necklace which also contained a copper reproduction of an ancient Cycladic goddess from the Aegean Sea he wore for good health; a cherished ornament Alexandria Tsoussis, owner of Porto Panormos, had given him almost ten years ago, had been caught on the gnarly rock. It was wrapped so tightly around the neck it enabled his head to remain above water. His precarious and questionable position required the medical examiner be brought in to determine the cause of death.

I received the results yesterday and while relieved it wasn't suicide, I was equally saddened it was his heart. Tests showed he had suffered an extremely high arrhythmia prior to falling or floating backward – something he hadn't experienced for at least nine years. Before making it to shore he collapsed after raising halfway out of the water, falling backward with the necklace catching on the protruding rock. He had not been choked by the necklace. I know it's a small consequence but thank God. I couldn't have handle the thought he had been strangled even if accidentally. And if the necklace hadn't kept him afloat he may have drifted out to sea and been lost forever. We never would have known what happened. At least this way I can say goodbye properly. I think we both know how he valued the send-off; for acknowledging a life well or not well lived and for the service to contain a mixture of solace and happiness to the few who really knew and understood him.

My heart is breaking, Chris. A few weeks ago he asked me to marry but I declined. While this decision appears mean and selfish, my deepest regret is we didn't commit earlier, back in '09 or '10. We should have but didn't. We could have had seven or eight fantastic, fabulous years together. I understood his concerns and appreciated them but damn, I should have been my forceful self. Why didn't I take the initiative? When he proposed six weeks ago he chastised himself vigorously for procrastinating, for not having the courage to leave his career, to leave America and to join me in Britain. As he always said, he had been on a mission since '08, 'to throw out his tiresome house of life', to become more bohemian, to be more unpredictable and to reject most materialisms. While he succeeded in numerous ways, I always thought he held back. What finally dismantled him ironically wasn't me but the state of America and its politics. He had come to realise that America had morphed into something so unsavoury it couldn't return to its guiding principles. He appreciated that regimes collapsed by their faults and own incompetence. All was drifting on the wind. As you're well aware, that's why he left for Fiskardo. He had concluded the only thing that made sense at all was to cling to what was good in life – something, Edward believed, that was worth losing everything for. That's what brought him to Greece. And the chance possibility of rekindling our relationship turned this philosophical – almost subjective truth – into reality. So in an important way, I suppose, he succeeded. That he attempted to rectify an earlier bad decision meant Edward accomplished his goal. It was my selfishness and the fruits of longevity that failed him.

I understand you are too ill to travel but, if possible, could you write a few words which I could read at his memorial service? He loved you like a brother, Chris, and greatly respected your intelligence and wise perspective. And, of course, your humour – which, I'm proud to say, – I experienced personally. Thank you.

I debated what to do with his remains but have decided because of Greece's space limitations I'll design and fire a

Greek-inspired stoneware urn to hold his ashes. Sadly it will be the first firing in the wood-burning kiln that Edward so proudly and energetically built for me in mid-October. He will be buried outside St Nicholas chapel on the island of Daskalio located between Cephalonia and Ithaca. It's a special but also painful place… it's where Edward proposed. I secured this isolated spot only with the able assistance of the extended Tselenti family, who worked tirelessly through the governmental bureaucracy and obtained a special dispensation. A fete is planned after the service at their restaurant, what Edward affectionately called 'the best unofficial jazz club' he'd ever experienced. I'm sure the reception will begin respectfully but end raucously, the way Edward would have wanted. Kastas and Vasilia Tselenti have assured me the jazz will be continual, it will be intense and it will be loud. The police have been terribly kind and are extending the noise curfew until 2-am. My God, I'll miss him. I'll miss him. I'll miss him.

Interestingly, Chris, while tidying Edward's files in the flat, I came across the attached letter to Christie and Day Publishing, London. Although never uttering a word except to say it was a 'work in progress', it seems Edward actually was in the final stages of getting the manuscript published [enclosed] that he had laboured over for a decade. It's so autobiographical – he didn't change any of the names – obviously I figure prominently as do you in the guise of his intellectual mentor. I'll contact Christie and Day Publishing soon and tell them what's happened. Although the content is overly personal, I nonetheless will do everything I can to honour his memory to get it published. I owe him that. The ending is incomplete so I don't know whether Christie and Day Publishing will leave as is with a postscript of what occurred or employ a ghostwriter. I'd appreciate your thoughts on the matter, Fritzy.

I also must tell you something disconcerting, Chris. Sitting atop the manuscript's cover page was a piece of paper with a few handwritten sentences. I think it reflected his state of mind after I turned down his proposal. While it lacks any surface meaning to the uninitiated, I'm worried my rejection may have caused irreparable damage to his heart, causing it to race uncontrollably. I thought initially it may even had been a cryptic suicide note but I think I've put that out of my mind. I recall when we met in NYC years ago, he said the doctor had warned that intense and unreleased emotional stress could initiate another incident without warning. His body wouldn't be able to recover. For the rest of my life, Chris, I'll have to live with the distinct possibility that I unthinkingly placed him in harm's way.

Here are the sentences. I'd appreciate your thoughts: **Nothing wrong with pursuing a life you feel compelled to live. To compromise, to question or to ignore the pursuit will inflict unasked-for pain on the man who loves you. It may be best, perhaps, to live alone than be married but feel alone and discontented.** These were his last written words.

Life will continue for me on this gorgeous, peaceful island but so will the void brought by Edward's death. The future is promised to no one... a truth you know far better than I. And while I'll continue living without rancour and without cynicism, I shall be plaintively aware whether married or single, emotional fulfilment is as fleeting as life itself.

Much love to you, Chris — we must stay in touch,
Sara

AFTERWORD

20 October 2017

Mr Reginald Cordings-Smyth
Christie and Day Publishing
Murrow House
84 Hallam Street
London, United Kingdom
W1W 5HD

Dear Mr Cordings-Smyth,

As discussed on the phone this morning, I am overjoyed you've accepted for publication, Grey, Red, Blue … Gone. And it's equally gratifying that you find it relevant in today's world. I certainly do, but I'm a bit prejudiced since several events were experienced first-hand. The ending hasn't been flushed out entirely but should be completed in the coming weeks. Only one conclusive element remains to be written. Rest assured, however, it will end happily. Grief abounds in the world today. Literature doesn't need another depressing tale of unfulfilment.

In an earlier letter you asked about the significance or meaning of the title. It's an emblematic colour spectrum of events in Edward Lee's life. 'Grey' reflected the overcast skies that hovered incessantly above and between Seattle's concrete and glass buildings. 'Red' symbolised the gingerness of Sara's hair. 'Blue' invoked the overpowering pull of the Ionian Sea. And, of course, 'Gone' described Lee's departure from America.

As time permits, I look forward to receiving your recommended edits. Use of email is somewhat restricted, so you may experience a considerable delay before receiving my comments and alterations. Once the editing process begins and if not too bothersome, I'd appreciate you forwarding corrections to the address below. Copiers also are scarce commodities so it would be easier if you could forward - via post - hard copies of alterations that exceed five pages. I thank you in advance for understanding and look forward to having the book 'on the shelves', so to speak, by year's end and in time for the holidays. Thank you.

Respectfully,

Edward Lee

Nitsa's Place, Flat B
Fiskardo
Cephalonia, Greece